ENGAGED IN WRITING
AND
THE FOOL AND THE PRINCESS

ENGAGED IN WRITING

AND

THE FOOL AND THE PRINCESS

BY

STEPHEN SPENDER

FARRAR, STRAUS AND CUDAHY, INC.

NEW YORK

TO
HANSI LAMBERT

ENGAGED IN WRITING

TO

NICOLAS NABOKOV

ENGAGED IN WRITING

I

WHEN he got out of the train on to the covered-over platform of the railway station at Venice, he heard the rain stroking the roof through the darkness. Carrying his suitcase, Olim Asphalt left the station and walked across a wide road or square of cars and buses, all at their terminus. At this backyard, wheeled things come full stop before the looking-glass wheel-less world of Venice. As he stood on the jetty—just across this yard—waiting for the vaporetto, he put down his suitcase and glanced at his watch. He was late for the banquet which would precede the week-long East-West Conference of European intellectuals organized in Easter Week of March 1956 by Dr. Bonvolio, head of EUROPLUME.

From the deck of the vaporetto, Venice seemed less dream than gleaming black-and-white-misted cinematography. The façades of palaces were ghostly shadows on transparent gelatinous negative. At every crossing of waters, the tall vertical ends of carved stone buildings were like the two sides of a stage which suspended between them a screen of mist. The slapping of waters and the groaning of the rope fixed to a pier where the vaporetto halted, were small squeaks in the European storm which swept up the marble junk of Venice into this little corner of the Adriatic.

Coming from Paris, headquarters of LITUNO, which he was to represent at the Conference, Olim Asphalt had

9

endured a waking nightmare all night in the wagon-lit, during which he had re-read Krushchev's famous speech to the Twentieth Party Congress (as much of it as was then reported in the newspapers) made only a few days previously. The train raced through wide darkness laid open to tortured political prisoners, deported populations, slave labourers, victims. Like a mediaeval woodcut of the Dance of Death, Europe was jigged over by near-skeletons; white skins, brown skins, no-skins, victims of thirty years of modern tyranny. Bones showed through bodies, blood poured out of orifices. Shot down, gassed, burned in ovens, driven out half-naked across freezing and burning landscapes, packed and canned in trucks of doomed trains.

'The b——s, the f——s, the sh——s,' he said aloud into the darkness. On his berth, his body seemed a parody of sleep. 'We must bloody well do something about it.' Force of remote habit even made him think: 'This meeting will decide.' Through the darkness he exploded with a rather melodramatically bitter laugh, as he reflected that the call to bloody action was a war-cry from twenty-five years back, when it would have been uttered at least half on behalf of those against whom he now whispered it in the darkness. This thought brought him up against a massive furious obstruction in his mind: that despite everything he would not even now blame Stalin as wholly as he had once detested Hitler. He started up on some frantic sums with corpses: seven million incinerated Jews against a great many more millions in slave camps or executed (but the trouble is that one does not ever know how many sands there are on the shore. And *slave camps* is itself the kind of rhetorical phrase one is ashamed to use). Finally one had to dismiss all this reality as unreal, because it was too vastly real to contemplate. And if one entered into it one would be annihilated—

  Annihilating all that's made
  To a green thought in a green shade.

The train took up the rhythm and offered reality on sleepers: *la douceur de vivre*, love affairs, America. One had to go on, improvising happiness from day to day, postponing doom by ignoring events that, happening over the rim of the horizon, were inconceivable here. Inconceivable. Unreal. That was better.

The private life—ha, ha! He let out into the sleeping car what sounded to himself more a histrionic yell than a laugh. Private life for him a week ago had been coming back into the Paris apartment after a night on the tiles, and finding Elaine stretched immobile waxen pale on the double bed, the opened bottle of sleeping tablets on the table beside her. Her beauty like an image of all her moments of innocence and purity concentrated into an impression of herself moulded out of her own flesh—that appalled him. It was a clear warning that if this happened—really happened—nothing of his own life would be acquitted.

Then the dynamo of penance had started rotating. At this stage of their relationship he could see the other side of the wheel at the very moment when he felt guilt on this side: the other side, when he would resent that guilt and feel that the very action that had made him sorry was an aspect of the deep hidden mechanism by which she drew him always back to her.

Thank God, really, for Stalin and Hitler. They were a vaster kind of machinery. In a secular age the spectacle of their most ambitious projects—their murders—was immensely comforting to all private left-wing sinners. If LITUNO let him speak the rhetoric surging up in his mind, what he'd like to say to the French intellectuals was that the Left to them played the role of the Ganges to Hindus. It was a great blood-washing stream, blood-

coloured itself, in which sons running from their
mothers, husbands from their wives, faithless women,
bandits even, together with saints, idealists and mystics,
cleansed themselves of guilt by the mere act of washing
themselves in the Left. *Le gauche, la rive gauche.* Now
he stood on the deck of the vaporetto contemplating
agreeable aspects of representing LITUNO, the literary
and cultural, sub-organ—some said an operable appen-
dix—of the United Nations. Travel allowance of fifteen
dollars a day (apart from tax-free salary); most meals,
presumably, provided by EUROPLUME. The only bills
would be from the hotel: say, five dollars per night. This
would leave ten dollars per day, or 7,000 lira, for
gondolas, aperitifs, entrance to exhibitions.

To eat: *lasagne, scampi, cotolette, osso buco,* and soft
shell crabs from the canal. To meet: the *chic*-est existentialists, Sarret and Marteau, from Paris; Sereno and
Longhi from Rome; Pobedin, Korovin, and Pomyalov,
three Russian intellectuals, provided with labels and
guarantees of the appropriate writers' organizations:
Csongor Botor, novelist, poet, and essayist, from the
Budapest ditto; and several others. To drink: *Soave,
Valpolicello, Lachrima Christi, Bardelino, Chianti*; he re-
cited to himself the soft names of Italian wines. To see:
all Titian's Danae marble flesh upon her Adriatic bed
of lapis lazuli, her canals blue veins, shower of gold suns
and silver moons falling upon her domes.

The vaporetto stopped at the landing stage in front
of a jetty leading straight to the main entrance of his
hotel. He was late for the banquet which preceded tomorrow morning's opening session. Not waiting to go
up to his room, he deposited his things with the hall
porter, and ran out into the rain. A page boy accompanied him, pointing out the Hotel Stella across the
piazza by the Biennale. 'There is always rain nowadays,
the season is ruined, it has never been like this before,

it is all due to the atomic bomb'—remarks pelted by a running figure like Boreas in a Botticelli, gaily puffing zephyrs through his mind.

The piazza was one great shallow bath of rain-water. When he came to the end of the colonnade opposite San Marco, Olim turned back to look at the duomo and the campanile—floating on the surface two inches above the pavementing: a 'shot' often taken by more sophisticated photographers (who sometimes catch the flat glassy mirrored image interrupted above by blurred crush-petal slightly out of focus pigeon wings. An effect impossible at night).

But what he treasured now was water bubbling soggily up through cracks in stones. He imagined deep down the rain welling above the log-heads of ancient piles on which Venice rests, crumbling logs driven into sand, soft shell crabs fed on dead men's eyes. Victims.

The banquet was in a private room in the Stella: a large, bare room with faded nineteenth-century murals, like the back of an operatic stage-set. It was now three-quarters filled by an immense round table covered with a white cloth, on which, among plates and cutlery, dead leaves and flowers were strewn. The guests, already seated in their scroll-back chairs, circumferenced an out-size sunflower disc. Waiters served from a long trestle table—oblong beside a circle.

Olim took the empty place evidently reserved for him —six o'clock on the dial. He deduced this from his opposite, indubitably figure 12, the King Arthur of the Knights of EUROPLUME, Dr. Bonvolio, bald-headed, beaming. His skull shone through the room like the sun the sunflower follows.

Sitting to Olim's left, was his old school friend, Alex Merton. Their profiles, they each might have thought, were scissored for one another by these kind of public occasions. They took it for granted that they would meet at conferences, congresses of 'the intellectuals'.

'Oh, you here!' Olim said in a tone that insinuated 'So you're in the racket too!' while also taking their joint appearance for granted. Alex Merton took in calmly Olim Asphalt's familiar botched face, with its self-parodying leer, the expression in which openness was fused with determined cynicism, like—like, he thought, one of those pieces of modernist iron sculpture, a good job of soldering. Their banter proceeded with a meaningful meaninglessness which would have shown the French delegates, had they been listening, that English intellectual exchange consists of imbecilities.

'You here?' Alex Merton echoed: 'How did you come?' 'By train.' 'Late as usual . . .' (this reached back to school). 'When did you arrive?' Olim asked. 'Well, actually, I've been here some days. I've been staying with the Princess Cassamassima. I thought perhaps I should give this meeting some sort of editorial attention.'

They did not pursue this obscurely competitive conversation further. Alex, having apparently scored a point, turned to his neighbour, Yves Borès, a French novelist who was also a familiar at such gatherings, on both sides of the Iron Curtain (Alex and Olim were only invited by 'the West').

Yves Borès appeared subtly quiet: the face of a writer who has discovered his 'philosophy of life' and won a literary prize, at one and the same moment. The most assiduous attender of conferences, he looked as if he did not belong here, radiating the quiet of pine forests and mountain peaks at sunset. 'What have you been writing?' Alex asked. 'A little journal of a voyage I have made on Lake Balaton. Nature is so peaceful there.' This roused Olim. 'How are the politics?' he asked crudely. 'Oh, *ça marche, ça marche. En effet, c'est très interessant.*'

'Indeed? I look forward to reading your journal,' Alex observed pleasantly.

Olim interrupted to tell Alex Merton that it was very like 'old Bonvolio', who regarded the English as in some way always sabotaging his organization, to put them together at the table as far as possible from himself. Then he turned to his right-hand neighbour, apparently a simple peasant girl in her plain smock, her doll head stuck over with little shavings of fair curls. In front of her, on the white table-cloth, a card recorded her name, place of origin, and function; MAGDA KARINTHY (*Hongrie, interprêtre*). When he made some remark, she did not answer but managed to direct a sharp hostile sidelong glance at him out of her left eye. This he took to be the first breath of the bleak Eastern wind of ideology blowing from across the steppes. He gave one of his splutters.

Right of the interpreter, was the nuclear physicist Dunstan Curlew, his head weighed down by a heap of yellow hair; a Jason out of science fiction, who by intensity of thinking projected from the adventures of his mind, upon his head, his private golden fleece.

Just now, Dunstan Curlew's immense white face was wrinkled with the tentative experimental creased smile he put on for extra-laboratory extra-Party-political-cell occasions. Through his complex facial entanglements, his eyes were tuned in to Magda Karinthy's out-raying charm. Without moving the elaborate instrument of his gaze, Curlew did just shift his eyes to take in the late arrival, with what Olim—inclined to feelings of persecution—took to be an expression of pained surprise. Olim quickly looked in another direction, to be confronted at about two o'clock on the dial by the pear-shaped tragi-comedian's face of Sereno.

Sereno had the three Russians between him and Bonvolio, the French being to Bonvolio's right. Out of his dead-pan gaze, Sereno looked impassively at Olim, shifted his black eyes to the Russians and then to the French. He looked blankly in front of him for a few seconds, then responding again to Olim's smile, his head and shoulders surged balloon-like a few inches above the table, and back again, anchored to their original position.

The movement was an immense shrug, and it communicated not only Sereno's feelings about Pobedin, Korovin, and Pomyalov—Sarret, Marteau, and Borès— but the excitement he was holding back. Ever since the famous Thaw, the renowned ex-Communist poet had pursued a cat-and-mouse game, of getting real live Communist intellectuals from behind the now lifted Iron Curtain and bringing them to the West, where he put to them ironic part-amused part-sombre questions. The voice he was playing was that of truth-will-out. And, as in tragedy, there was a comic almost farcical element in the procedure. The jack-in-the-box truth pops out; the roar of laughter is a roar of tears.

Sereno looked back across the jerking puppet-like figure of Bonvolio to the French, and Olim, understanding him, followed his direction. Already, Sereno was indicating, the French had the meeting well in hand. French would be the language spoken, French the ideas discussed, French the terminology, and French the elucidation of any un-French ideas which happened to be thrown up during the discussion. There was Sarret with his aqueous eyes behind his goggling spectacles, his gesticulating hands, the gasping movement of his mouth when he spoke, emitting each word as though it were a bubble, already explaining, entertaining, astonishing, with his segments of analysis—each produced and exhibited like a section put on a slide under a microscope. His jokes exploded like small crackers in little bursts all round him.

What specially excited the comment of Sereno's indicating eyes, was that Sarret and Marteau should appear to be on such good terms. For, as Olim must, from his centre in the Paris headquarters of LITUNO, know, only yesterday—they had left their audience—the Boulevard Saint Michel—violently divided by the Sarret-Marteau split following on Krushchev's denunciation of Stalin, yet here they were, Sereno seemed to comment, shamelessly *tu-toi*-ing.

In *L'Hebdomadaire*, Marteau had pronounced that after Krushchev's revelations of twenty years of murder, torture, imprisonment on false charges, deportations, and forced labour, anti-communists need no longer be denounced wholesale as unrelenting enemies of the proletariat. Distinctions could be made. He went so far as to coin the catch-phrase: 'Amnesty of the intelligentsia'. He laid down the rules of a new game which might have preoccupied the Boulevard for several months: discriminating between those 'premature ex- or anti-communists who were "genuinely of the left" and those who were "implicitly of the right".' The prospect of this general intellectual exercise was upset by Sarret switching the controversy back to the familiar Sarret-Marteau dingdong, with a stinging attack on Marteau for introducing into his politics 'the spirit of cynical post-mortems'. Sarret pointed out that Krushchev's admission of the errors of Stalin was no evidence that premature anti-Stalinists had been any the less pro-American bourgeois capitalist sympathizers. The anti-communists, Sarret wrote in his review *O Tempora*, should now be contested more rigorously than before; for there was a danger of the good faith of Mr. Krushchev being used to bolster up the bad faith of 'anti-proletarian bourgeois proto-anti-Stalinists'. As for Marteau's idea that certain people could, before the Twentieth Congress, have been anti-communist without being of the Right, this was precisely the fallacy that Sarret had spent years exposing. He had always insisted that to be anti-communist was by definition to be against the proletariat, that is, to aid and abet the Right; and the more successfully the anti-communist deceived himself and others that he was 'leftist', the more useful he could be to Reaction. Nothing had happened to alter the fact that, until two weeks ago, to be anti-Stalinist meant to be anti-proletarian.

However, in spite of all this, while Sarret was talking, Marteau looked at him with an almost affectionate smile. And when they were not mutually *tu-toi*-ing, Sarret and Marteau were paying courtesies that looked at this distance, quite oriental, to the Russians. Above the snow-white-clothed table, Pobedin, Korovin, and Pomyalov seemed fixed like mountains on which famous public figures have been carved, with faces that express eternal benevolent attention. They were natural objects, or perhaps just living models for social realist art. Pobedin, the trotted-out romancer, whose revolutionary writing preceded the revolution, stared straight in front of him, his tired worn leathery face resembling that of some prehistoric animal, overtaken by zigzags of evolution, still fastidiously surviving. Vassili Korovin had a different alertness: that of a boy who, never losing his innocence, has believed everything and alienated no one. Boris Pomyalov evidently belonged to a new generation of self-promoters rather than survivors. With his bashed-in left eye and his pugilist's nose, he had an air of being something of an intruder on literature.

The Russians, behind their barriers of language, ideology, and imperturbability were not very rewarding objects of scrutiny. Olim turned back to Magda Karinthy, but here there was still no sign of response.

Being fairly accustomed, one way or another, to receiving snubs from misses, and having drunk several glasses of the chianti, he gave her a nudge and asked: 'Why are you so hostile, mademoiselle?' She looked at him with her very clear pale eyes, and objected: 'Not at all. I am not hostile.' 'Well then, why don't you talk?' 'I was talking to my neighbour.' 'Oh, to him,' said Olim, pointing a stubby finger at Dunstan Curlew. 'Is it he who's been putting you against me? Well, that's very wrong of the comrade. This is an unofficial gathering, and we're all supposed to be friends—under the aegis of Doctor Bonvolio up there. I'm a representative of LITUNO, and I don't take any side,' he went on, 'so you shouldn't take sides against me—though you may forget that I'm an official.' She looked as though none of this could possibly concern her, and Olim began to suspect still more strongly that Dunstan Curlew had been denouncing him—perhaps as a 'traitor' even.

He decided to put down a barrage of interference on Curlew's wavelength. 'Good evening,' he called across Magda's form, unresponsive as an effigy. Curlew's great head swayed back a few inches, and his eyes tuned in Olim-wards. 'Delighted to see you,' Olim boomed. English, in his public school accent, sounded even to himself like a subtly aggressive language specially invented for the purpose of insulting compatriots abroad. Dunstan moved his eyes and the general direction of all his receiving lines—alerted to some new danger, some potentially 'reactionary' move. 'Where are you going after Venice?' Olim persisted. At this Dunstan blinked, and suddenly imparted information which seemed to tumble from him like all the coins out of a slot machine. 'I have another meeting, also of intellectuals, but of scientists, to attend in Vienna.' Olim had hit the jackpot.

Olim wondered whether superlative intelligence had enabled Curlew to perceive in a flash that his suspicions were foolish, or whether he had some irrational Achilles' heel of personal vanity. The idea that this completely objective observer of facts might be immensely vain, fascinated him. These speculations were interrupted by a pronouncement beamed across in all directions, like instructions on a loudspeaker system in an airport, by Bonvolio. They would meet tomorrow at ten sharp at a room in the Ducal Palace specially set aside by the Commune for their labours. The banquet ended without further explanations or introductions. All the intellectuals shuffled to their feet and only stood around, in the narrow space left by the immense table, for as long as it took to get their coats.

Walking over to where they were now standing, Olim greeted Sarret, Marteau, and Sereno, whom he knew well from previous congresses. The French writers, none of whom had a word of any language except his own, nevertheless were aware of Olim Asphalt as one of ' *les jeunes romanciers anglo-américains*': Caldwell, Mitchell, Capote, Mitford, Vidal, Faulkner, Waff, Steinbeck, Greene, and Green. Sensitive to the risks of the *deuxième métier*, they saw here a case of one in whom the means of livelihood had swallowed up the primary vocation—*ce pauvre type de LITUNO*, their eyes said. They approached him as one attending the funeral of his career. He did not altogether reject their sympathy. It satisfied his self-hatred, relieved him from having to enter into long intellectual discussions in difficult French, and gave him a subterranean feeling of potential revenge. He felt that with his newly acquired lack of recognition, he had put on a cap of invisibility which enabled him to observe them unawares.

A voice said: 'Am I interrupting?' and, looking round, Olim saw a late arrival. 'I just got here,' Csongor Botor explained.

Csongor Botor was an over-size shambling figure with grey hair stuck up all round his head like some

unbrushed boy's. Olim was shocked by his having aged
far more than the ten years since he had last seen Botor
in Hungary, much longer than the distance from Budapest to Venice. His very last glimpse of him was, in fact,
of Botor standing astride a barrel of new wine (called
Badacsony—he clearly remembered), brought into the
subterranean cave of the surrounding vineyards where a
gathering of the liberated post-war anti-Fascist Hungarian poets and intellectuals assembled for the tasting.
They had driven out from a baroque castle of the time
of Maria Theresa, on the shore of Lake Balaton. The
castle was once the property of a great landowner who
had put himself beyond the pale of human consideration:
he was suspected of Nazi sympathies. It was a duty to
take over his property and fill its hundred-odd rooms
with novelists and poets living and working together in
communal creativeness. The Writers' Association invited Olim Asphalt, representing LITUNO, to approve
and disseminate their idea of taking over the more
reactionary castles, and filling them with approved left-
wing intellectuals. The castellated writers wined and
dined Olim, explaining as they did so that here, in their
new democracy, the spirit, in all senses of the word,
inherited the earth. They certainly had the air of con-
suming their freedoms, frantically almost. They were
less ideological than cynical. For instance, up there on
the barrel, Botor stuck his fingers into the large hole of
the stopper and, waving his free arm, addressed the body
of the barrel with the words in (for Olim's benefit)
broken English—'My dear, you have no idea, I'm sure,
where we were last night!'

Olim reported well to LITUNO of the castellated
ones. He saw that if intellectual life had to be 'protected',
castles in rolling scenery among vineyards compared
favourably with the urban beehive offices of subsidiaries
of the U.N. A few months after his visit, a notorious

curtain had fallen, and he heard no more from his eloquent Hungarian colleagues, whom he liked to think of
always in a Bacchic frenzy practising social- while living
sur-realism.

Now, ready to let rip a roar of reminiscing camarad-
erie, he went up to Csongor Botor. Botor looked at him
with a dazed, distancing, distanced expression. 'Don't
you remember me?' Olim asked. Botor seemed at once
locking down from the wine barrel, and through the
perspective of a gun barrel, as he said, in an old man's
voice, 'Why, of course, I remember you—on Lake Balaton—I remember perfectly, perfectly. You were the
representative of LITUNO, weren't you?—at that very
interesting discussion we had. A pity it didn't come to
anything. . . .' And with that he shuffled off towards the
door.

Olim next sought out Sereno, standing alone by the
long sad trestle table now almost denuded of plates,
staring across the room with his abstract melancholy
gaze. Seeing Olim, he started, as though woken from a
dream. Lasting about a second, a smile flashed across his
face, which then relapsed into its usual look of blankness.
'It should be an interesting meeting,' said Olim, sobered
rather by the encounter with Botor. Sereno looked at
him as if to say that was assuming altogether too
much. 'It depends. It depends on whether *they* say anything.' 'Who?' 'The Russians. Csongor Botor, that
Hungarian.' 'Do you think they have come all this way
to say nothing?' 'They will say what they have been
told to say. But when the time is ripe, I will have some
questions to put to them.' He tapped his side pocket.
Then, looking back across the room as at a cast totally
unfitted to play the rôles he would gladly have written
for them, he said: 'And Sarret. Sarret. That is a bad
business.' 'Why?' 'He will only say that there is
nothing to say. And at enormous length.' He sighed,

and as Olim looked unsatisfied, added: 'Don't you understand? That is his philosophy. The philosophy of incommunicability, which he communicates interminably. The philosophy that—since there is no deity but only a Situation—Sarret is the only person who can communicate anything. With Marteau perhaps allowed to prod him on.' His smile switched quickly on and off. Then he touched Olim's sleeve. 'But look. You see? Just what I had expected.' What he had expected was the incursion into the room of three small, unshaved officials who had taken the Russian representatives aside into a corner. 'They must be consuls, police agents,' muttered Sereno. 'Excuse me, but I must protest,' and he went over to Bonvolio.

'A brief walk is indicated,' Alex said, coming up to Olim. As they left the room, they heard Sereno saying to Bonvolio in an Italian simple as a first lesson, that all discussion would be impossible if police agents from consulates and embassies were allowed to intrude their advice on their nationals. At the door they were confronted by the bewildering spectacle of Dunstan Curlew. Thinking he was perhaps lost, and that the English would surely all be at the same hotel, Olim asked the scientist where he was staying. Curlew squinted at him with a look like a squeezed lemon, as though he were not going to give him one split atom more of information, and scurried off downstairs into the outer darkness.

Alex and Olim lingered at a convenient distance. Outside they walked directionlessly for a time through the chiaroscuro of the streets, occasionally interrupted by a piazza—pale-brown stage-set lit by spot-lights that hung in the centre of the scene. The weather had cleared, and the soft stone blackness broken by swooping beams from street lamps, golden lines incised by edges of windows and doors, reflections from water, echoed with footsteps on pavements, murmurings, instruments, and the pizzicato laughter of seemingly ever awake children. Above their heads carved scrolls on the façades of churches stayed like spread angels' wings. They crossed a bridge alongside a concourse of canals that formed a minute intown harbour where a huddle of pitchy gondolas raised the axes of their prows. Then they walked down a wide street with shop windows bright as the lit tanks of an aquarium, containing fruit, shell fish, beads, clothing, surgical instruments, all looking like rare specimens on exhibition, museum pieces, garish and gleaming, obtained one by one with immense difficulty, from the mainland.

'Today I am fifty,' said Alex, when they came to the door of a bar. 'Let's go in and have a drink.'

They went in. The door of the bar shut out Venice and they were in a joint that might have been in any of the States. There was a long counter with bottles and an Espresso machine, and two girls standing behind. In front lolled two Americans, G.I.'s on furlough, one black-haired, hirsute, the other ginger, freckled. They had with them a Venetian boy they called Giovanni. The dark one from time to time lunged amiably at Giovanni, who called him ' Yank'.

Olim and Alex sat down at one of the four tables in the bar. Alex ordered cognacs, raised his glass and said: 'To your fiftieth birthday.' He had the same smoothed-back hair, the same accomplished glance, that had made Olim feel he was enviable, thirty-five years ago, at school.

Suddenly Olim was depressed. The beaten-dog's look on Csongor Botor's face still hung before him. And here he was with Alex, a school confabulation. He hovered between a prison boyhood and the prison of middle age. There had been a moment when the door seemed open— but that was onto a freedom that proved a worse prison.

'To our fiftieth birthday,' he said nevertheless, raising his glass.

Alex said briskly: 'The obvious banal thing about being our age is that everything is different from what one expected, exactly to the extent that one feels so much the same. I mean—one expected to feel old: one feels the same as ever: that is surprising.'

This was the same kind of thing as he used to say at school—only brighter, really.

'Sometimes one feels damned old. I felt old ten minutes ago when I saw how Csongor Botor had changed in as many years.'

'Ah, that's why one resents one's contemporaries. They are mirrors that certainly give one unpleasant glimpses of increasing girth, falling hair, false teeth. They let one down pretty badly at times.'

'You know perfectly well, Alex, that the fact is that things change. One feels young because one refuses to change with them. It's refusal to change, Alex, that gives you the illusion that you are young. If one grew older with things changing all round one, one would not feel or look young, but perhaps one would be young. For instance, one would understand the young, instead of simply understanding how one felt when one was young. One is old through pretending to be young: because one remains attached to one's youth, and unconscious of change. It is the fact that you feel and look young that makes you old, Alex.'

Olim said all this heavily and precisely as though each word were a stone he carefully trod on.

'I take a more cheerful view,' said Alex, wondering how drunk his colleague was. 'I do insist that one is more like oneself than one had anticipated being. Why, when I was twenty, I would have thought it indecent that, at fifty, I would still enjoy going to bars like this, not to speak of things like falling in love.'

'What you forget is that they may not enjoy you,' said Olim looking round the bar. 'Only this evening, sitting next to me at table, there was a damned attractive girl. Magda Karinthy her name—I took it down. I certainly haven't changed in that I'd prefer spending this week with her in a gondola, to my platonic life with all you intellectuals. Where things have changed is that she wouldn't feel the same about me. And certainly it's damned hard to realize that. The absurd thing about being older is that just now I couldn't understand why she didn't respond to me. . . . Being with her, I felt myself her age.'

'At twenty though, you would surely have expected that at fifty an intellectual discussion between distinguished men of letters from two opposed ideological camps would realize the sum of your desires?'

'Anyway,' Olim said, harping on the idea, 'myself at twenty would find the picture of myself at fifty with Magda at twenty-five—repellent. And ourselves at twenty may be right about that, old boy.' He grinned nastily.

'I can put yourself at twenty right about that. He had illusions about the Great. He imagined that to spend a week with "the intellectuals" would be like bathing in the precious life blood of master spirits. What he didn't know, you and I now do know. Milton meant to be ironic. Master spirits, by the time they've become famous, don't have any life blood, apart from what they bled into their books. Even the photographs taken of them are the precious life blood of their looks. Tape-recordings are the precious life blood of their voices.'

'Have another cognac,' Olim said. He looked with reddened eyes across the table, and then towards the bar, at the bottles with pink and amber and green liquids in them, the Espresso machine, the barmaids flirting with Giovanni and the Americans. He seemed to take in contents and inmates as potential life to be exploited. He said:

'All the same, this meeting isn't going to be the same

as all the other intellectual discussions and conferences
we've attended.'

'I can't see the slightest difference,' said Alex. 'Everyone present has taken up his position ages ago. I can
assure you that not one speech will be made that an
efficient machine, fed with the Sarret formula, the Marteau formula, or the Soviet point of view, couldn't
exactly forecast.'

Olim became flustered and annoyed. 'I refuse to
accept that statement—utterly. After all, there isn't a
person here who doesn't realize that tens of thousands of
Russians have been legally killed—by laws without the
slightest justice. The whole fabric of ideology has been
rent—don't you see that? You must see it! All the
assumptions of the past thirty years are seen simply not
to exist. We're left without a single theory or argument,
but just brutal, stinking, ugly facts.' He stared round the
bar again, snorting—a bit over-acting his role, Alex
thought.

'I couldn't agree more. That is, I agree about the
situation. But I don't think our colleagues will take
much notice of it—not as it affects their theories. What
you forget perhaps is that they are intellectuals who are
also writers.'

'What difference does that make? All I require, Alex,
is that they should be human—like you and me!' he
said, accusingly almost.

'They are all people who began by being moralists
and who then derived from their moral passion a point of
view that could be converted into literature, which they
then sold to a public.'

'That's too difficult for me, old boy. You'd better
elaborate on it.'

'The writers here have two things in common—that
they all have pasts rooted in some kind of moral relation
to an immoral public situation: and that they all have

palpably rootless presents, connected only with meetings with other rootless writers.'

'Go on, go on.'

'I assume that Pobedin, Korovin and Pomyalov in 1920—say—genuinely cared about the revolution of the proletariat. Today, they are just government property and organs. I suppose you wouldn't dispute that. Sarret once was a rebel of an outstanding kind. Today his rebelliousness is inevitably an attitude required of him by his readers. The moment a bureaucracy in the East, or a large reading public in the West, takes over a writer, he loses contact with his reality, which simply becomes one of his personal assets. He's swallowed up by his reputation. The doubts and questions attached to his moral being—in which a person's reality lies—have been taken over by his public name. Every French writer has to be *angoissé*. He wears his anguish like a medal. His personal qualities cease to be good and bad. They are simply elements in a formula that goes into the work. Before Gide wrote *L'Immoraliste*, it was possible, in a real sense, to regard Gide himself as involved in a moral conflict which might make one decide that he was immoral. The moment *L'Immoraliste* became one of the modern French *œuvres* that everyone ought to know about, the immorality (if it was that) became a peculiar virtue attaching to that product of the work—his reputation. It's the same with Sarret. Imagine Sarret at school: a tough proposition, you'd say. A rebel, a debater, the leader of a gang. What would make him real would be the moral doubt attaching to his behaviour. It would seem to his professor at the Lycée that Master Sarret would prove himself wrong or right, by the moral choice that he finally made. But actually, what happened was that he made the choice irrelevant, by becoming a famous writer. All doubts were removed in the great dissolvent and stain remover—success.'

'That's a very pretty thesis for your editorial, Alex, but it doesn't take life into account. One's reputation can't take over one's life—unfortunately. One still goes on having a mistress who swallows a bottle of sleeping tablets because one won't marry her. One can't absolutely shut out the facts—the millions of stinking corpses One wakes up at 3 a.m. and realizes that what one has done is no use. One is still a body that is going to be shoved into the ground, however little or much one is read—or red!'

'And all those things,' said Alex, 'are perfectly good grist for the mill of literature. A writer is like some country which contains a great many products, some good, some bad: but it manages to export the whole damned lot, and thus convert good and bad, beautiful and ugly, into some universally acceptable respectable commodity—say Swiss francs.'

'*Piu di vino!* Giovanni,' yelled the dark-haired G.I., seizing Giovanni by the arm. Giovanni shoved him away, laughing: 'I no gi' you wine, Yank, if you fight me; then I know you have wine we all fight.'

Olim took up the cry, '*Piu di vino!*' he echoed. He shouted to the Americans, the waitresses, Giovanni, everyone—'Come and have a drink with us.'

They sat down, they went on drinking. Olim discovered what States the Americans came from. He liked all of them, hoped they liked him. Then, as if taking up the grown up conversation where the children had interrupted it, he lunged at Alex: 'You can't get away with it, you know. If no one else speaks, you'll have to say something at this conference. You'll have to tell them something.'

'But what?'

'That all their ideas lie buried under murdered corpses. That there aren't any ideologies left—or won't be soon: only heaps of facts like stinking fish. They have to nose their way out through the heaps. That will do to say as a start.'

'It seems to me that you are perfectly capable of saying all that yourself.' Alex was a bit affronted.

'What is so characteristic of me, and so utterly ludicrous, is that I'm the one person here who isn't allowed to express an opinion. I'm here representing LITUNO as what's called an Observer. Since the purpose of LITUNO is to improve international relations among intellectuals, that means that its representatives are not allowed to take any side among them. Points of view always worsen relations. Isn't mine worsening ours now?'

Alex smiled pleasantly. 'My dear Olim, you mean then that LITUNO actually puts a padlock on your mouth? You sit at these meetings like Papageno, only saying Hm Hm Hm Hm?'

'Yes I do. You'll see. You'll see. I was a prefect once, you remember. At the very end, I shall be requested to make a statement about the kind of economic aid LITUNO can offer to the second East-West reunion, proposed by Bonvolio. I might, of course, jump over the traces then.'

'What form would doing that take?'

'Well, I might resign. Elaine doesn't like me being away at conferences, and I'm not really cut out to be an official, you'll agree. I did go through a ludicrous phase when I really thought that the fight against illiteracy, international exhibitions, the United Nations and its sub-organizations, were Good Things: you know, the Cause we all hanker for, because we haven't kept up with Change, which has buried all the Causes under Corpses. But I soon saw all that was abstraction, generalization. So now I'm back at believing in minute particulars. . . .' He looked round seeming to take in every object, then he took a swig straight out of the

bottle, and grabbed at the waitress, with a paw-like hand.
'Wine, smoke, sweat, flesh, blood, sex, corpses—I've
come full circle.'

'We'd better go,' said Alex. He stood up. Rather to
his surprise, Olim stood up too.

'Why don't you join us? Why don't you have fun?'
asked the dark-haired G.I.

'Because I'm a prefect,' said Olim, 'and my friend
here's a prefect too. We have to get up early and go to a
prefects' meeting.'

'Come with us. Help us finish another bottle,' shouted
the ginger one.

In the street, Olim looked back at the shut door of
the bar, and said: 'All the same, it might have been
wiser to follow them to the end of their night.'

As they went under the arcade leading into the piazza,
they heard the voice of a youth calling 'Gondola! Gondola!' 'There you are,' said Alex, 'for you and Signorina
Karinthy.' 'I'm not her idea, or, rather, her ideology.
But still I'll remember.' He looked at the gondolier,
who immediately started coming hopefully towards
them. He was dressed in close-fitting dark blue clothes,
and his hair jutted like the peak of a cap over his forehead. 'Gondola! Gondola!' he said. They explained that
they could not go out tonight. He told them he was here
every evening at the same hour.

After the cell meeting, Csongor Botor had walked by
himself for an hour along the sides of canals, over
bridges, into little piazzas, trying to recapture something that he had lost. Gazing across the great empty
square at San Marco, he heard the same voice call
'Gondola! Gondola!'

Walking shamblingly up to him, he turned towards
the boy his heavy face of unfathomable profundity.
'*Gondola! Gondola!*' the boy chirped rapidly, like a
cicada. Botor shook his head. The night. The canals,

dark passages leading into deeper darkness. Leading
under ground. The great cold space of the shadowy
Laguna. '*Troppo freddo questa notte.*' Besides, it might
rain. Lifting his head up to the sky the stars seemed
moving chips of misty light. The boy saw what he was
thinking. 'No, no. It will not rain. Everything's changed.
The good weather will last. At least till Easter.' 'Tomorrow. I'll come back tomorrow. At the same time,'
Botor said, turning away heavily. The boy looked after
him, but did not follow. This reassured Botor. He
actually came back, walked up to the boy once more and
looked at him silently. '*Gondola! Gondola!*' the boy was
all ready, started moving in the direction of his boat.
Botor shook his head and repeated, 'Too late. Tomorrow.' Then without smiling but with a kind of im-
ploring curiosity he inquired: 'Your name?' 'My name?
Carlino. . . .' He added that he was always here, would
always take him out, was always ready, etc. 'I wanted to
have your name,' Botor said, and then with the scruple
of a poet, 'I mean, I wanted you to have a name.
Carlino,' he repeated, and this time when he had gone,
did not come back.

II

At ten the next morning the intellectuals of East and West walked up the great white marble Staircase of the Giants, in the courtyard of the Doges' Palace. Olim lingered, watching them trail up the steps. From below, he got a perspective in which the drab coats and macintoshes, the faces like bunions, the limbs like carrots, of the intellectuals were silhouetted against the thighs and stomachs, strong yet reposeful, of helmeted Mars, and of Neptune, whose curled marble beard seemed blown to one side by a chiselling wind. The dim procession of macintoshed moderns with the marble figures towering above them, looked as though they were going to enter a hall where the Past had set up an inquisition to examine why they dressed as they did, looked as they did, thought as they did.

At the top of the stairs, in the gallery under the arcade, he turned and looked down at the back of Mars, weather-stained, with apple buttocks separate-looking from the rest of the figure, streaked and pale as the milk-white silky testicles of the bull that raped Europa.

Then, looking up from below, he saw—a last-comer again—Csongor Botor. Botor's long, untidy hair had been shoved distraughtly, rather than brushed to one side across his head. At first Olim thought it was this, together with the deep incised lines of his forehead, which gave him—in such contrast with the other intellectuals—the look of the Neptune above, with beard hewn sideways. Then, following the direction of his eyes, he saw that Botor was looking at the Neptune—

with that gaze which was like an inhalation, a great, deep inbreathing of the sight.

The reunion was in a room not open to the public. Dark, it contained a dull, stained magistrates' bench under a vast painting of armoured warriors leaning on spears in company of naked gods and goddesses. They surrounded two helmeted leaders, ceremoniously clasping hands. Called the Reconciliation, this allegory celebrated a peaceable meeting of Byzantines and Venetians.

The room, perhaps at one time a place where penalties were imposed, seemed something intermediate between the most splendid chambers and the worst dungeons.

In poses that scarcely rivalled the indolent heroes in the mural, the intellectuals stood around, looking at one another. Each recognized in some other a face of intellectual power, genius even, but not youth or novelty. The youngest delegate must have been nearer forty than thirty. The unstated qualification for being here was familiarity with the terms of a debate which had gone on for the past twenty-five years, about the ideas of the Left. There was something about the assembly of an Old Boys' meeting of seminarists, who had passed a lifetime finding and losing their faiths, of 'clerks' who hovered for ever on the controversial verge dividing loyalty from betrayal. They seemed a much fingered greasy pack of cards, with Sarret's squat figure, faces at both ends, king of trumps.

Apart from the ideas involved, the nagging altercations, there was curiosity about those who were not there, colleagues shot down escaping or who had joined some side everyone agreed to be worse than the several shades of rightness and wrongness that qualified each here.

Yet perhaps what seduced the Westerners most of all was that which they least admitted: an insatiable curiosity about what was happening 'over there'. There was

a great dish, and what hid it was not so much an iron
curtain as a silver cover. Under this, they knew there to
be a course consisting of the irresistible historic mixed
grill: revolution, murder, personal power, oppression,
and a sauce of reform. The steam of gossip shooting out
on all sides was sanctified: every rumour a specimen,
sniffed over, analysed, and metamorphosed into abstractions that could be measured against other abstractions.

So in spite of everything that had happened, the
Russian delegates still had the aura of a priesthood not
wholly discredited. The grey fatigue of Pobedin's face
looked mysterious, Korovin's expression of retarded
puberty ardent, whilst the ebullient Pomyalov combined the audacity of a bandit with the authority of a
somewhat sinister policeman, and the jollity of a gypsy.

To open the proceedings, an educative Minister,
specially imported to welcome intellectuals, made a
speech. Rincontro—for that was his appropriate name—
had an oval, wide-open face, swept somewhat bare by
public virtues, but nevertheless garnished with some
amiable Italian trimmings. He spoke of Venice as a
symbol of East-West union—and in the scrolled Italian
tongue scooped out by curving flourishes of his fat little
hands—he seemed to hew words in commemorative
lettering based on some fine Renaissance calligraphy.

*Venetia extends her welcome to the delegates of Eastern
and Western worlds—and in doing so she, the jewel on the
shoulder of the Adriatic sleeve, finds nothing unfamiliar—
for her rôle has ever been the union of Latinium and
Byzantium.*

*In her, East and West have been transformed within the
exalted synthesis of Art—and Intellect is not foreign to her
either—the very stones of this palace and every pillar and
column of St. Mark's celebrate such an union.*

*To make the earliest mosaics which in their primitive
abstract gold stiffness adorn the Baptistry, artists were*

brought from Byzantium; and to each Byzantine were attached two young Venetians who soon learned from the East that skill which became a new form of expression for the West—

He had raised his hands as though releasing pigeons; and indeed his theme almost flew out of the window, across the courtyard to the Duomo, and back several hundred years. Then he had a gesture of revolving his outstretched hand as though to call the fliers back into the room, and he resolved twelfth-century Byzantines and Venetians into a metaphor of our times. It creaked rather, Olim thought.

EUROPLUME, which has its seat in Venice, has brought here in this great conference of the intellectuals representatives of the two parts of our divided world, who will sit together at this table, making their mosaic—the picture of a world where ideas meet and dwelt together in harmony. I, a Venetian, sitting at this table, will listen to their ideas and hope to learn their skill so that Venice may become the image-creating centre of unison in a divided century.

He raised his arms in a salutation, a blessing, almost episcopal. The ingratiated applause had scarcely died down than Bonvolio jumped up, eyes shining behind shining spectacles. Here was a man with a mission. They had been brought here—he left no doubt—to be converted to the Bonvolio Doctrine, or the Instrument of EUROPLUME.

Bonvolio knew he was dealing with logicians, so he surrounded the centre of his thought with an elaborate carven gilded frame of logic, bristling with 'preciselys' and 'concretelys'.

'I wish to make clear very precisely and in the most concrete way possible,' he began, 'that our programme here is to have no programme. Certain of you may have objection to this programme—or, you may say, this lack of programme. But the aim of this meeting is, simply and exactly, to arrange another meeting. And for the purpose of that other meeting what we have to discuss is whether we can meet and, if so, precisely what discuss. In order to discover this, it seems best that we should examine ideas of a general order, to discover what grounds we may have of agreement, or, if I may so put it, of our agreement to disagree.

'What I am laying before you now, is, if I may use the expression, the Philosophy of EUROPLUME, which is in turn, if I may be personal, my own philosophy, *Bonvolismus*, for like our friend M. Sarret, who is here among us, I feel entitled to a philosophy. *Bonvolismus* or the philosophy of EUROPLUME, is that whoever meets within the terms of EUROPLUME does, precisely, agree to meet. Therefore each one of us represents this agreeing to meet more than any other cause which might possibly imply disagreement. Everyone here accepts the Concept of the Dialogue.'

Waving his arms and jerking his head occasionally to take a rapid glance at his prospective critics, Sarret, Marteau, and Sereno, Bonvolio looked not unlike the conductor of an orchestra. Nor would this metaphor have struck him as less than apt. For was he not conducting the International Symphony of Harmonious Cultures? His nod in the direction of Sarret or Marteau or Korovin was that of the conductor who encourages a drum here or suppresses a piccolo there. He now burst into his coda:

'Because we are as VOICES within the HARMONY of EUROPLUME, we enter into another, a transcendent kind of politics—what I call Secondary Politics—the politics of the man of culture, defending his position as man of culture—against every other kind of politics, against precisely what I term Primary and External Politics. He may well make alliances with External or

Primary Politics but only for the sake of the Secondary and Interior Politics of Culture.'

He went redder than those unaccustomed to him would have thought possible, waved his arms still more, and started shouting at the top of his voice:

'Precisely for the reasons I have given, the Intellectual, the Man of Letters, has to be IN public life, IN politics, the politics that are FOR or AGAINST us. In my Thought the Non-Political has no meaning. Today, I say, it is the first duty of every intellectual to be PUBLIC. Everything else comes after that, because everything else depends on it!'

There was a hush. The Russians, to whom all this was translated by Magda Karinthy, gazed ahead of them non-committally. Across the table they had a remote staring air, like a range of mountains viewed from a distance. Alex Merton looked intently down at a sheet of paper on which he had done a miniscular drawing. Dunstan Curlew's head seemed weighed down under the burden of confusion actually penetrating his brain cells and causing him physical pain, Sereno's face expressed the nothing which was a very great deal, the other Italians looked as if, brought up on Croce, they were able to cope with this kind of thing. Csongor Botor appeared to be cutting his initials in the table with a pen. Borès, the most earnest of the French delegates, had reduced Bonvolio's thoughts to two neat columns of notes.

Sarret turned to Marteau and appeared to utter what looked like an exclamation of wordless astonishment enclosed in a bubble of air that floated, outlined in light, to the ceiling. Marteau laughed and whispered '*Chut!*'

Then Sereno heaved a sigh which seemed to convey that since no one else would undertake the task, he must begin constructing foundations on which to build from bricks that Bonvolio had let fall. 'We are certainly very recognisant—recognisant,' he repeated, 'of the Chairman's suggestion that there should be no fixed programme—' With a movement suggestive of deftly picking up a brick, he went on: 'I myself appreciate fully the importance of giving a good deal of time to exchanging theoretical points of view, because there has been a rift, yes, a rift. In consequence of the separation which has lasted so many years we might well discover that we are using the same terms and applying the same concepts with an entirely different meaning, according to whether we come from East or West.'

He stared rather heavily across the table, including them all at the end of his intervention in a glance that said: 'Put up with this folly, so that we may now come to the real subject of debate.'

Here he paused, and seemed even to have finished, but just as Bores raised a finger like a pencil preparatory to making some minute tick or underlining, Sereno uttered the single word 'Thaw'—'dégèle'. 'What we most want to hear from *Them*, our Soviet friends, is the effect on their lives, as writers, of the Thaw, if this term is recognized by them.' When he finished, his eyes seemed to become detached from the words he was using, as though they looked across them to the reaction that one phrase—the Thaw—produced.

He fell silent, looking up at the ceiling.

Borès jabbed the air again, and took up his notes. The appeal to be practical had not, in his case, fallen on deaf ears. He had taken the journey to Congresses on a couple of books on the Resistance in the Mountains, and a great many articles. He still had the narrow-scale eagle glance of the Guide, and, if one was romantic, one could imagine him throwing all this stuffy air up and going back to his hills. His constructive rôle was to show the way up peaks indicated by Bonvolio, who said: 'Excelsior!' What was necessary, Borès ardently said, was 'to define our terms.

Unless we know what we are talking about, we shall not know what we are talking about. To begin with, we ought to know what we mean by the word Culture. If we define our terms we shall measure the gulf between us, and perhaps, throw across it a rope.'

To be practical or not to be practical; to define or not to define; to use terms or not to use them; to have a programme or to have none.

The Russians began to show signs of discontent. There was an apprehensive feeling that they thought all this talk Western decadence. There was a stirring among them, like breezes moving in boughs of pine trees. They talked with one another in low voices, occasionally studying reports on the progress of the discussion handed to them by Magda Karinthy. Finally, after the third or fourth intervention by Borès, Pobedin put up his hand, and produced an attentive silence. Leaning forward, and gazing across the table as though he were the first of them to sight the Grail, he spoke earnestly and slowly, pausing at the end of each sentence to let Magda Karinthy interpret his words. Pobedin said that he and his colleagues believed in cultural exchanges, exchanges of points of view, exchanges of personalities, exchanges of works, 'in every possible manner and way'. Nowhere would such exchanges be undertaken more favourably than in Venice which, if not the mother, was at any rate the elder sister of European culture. 'Culture,' he said impressively, 'leads to communion between men and to mutual respect between man and society.'

Sereno gazed at Pobedin's distinguished grey head of hair, his expressive eyes in his totally inexpressive face, contemplating this Lazarus come back from the dead of Stalin, to say with a sepulchral solemnity: *Culture leads to communion between men and to mutual respect between man and society.*

Bonvolio was ecstatic. M. Pobedin's definition of culture—which, indeed, he repeated—was his own thought expressed with a happiness to which he could not aspire. 'We are all of us agreed then'—he cried rapturously 'to integrate Pobedin's meaning with that of the rest of the meeting—that culture means communication. But if we are to know what we are communicating, we must understand our means of communication. Concepts, categories, backgrounds, histories, beliefs, philosophies, theories—all these we must establish in their East-West relation,' he exclaimed, raising an arm as though pouring prodigious fruits from a cornucopia.

'Surely,' Alex Merton protested urbanely, 'desirable as it may be to relate so many different terms, we ought also to eliminate. We need a clearing house as well as a Bourse.'

'What terms does Mr. Merton think should be disposed of?' Bonvolio leaning forward in his chair with a ferocious expression, positively shouted.

'Well, let me explain. Terms, I should say, that are used by each side in exactly opposite senses. Well, let us take instances—Peace, Liberty, Democracy.'

Then, appalled at the silence his words had produced, Alex went on: 'Lists, lists, that's what we want. Lists of books that you know and we don't, that you don't, and we do. Names of writers you'd like us to send over for you to meet, books you'd like to read.'

He leaned back, lolling one arm idly over a chair, and smiled pleasantly, humorously, at Bonvolio.

'Mr. Alex Merton flatters us over here if he imagines that we have any knowledge of names he might suggest to us,' said Botor.

'Just so, just so, that's why I made the proposal. Lists, I repeat, that's what we want, to draw up lists of what you think important and I think important and show them to one another.'

Csongor Botor ignored this. He looked not at Alex

Merton but at Olim Asphalt and said in a loud harsh guttural tone of voice: 'We know nothing of one another. We have forgotten one another—we have been separated by a gulf not of time nor space but of ignorance. We suppose this time means nothing to you, living in your world where *plus ça change plus c'est la même chose*'—he emphasized the French with an altogether over-weighted, quite embarrassing irony—'I can assure you it has been eternity for us. However, if we do meet here, we meet as men, as human beings. We cannot and should not avoid using words that appeal to man: least of all, the beautiful word PEACE.'

At that he flung down the pencil with which he had, while he spoke, been doodling, and directed towards the Russians a glance transparent in devotion. They did not look back at him.

For the rest of the morning they went on discussing whether or not they should use terms knowing or not knowing what they meant by them; and whether they should devote themselves to principles or what they called 'concretizations'. Bonvolio summed up the morning's labours by saying that their disagreements were what he called Secondary and did not matter, because the purpose of the meeting, on which they all agreed, was to discuss what they could discuss, and precisely and exactly, this is what they had been doing.

III

That afternoon, when they had returned from luncheon (in order that there should be no escapes, the
politically-conscious organizers arranged that all meals
should be held in the Hotel Stella private room, at the
great round table), there was a feeling that the pro-
fessionals must weigh in. Perhaps someone had 'spoken
to' Bonvolio during the interval, because he said nothing
whatever, opening the meeting with a nod to Marteau.

Marteau's very appearance transformed the atmosphere from the weighted inwardness of Bonvolio-
directed programme music, to cracking outdoor painter-
liness.

He was a speaker who combined eloquence with a
kind of public intimacy. He seemed always to talk person
to person. Now, he was demonstrating how he could
avoid some obstacle. Now, he was making a glancing
aside that caught the listener like a smile straight to the
eyes. Now, he was asking a question which, though the
reply was indicated, flattered the other's assumed ability
to make it.

For Marteau, speaking was a demonstration using
every aid and instrument: scalpel, operating table,
brushes, lantern slides. He began clearing away with a
movement of his hands, pushing the morning's rubbish
resolutely, gently aside. 'I listened this morning to what
was said with the greatest interest, but am I right in
thinking that something essential was left out of the
discussion?'

Then, permitting one object of discussion to remain,
to be looked back at and examined: 'Our good friend
Sereno certainly introduced what ought to be the main
topic of discussion—the Thaw. But—' here he turned
and addressed a smile to a blank wall with two eyes
painted on it—Sereno's face—'you made a statement
when perhaps you should have asked Them'—pointing
to the Russians as to triplet Ural peaks—'a question.
Do they accept this term *Thaw*? And if you asked them
that—might not They put the question back to you—
what about *your* Thaw? Doesn't the idea of the Thaw
apply to both sides? Doesn't it imply the need of a
change of position for both?'

He pushed back his chair now and began, like Des-
cartes, or Pythagoras, or someone of the kind, to demonstrate that piece of geometry which he called the Thaw.
The tubular form of Sarret was all alert, with bulging
eyes fixed on Marteau's face, and a look as if ticking
machinery of a bomb inside him was getting ready to
detonate. The Russians watched these goings-on with a
mild dazed interest, as at the performances of unnecessary seals.

But first of all, before drawing the neat lines of an
abstraction completely worked out, Marteau proceeded
to make a brief historic exposé.

There was—there had been—a long time ago—before
the Russian Revolution—Marxism—different from
Stalinism. Now Marxism allowed the artist or writer
considerable freedom within that system of ideas which
explained and determined the rôles of almost every
activity within society. Did not Marx have a conception
of Greek art which exalted it almost to the sphere of
absolute values?

(They saw statues, they saw vases, absolute forms, on
which a profile, a nude, a wing, shook lines with lines of
Picasso.)

And in the early stages of the Revolution, Lenin had given considerable freedom to poets.

(Alexander Blok was allowed to trail through Leningrad twelve Red Army soldiers who turned out to be led by Christ. Mayakowsky was allowed a peep at a cloud that wore blue trousers.)

What happened in the period called Stalinism? Marteau put aside the colours and took up his scalpel. He extracted an abstract formula from a million corpses.

An external rule, dictated by what its leaders conceived to be the necessities of the State, was imposed on art and invaded the interior activity of each writer.

Good. Accepting this principle, now let us look at the results. Poor little Soviet poet, subject of Stalin, member of the Union of Soviet Writers, criticized in *Life and Culture*, *Red Star*, and *Pravda*, ordered about by Zhdanov, six suicides behind him, his best friends sent to Labour camps: *'Shall I, when I witness suffering all round me, reveal the truth of this suffering which is so striking to me that it has become my own interior truth, or shall I, out of recognition of the external needs of society (which are the component parts in the construction of a better world), deny this truth?'*

Stalinism. The total pressure brought on the artist to deny his interior truth in the interests of the construction of the better society. How inviting!

His argument sped easily, delightfully across crisp blue waters. The course he took was held in his eyes, on each side of his nose, strong and buoyant as a figurehead, above the mouth lifted to meet the waves. There were splashings, breaking white foam, sparkling asides. He never lost the pleasure of his mental journey.

Marteau was overjoyed with the intellectual clarity with which he used concepts to depict a vivid scene full of murders, imprisonments, deportations, thrust upon a whole population, accompanied by the demand that no one with eyes to see or ears to hear should say what he saw or heard, because to do so would be to make things more difficult for the tyrant, whose declared aim was to improve conditions and make a better world.

(*But the air was becoming thick with the ghosts of the murdered and the suicides, those removed by the intellectual premises of Stalin. Sereno appeared to be staring at these ghosts. The Russians did not see them, because they were several pages behind in following Magda Karinthy's translation. Sarret did not see them, because he was occupied with thinking out the arguments which he was shortly to produce in answer to Marteau.*)

Although Marteau believed oppression to be wrong he did not appear to doubt for one moment the good will or honest intent of the tyrant. And the reason he did not doubt these was because, for the purposes of the argument itself he had to treat murder as an abstraction.

If the tyrant were simply a tyrant then there would be no delightfully clear-cut sides to oppose one another in argument. The argument could only develop if you granted the tyrant a philosophy and you were prepared to treat murder intellectually not as murder, but as a system of thought. The tyrant murdered suspects without trial, sent workers into slave camps, liquidated peasants, and demanded that no one should mention these items on his political programme, all because he was working out in action what Marteau considered to be a purely intellectual hypothesis: that the general good was served by these logically inevitable methods and must not therefore be challenged by the particular corpse.

For the purposes of arguing, Marteau accepted this hypothesis, suggesting that what we were witnessing today was a slight modification of the original premises. The particular and private truth of the artist who happened to notice that people did not like being murdered in the service of an abstract concept of Necessity, was

now being gradually reintroduced into the argument of
the State. There was a possibility that it could even be
reconciled at some point with the general social good.
This was, he suggested, the concept of the Thaw. In
view of which, he said, he would like to put a question to
their Soviet colleagues; and turning towards them, he
inquired with all the force of his charm: 'Would I be
correct in assuming that the philosophical meaning of
the Thaw is that, as a result of it, today *the autonomy of
the inner rules of Art have been reasserted within the single
work*? That is the question I would like Them to
answer.'

This question produced a great rustling of papers,
and baffled looks, among the Russians, It seemed to have
fallen among steam rollers. Pobedin looked harassed,
and Korovin like a schoolboy trying to follow some visiting dignitary's strange idiom. Pomyalov, for some
reason, seemed extraordinarily amused. Magda Karinthy was occupied in passing papers on which she had
scrawled sentences, to Pobedin. But with a gesture of
his hand he let Marteau's question pass.

Marteau now introduced into his argument a new
concept, that of universals. If it was true that the neces-
sity-dominated benevolent central government no longer
imposed a self-denying ordinance on Russian writers,
and that the voice of the individual with his private truth
could again be heard, then such truths would sometimes
coincide with those of individuals in Western countries.

The world, in effect, was indeed divided into two
seemingly irreconcilable camps, but certain truths were
probably beginning to be admitted by both sides. He
pictured them as escaping from the context of one ideology and entering into that of the other, to discover
themselves, apparently much to their surprise, accepted
by both. Olim saw a no-man's-land between two irreconcilable armies. By night two times two equals four

escapes from East to West, or from West to East, to discover itself accepted on the same terms by Marteau and Sarret on one side, the Union of Soviet Writers on the other. Beauty is truth, truth beauty, was receiving a more dubious reception in the East, when Olim awoke to discover that Marteau was entering on what seemed to be a peroration. In this he introduced an entirely new concept—that of Engagement. For just as a conjurer producing a scarf or handkerchief from his pocket reveals that it was really a bowl of goldfish or a bunch of flowers, it turned out that all the time, really, Marteau had been leading towards Engagement. Did Engagement mean that the writer's duty lay in the direction of telling the truth about what he saw, or of carrying out governmental instructions which were component parts of a better future? That was another question for 'our Soviet friends' to answer.

Bonvolio was suffering enormously, could contain himself no longer. As if choking, he cried out that after the speech they had just heard, he felt the need to clarify, to develop, to carry if need be one stage further, his own Thought. Marteau watched him with that attractive, impertinent smile which made two hollows in his cheeks, like a boy's dimples.

'Buzz, buzz, buzz.' This graceless interruption, said most gracefully, came from Alex Merton. 'Bees, bees,' it resolved itself into. 'Much too much has been said to suggest that we are all agreed that literature has to be political. Is it true? Every work does not have to take sides or even attain universality by flitting from one side to the other, in and out of different camps. For instance, the bee-loud grove and I will have a hive there, and I will have some honey, or whatever that is—'

Olim, though not allowed to speak, knew all the arguments about the literature of bees. It could encourage interest in agriculture, the production of honey; alternatively, it could be reactionary, in upholding the nostalgia of pastoral as against industrial life. Orthodox priests, in Eastern Europe, often kept bees.

Just then Dunstan Curlew's great head started swaying to and fro like a pendulum. It was supported by his hands being held over his ears and pressed so close that they were a hub on which the head rocked like a cradle. At the same time he gave forth a great soft howl which, when Olim looked anxiously in his direction, translated itself into, ' I've never before in my life been to a meeting like this.' Bonvolio, huffed, called upon the scientist to make a 'constructive contribution'. ' I hesitate to do so, not being a literary man,' was Dunstan Curlew's excuse. Pressed, he doubted whether a mere nuclear physicist could contribute to such a poetic discussion. Well, perhaps he would speak: 'Sometimes the nonexpert can shed light on subjects of which he knows little or nothing.' To begin with, he had to say that he thought these questionings about the social function of writers were made largely irrelevant by the state of modern knowledge. This observation opened into a kind of prelude: a terribly simple introduction to Marxist theory mixed with some scientific substance (heavy water?) to drive out all objections.

Man moves in society.

Man always has moved in society.

Man is a social force in society.

Man always has been a social force in society.

The difference between man in the past and man today is that in the past man was unaware of himself as a social force. Today he is aware of himself as a social force.

Therefore he has no excuse for not being aware of himself as a social force.

And this blessed state of consciousness is thanks to Karl Marx.

Amen.

The self-satisfied smile of one mounting his earliest
hobby horse, and finding that it still could trot, spread
over Curlew's face, as he broadened his discourse to
include theology. For he had begun as a seminarist, and
it gave him subtle titillation to fuse the dogmas of his
Jesuit training, purged of superstition, with the dogmas
of dialectical materialism. 'Theologians distinguish between absolute ignorance of something vitally important
that you have no means of knowing, and wilful ignorance, of that which you could know if you did not will
not to do so.' Curlew's face had a complacent smile that
showed his extreme satisfaction at hearing his lecturer's
voice purring through his body, like a well-running
engine. 'In the future there will be no such thing as
absolute ignorance of social and political responsibility.
Every writer will be conscious of whether he is moving
for or against the progressive development of history.
But today we cannot be said to have attained that state of
total permeation of consciousness of our historic duty.
There is quite a lot of absolute ignorance still hanging
around. All the same, we can be sure already that the
idea of complete individual freedom is false, because we
have knowledge of living within conflicting social forces,
and therefore to refuse to act upon that knowledge is
irresponsible. Our duty is to associate ourselves with the
progressive forces working towards social good. . . .'
Everything appeared to Curlew extremely simple. The
only things that prevented the future immediately re-
replacing the past and present, like new and better
machines superseding old and bad ones, were human
blindness to scientific opportunities, and the surprising
difficulty of organizing human beings for the better
world. The latter could be corrected, however, by minor
adjustments. He had a kind word for the victims of
Stalin: 'In future we should not allow the State to under-
mine Society,' he said, looking serious as a headmaster.

This formula disposed of the errors of the past thirty years.

Ghosts. Visions. Words. Words. Words. Filled the room like the bees in the bee-loud glade. *Nine bean-rows will I have there.* Olim wrote on the sheet of paper he was using for his notes. The ghosts of the murdered were as present as the figures of gods and goddesses, princes and warriors, in the Reconciliation. He saw them. Sereno saw nothing but them. Who else? Csongor Botor wore an expression of ironic boredom which did not preclude ghosts. The Russians took them for granted as part of the ectoplasm of ideology. They had existed once, then they had been wished away, now they were being conjured back again out of the air by a suety little magician. It was interesting that one was oneself alive, that was all that mattered.

There was the faintest discernible uneasiness about Curlew, as though the shadow of a doubt had crossed his mind. The scientist does not believe in ghosts. There are only fantasies, and these he was smothering in what is permitted, the Science Fiction view of the Future. A Grail, he was occupied now in attacking poets for their purity, he was occupied now in attacking poets for their lack of vision: 'The reason why, as a scientist, I feel contemporary literature is the work of lesser artists and *petits maîtres*, is that poets show absolutely no awareness of a Future which opens the most wonderful prospects in history for benefiting mankind, through science. We may say, that if the world's resources were not wasted on armies and armaments, for the first time in history it would be possible to envisage all humanity benefiting without the necessity of revolution or wars.' Letting himself rip, he began to describe the inventions which could change the lot of all mankind. Instead of wasteful, damp, uneconomical houses, over-cold in winter, and over-hot in summer, unadapted to the physical movements of those who occupied them, science could perfect machines for living in, with rooms of perfect dimensions, walls of perfect thickness, temperatures of perfect equability, air of ever-renewed freshness, material of perpetual resilience—all attained by the experimental method of building several different types of dwelling, putting into them average families, and then measuring the needs and reactions of these by concealed instruments. Such houses, made mostly out of slag and rubble, would be cheap and easy to build. It was quite possible to conceive that within a generation the whole of humanity would be housed in ideal dwellings constructed from the rubble of past wasteful, ruinous, unhygienic ones. Wishing doubtless to light a flame which would inspire poets to less miserable flights, he went on to envisage improvements which could be made in communications —waterways, shipping, and aviation. Beyond the transformation of the means of living he foresaw nothing less than the improvement of the human race itself, by a cocktail mixture of hygiene, birth control, and eugenics. And standing on a pedestal, in his mind's eye dwelt an image of a woman bred part-organically, part-mechanically; tall and strong, incapable of reproduction, without feelings, but lubriciously satisfying every response psychology and physiology could, through their exhaustive researches, discover in the most exacting male.

When Curlew stopped speaking, the writers for at least ten seconds saw themselves as grubbily dwarfed under the towering and flying future as they had been by the past, when earlier in the day they had walked up the Steps of the Giants, past the figures of Mars and Neptune. The cloud passed.

During the murmuring pause that followed Curlew's speech, Olim said to Alex: 'He seems to have left out Science Fiction.' 'Leapt out of Science Fiction, did you say?' said Alex, playing at misunderstanding—'He—a

real scientist? He couldn't be!' 'That's where we really
are rather decadent,' said Olim. 'They nearly all think
like he does; that the world should be their laboratory.
Just think of the things they say! Just think of the
women they like!'

It was time now for the writers to play the Ace of
Trumps, Sarret. Everyone seemed aware of this, and all
eyes were turned to him, where he sat looking not unlike
a diver, with the lenses of his glasses distorting his eyes
so much that they, rather than his spectacles, looked like
goggles. By now the room had become so much the
malleable material of the speeches that took place in it,
that when he spoke it was as though the smoky, waver-
ing atmosphere was the water inside an immense tank
through which he sank, with boots that had soles of lead,
and with a chain of bubbles rising from the top of his
helmet. He had jumped in at a point which brought him,
on the table or floor, metaphorically speaking, beside
Marteau. He was back at their current subject of
altercation—the Thaw (and, indeed, for Marteau and
Sarret, Venice was only the extension of a Parisian
café).

'Marteau,' he rapped out, in his sharp, croaking voice,
'Marteau spoke of the philosophy of the Thaw. He
applied, it seems to me, his systematization in a very
partial manner. The Thaw—he indicated—was pre-
eminently something that happened to Them, to that
half of humanity which is Communist. True, he said he
wanted Them to help us correct our picture of Their
thaw—but he seems to have missed what I believe to be
the essential thing, that it is as impossible for Us truly to
thaw as it is for Them to thaw.'

On this he paused, looking at Marteau, who looked
back at him, pencil raised in air, excluding everyone else.
Marteau knew, of course, his offence. He had tried to let
some air into Sarret's airtight theory: his faith that each

person, isolated within the environment to which he
belonged, lives completely conditioned in all his thinking and feeling—every fibre of his being—by that conditioning. The division of the world into communist and
non-communist, the bourgeois and the proletarian interest—ideologies that could never enter into one
another's ideology—was a perpetual stimulus to Sarret's
powerful intellectual imagination. What was particularly inspiring about it was that, although himself a
totally conditioned self-condemned bourgeois, he believed that the communist cause—the one he could not
enter into, the one that spelled annihilation to his consciousness—was indisputably 'correct'. He condemned
every idea in himself and others that was critical of the
communist ideology as being bourgeois, and the secret
he shared with Marteau was the understanding that
whatever polemical attack he made on his colleagues
was *really intended as condemnation of himself*. Thus his
intellectual life was based on the extraordinary feat of
entering into points of view which, by his own definition, it was impossible for a person with his background
to enter. This gave him great confidence in his own
exceptional genius, and a peculiar excitement that was
almost metaphysical: for he had converted his own
materialist philosophy into a belief that he himself lived
by a miracle of self-condemnatory analysis. Marteau
realized all this. Their loving attacks on one another
were like a hate affair between Siamese twins.

'Everything that has been said so far demonstrates,'
Sarret reiterated, 'that it is as impossible for Us to
Thaw in a way which enables us to understand Them as
it is for Them to Thaw in a way which enables Them to
understand Us.'

'And if you ask me why this is so, the reason is very
simple,' he exclaimed, with enormous pleasure, as if he
had gone through a tunnel and arrived at an enchanting

point of view—his own. 'The reason is that we have a Bourgeois ideology, they have a Communist one. It is therefore quite wrong to speak, as Marteau does, of universals that can pass from one camp into the other. They could only do so if they were transformed into the terms of the other. Everything They say comes from within the context of THEIR ideology, just as everything WE say comes out of OURS. The two points of view do not conflict even. They move in opposite directions along parallel lines.'

The only exception to the rule of non-meeting was, it appeared, Sarret himself, who could, at moments, become de-bourgeoisified. He became autobiographical: 'I find that—just occasionally—by an act of the will, and perhaps of the imagination—I can—for a few seconds—enter into the context of Their thinking—which is totally alien to mine—about some specific idea. When I achieve this imaginative effort of transposing myself into the other camp, then, in my view, I am making an act of Engagement. Engagement is, for me, the momentary de-bourgeoisifying of myself.'

He jumped up and down in his chair, jerking his hands. In spite of his rasping voice, there was a kind of gaiety about his polemics, a certain warmth which made his logic and even his pessimism attractive.

The impetus of his own speech carried him through to what he called 'the very furthest point of the problem of culture'. What everyone else had 'missed', was that 'Each culture is also an ideology'. The fact that no one else had mentioned this proved to Sarret that it must be true. Everyone else was so enclosed in ideology that he did not remark on it, any more than a fish (and Sarret really looked more than ever at the bottom of a tank) was likely to comment on the water it swam in.

Sarret was never so happy as when attacking those whose position he identified with his own. And now,

with a jabbing finger, he pointed '*j'accuse*'-ingly at his
fellow delegates from the West: 'You,' he said, 'You
. . . all your ideas, all your activities, all your creation,
all your appreciation, all your ways of seeing and listening and witnessing are permeated with your own self-
interest, conditioned by the ideology that surrounds you,
just as much as those of the East are conditioned by
Soviet ideology. But whereas your conditioning leads to
nothing but the extension of your illusion of bourgeois
freedom, theirs is a component part of the advances made
by a socialist society. So what we should seek is a discussion of their ideas, with them, in the context of their
Marxist ideology. We should examine how far we can
understand these, while making allowance for the context of our bourgeois ideology.'

With pieces of paper on which they wrote notes
shuffled from one to another, with scratched heads and
scratching pens, the Russians tried to follow the Master's
justification of the water in which they swam. Finally
they seemed to abandon the endeavour, withdrawing
under rocks in their tank of ideological incomprehen-
sibility.

Of course, the fact that the Russians understood
nothing of what he was saying, did not trouble Sarret in
the least. Indeed, it proved that which he wished to
demonstrate: that he, a bourgeois, was incomprehensible to them, brought up within the context of the proletarian ideology. They need not do anything except
fail to understand, to show that they agreed with him.

Everyone, indeed, gave up the attempt to follow Sarret, chasing like an electric hare through the room,
except Marteau, to whom, in truth, Sarret's remarks
were addressed. *Ideological Unapproachabilities* was a
parlour game the two of them played, and now it was as
though they had taken over the table, across which they
shoved their counters and their counter-counters. Mar-

teau denied that he had denied that there is opposition between ideologies. 'Ah! Aha! But you did mention the little matter of Universalities which passed from one camp to the other?' croaked Sarret. 'I spoke of Universality to describe Universality. For example, you yourself are speaking "universally" when you speak of the conflict of ideologies: this is an account of the current state of affairs which would be accepted by both sides.' 'Ah! Ah-ha! That is because I am a little bourgeois who entertains the bourgeois idea of diversity.' He burst into self-mocking laughter that mocked them all.

So it went on. At moments it was interrupted by Bonvolio. 'You have forgotten, gentlemen, that no one here represents an ideology coming from the outside; everything in this room is subsumed within the ideology of the Dialogue, the philosophy of EUROPLUME. EUROPLUME is precisely and concretely, a BRIDGE, not a GULF. There are no communists here, and no anti-communists, gentlemen, I implore you to remember this.'

But they went on and on, now not so much playing tiddlywinks or draughts, as running down the table, which had become a field, and passing the ball from one to the other. Their ideas changed from being words, into paintings, nature even, the misunderstandings of the Urals with the Alps. They discussed whether Marx was not a universal: a bourgeois reading Marx was surely entering into communist ideology. Marteau, who had baffled Sarret with this, followed up quickly with Freud. Ah, but Freud was a clear example, said Sarret, of what he meant: he could be integrated perhaps into communism, but not simply transported. . . . At this point, to Olim's vaguely translating ear, they seemed to be making speeches in blank verse—minor lords wagging their beards against flat scenery, in an Elizabethan historic play.

Marteau

In order that Freud should be integrated
First he must be comprehended; not
Devalued with a single catch-phrase as
—Ideologically bourgeois.

Sarret

But Freud *is* bourgeois. That's a fact. And yet
He could be liberated from the bourgeoisie
And integrated into Marxism.
Now bourgeois, by its limits and negations,
Psychoanalysis could be finally freed
If it were subsumed into a totality.

Marteau

That would be transubstantiation.
In any case, you have to recognize
That Freud, though bourgeois, hit on something
Beyond theories or ideologies.

Sarret

Anyone can discover similarities
Of detail in opposing ideologies:
But if one such should pass into another
It has to be absorbed and integrated.
And as I've found, speaking with Communists,
This should present no final difficulty
Provided details fit their Marxist context.

Marteau

Everything's possible in conversation!
For years we've talked with Communists
Intelligent and frank in conversation.
But when it comes to other things, to actions,
Oh, how the situation changes!

Sarret

All I demand of us is this—
Instead of aiming at some coexistence
Fitting in one piece here, and there another,
As my friend Marteau seems to ask of me,
We must admit one coexistence only:
A movement of dynamic integration.

The carafe on the table in front of Olim suddenly
resolved itself into chains of criss-crossing diagonal lines,
moving in opposing directions, ovoid, and cojoining at
neck and base. Diamond shapes dazzled light emanating
from its core of water. The carafe became a vision with
centre and circumference, immensely complex, utterly
simple, revealing, and yet tactfully withholding, innumerable reflected lights, faint shadows, conforming
lines, minnow-like dartings of rainbow colour. It related
mystically to the sloping spears, the gleaming armour,
the vessel-shaped bodies of Mars, Venus, warriors,
Venetians, Byzantines, that shone over-ripe through the
dim background, the Reconciliation, the colour of the
purplish bloom of a plum. Olim took up his pencil and
tried to draw the picture in his mind, the vision of the
secret relationship, connected by light moving through
water, of the banal modern cut-glass carafe with the
Venetian High Renaissance. The work he produced
would be abstract and dry, human in its irony. It would
make the carafe a comment on the Reconciliation, the
Reconciliation a comment on the carafe. He toyed with
the idea—which would show the influence of James
Ensor on Olim Asphalt's most recent work—that the
carafe might also be a crystal gazer's ball of glass, drawing to its centre distorted ape-like leering faces of the
conferenciers, while the dark shadow at the base suggested a catastrophe occurring in the catacombs at the
very moment when they were discussing whether they

should or should not attempt to define what they meant
by Culture and Engagement.

Bonvolio, rattled, was talking wildly. 'Gentlemen, the
Dialogue cannot be pursued if those present allow the
discussion to be canalized into debates transferred to
Venice from the *Rive Gauche*. If we go on in this way, we
will find the debate becoming a series of private conferences between dissident members of the French Left, the
Italian Nenniites and Morandini, the Gaitskellites and
the Bevanites. There are references, there are concepts,
there are names, there are topics, there are conflicts of
personalities, well known to us all in Italy and France,
but of little general interest here and perhaps altogether
unknown to our friends from the Soviet Union.' Losing
grip, he splashed around wildly. 'Let us admit—to take
a precise and exact example—that the dodecaphonic
system of musical notation does not fit into the Five
Year Plan—let us be bold and admit that—all the same
we can clearly and precisely envisage a Five Year Plan
to the accompaniment of dodecaphonic music. After all,
in Greece there was the Lydian mode, the Doric mode,
in Sparta . . .'

'. . . There were military fanfares,' commented Sereno, who had his hands folded like a church steeple in
front of his face, watchful and listening as a cliff.

'Oh yes, oh yes, there are all sorts of music! I don't
deny that! And there are all sorts of links, and connections, and disputes in politics that don't concern us
here. But let us return to the topic under discussion—
Engagement. And then'—Bonvolio broke off with a
wild inspiration—'there is censorship! Why have we
not considered censorship? Every censorship is a juridical order, and as responsible intellectuals, we can't
refuse a juridical order. So at this point,' he cried, turning triumphantly to Marteau, to Sarret, to Curlew, to
the Russians, 'I agree with you. But I don't agree with

you'—he confronted Sereno with an 'at bay' expression
—'because I think you imagine "Engagement" means
being on the side of victims—always. Now if we are
juridically responsible individuals, this can't *always* be
so. Do you ask of me that I should always be on the side
of those who are defeated?' he demanded, with pathos.
'Must I always support the weak against the strong?'
he asked tragically. 'The oppressed against the oppressors? But that is unconstructive. Constructiveness lies
with the State. The State needs Culture, and Culture
needs the State. We must not be completely pessimistic,
Signor Sereno. No, no, we must not. We must also con-
struct what, in the terminology of my Thought, I call
The Optimism of Culture.'

Engagement. Engagement. Engagement. Putting
down his pencil, and abandoning his career as post-
cubist Tachiste, Olim Asphalt had taken in the word
Engagement. Engagement. Damn their eyes. And now
infested not by their words, but by Bonvolio's excitement and the silent rhythm of the rhetoric boxed up like
an engine ticking under a bonnet in each, Olim's thoughts
posed the question—What is Engagement? Engagement, he shouted inside his own head, to himself his
audience, is, for a writer, identification of soul, heart,
mind, with conditions he witnesses, together with his
determination to record the truth about them transformed within his art.

Engagement. The body, that is the rub, because the
flesh is weak, and cannot sustain the strong spirit.
Engagement in this time is to hurl myself into battles
on the side of the lesser, against the greater evil; to be
starved with the starving, burned with the burning;
shovelled into gas ovens and sent wandering over
deserts; put in cattle trucks with the deported; driven
across borders with the refugees. Engagement is to lose
my freedom, and to find it again; to sacrifice my life

even, and yet retain my sensibility, my nerves, my art; to be a skeleton, a cinder, yet to witness and create.

Engagement! He boiled, he burned, he felt hungry and parched. For an authentic moment, he really felt engaged. (But, of course, he was just sitting here; he wasn't.) If one were engaged in writing here, for example. How could one be engaged to describe this scene, describe these shadow men sitting round this table ?

Silent, roaring with his own secret howling, not allowed by LITUNO to speak, he glowered maliciously round him. What was he looking for ? One would have to discover, one would have to invent some point of individual sensibility, one of us here, connected electrically with that world of the damned: a pure receiver of that reality. Tormented, destroyed, terrified, conscious, and in the centre of his abjectness, heroically full of creation.

The fact that Olim Asphalt was thinking these thoughts, did not prevent the discussion continuing relentlessly with occasional halts for taking on new passengers, putting baggage aboard, like the vaporetto.

Now the whole meeting appeared to be in a liquescent state of perpetual transformation. Anything might change into anything. Voices from far places began to roar in Olim Asphalt's ears. He was in telepathic communication with Elaine, and explained succinctly and comfortingly why he would never marry her. He was in the office of the Director-General, describing to him the course of the meeting. Bonvolio was like a stag bayed round by hounds. And now even Sarret and Marteau had fallen silent, exhausted. In the hush that followed, the meeting seemed to disintegrate into shuffling, whispers and drawing lessons. An old Italian poet seized the opportunity to make a speech. He adapted a famous phrase, and declared: 'Beauty, like peace, is indivisible.' This made no great impression on the meeting, which, generally, lacked reverence for the venerable and the faithful. Leonardo Longhi, a younger Italian writer, protested that Dunstan Curlew would not have made his strictures about the lack of progressive modern writing, had he read Leonardo Longhi's novels. Dunstan Curlew confessed to negligence in respect to Longhi's books, which he nevertheless 'admired at a distance', and launched forth upon a lecture on 'a neglected branch of literature—so-called Science Fiction'. For Dunstan Curlew already began to show grave symptoms of omniscience. He filled in what appeared to be a completely blank half-hour by contrasting the 'popular' literature of the communist world, with that of the West, which 'only appealed to a microscopic highbrow audience'.

Next, there was an urgent question of conscience brought up by M. Borès. Should he—or shouldn't he? Should he, if moved by a public injustice, remain silent, in order to preserve his aesthetic purity, his grave integrity as artist and intellectual, or should he protest and thus, in fulfilling a moral obligation, lose his detachment? Alex Merton said that if he did not wish to compromise his art (the question of what Borès' art was, he did not go into) his protest should take the form of a letter to the newspapers which he need not consider as part of his *œuvre*. In England, there was a newspaper, *The Times*, which existed for the purpose of publishing such letters. If, however, he felt so passionately about the public cause that he could identify it with his deepest personal feelings, then probably his protest would transcend itself in art. Sarret considered that there was no essential borderline dividing art from journalism, and journalism from propaganda: in his own case, public passion often produced his best work.

Then the French philosophers with the ball at their feet, were back again on their favourite topic—Engagement. It began to sound like the preliminary to marriage, though they would have treated marriage with less reverence. Marteau said that Balzac was engaged (had he ever married? Olim could not remember). Sarret said that André Gide had objected to Engagement. This sounded in character. Had Proust ever been engaged? Unlikely. In a sense perhaps, yes.

The dialogue between Marteau and Sarret was resumed, the polemical tone less evident, being replaced by one of gossiping intimacy. They discussed their journeys, their earnings, their lectures, their articles.

Sarret recalled the request made to Chinese writers while he was in Pekin—write stories for children. He posed the question to Marteau (the meeting had come to resemble a broadcast dialogue between them, with the others a studio audience invited in to listen and applaud) —'Would you, Marteau, if you were requested to do so by the government, write a children's book? I confess I would be greatly perturbed by such a request.'

Olim passed a scrap of paper to Alex, on which he had written: *If you were a Chinese child would you wish to read a story written for you by Marteau?* Alex passed back: *I would regard it as the People's Chinese Torture.* Olim scribbled: *If I wrote such a story, I would be careful that it pleased the Chinese Children's Government.*

Korovin, the second Russian—as they now thought of him, with his skull like the shaved head of a twelve-year-old with very ancient parents—remarked in a gentle voice that in Russia today writers were invited, *invited*, but not commanded, to write plays. Jolly Roger Pomyalov said that the position in Russia, like that in China, was that there were too few writers for too many people.

Then Pobedin, his lock of grey hair falling over his forehead, said, looking earnestly across the table at Sarret: 'It will not be possible for us to reply to the extremely interesting and important remarks made by

M. Sarret until tomorrow. Meanwhile, we would like
to underline how important we think meetings of this
kind are. We feel that, as M. Sarret has said, there have
been misunderstandings, but we also feel that these can
be healed by exchanging points of view frankly and sincerely. We are, as I said before, particularly glad to be
here in Venice, which we all treasure as one of the gems
of World Culture, and I can only repeat how appropriate
it seems that EUROPLUME should be situated here.
Speaking for myself, when I walked through this city
today, tears came into my eyes, as I reflected that this
beautiful place, which should be the possession of the
culture of the whole world, can now be seen only by the
privileged few when it ought to be the joy and recreation
of the oppressed masses.'

Bonvolio drove phaeton-like across the table with
some remarks about the difference between being for,
with, by, and from, culture, between 'an intellectual
engaged with culture, and engaging his work for culture'. Olim buried his head in his hands.

Then, superseding the sound of Bonvolio's voice,
which he had muffled till it seemed but the Adriatic
wave murmuring in a conch, he was awakened by the
harsh disgusted voice of Csongor Botor. He looked up
and saw the President of the Arts and Literary Academy
of Budapest sitting up very stiffly in his chair, his hands
laid on the table as though grasping the sides of a desk,
and the voice coming out of a face wooden as a ven-
triloquist's doll. There was a kind of pointless, automatic
irony about the way in which Botor said he hardly knew,
listening to what had been said, which side he was on,
though he supposed M. Sarret supposed he was one of
what had been referred to as Them. 'However, it is
possible even for M. Sarret to be wrong,' he went on
gutturally, 'and it is still possible to be in the middle
even when, geographically speaking, one is placed in the

area where no one is supposed to be able to understand a single thought emanating from the other side. Maybe, I am one of M. Marteau's universals, banished to a particular camp. Anyway, I am not a member of any political party, and I have to agree with my enemies when they call me the anomaly of a bourgeois living in a socialist country. All the same, in that place, where, according to M. Sarret, my speech, my appearance, my writing, and my whole existence should be totally inaccessible to the ideologically transformed populace, my books sell in thousands, they are read, I may say, by factory workers and peasant alike. . . .' He now started boasting, quite pointlessly, in fact everything about this speech seemed, almost deliberately, pointless. 'The situation may be even more complicated, much more subtly interrelated than one would imagine from the way in which M. Sarret with all his famous subtlety, has formulated it. Does M. Sarret imagine that he is flattering us in our Eastern fastnesses when he declares that we cannot think in any terms save the ideological ones he has laid down for us? Does he think it impossible that the divisions which he thinks of as intellectual might be geographical, even physiological? Would not it simplify things if M. Sarret stated baldly that *over there the trees and grass are blood-red, the sky flaming yellow, cows and sheep are bright blue?* Yet might it not still be true that inside men are what they are, and what they are is for them to know and decide, and no formula invented by philosophers hundreds of miles away can, however ingenious it be, enter into their innermost minds and discern there an automatism of ideologic thinking which is the opposite of whatever anyone is thinking over here?'

Then from being aggressive he suddenly changed his tone to an almost embarrassing sentimentality. . . . Striking the table with his hand—'We must try to

understand one another, we must try to accept the fact
that we are forced to assume certain positions. We must
try to see what we REALLY are. If with our dear Soviet
friends, we are able to arrive at an understanding that is
analogous, then we will have made real progress. . . .'
Olim thought he was about to burst into tears. But he
ended with his face directed to the Soviet writers, an
oleaginous smile.

So this is the man with the gaping hole in his side,
this is the one who is truly engaged, Olim thought. But
is he his own writer or his own hero? Evidently he himself does not know. He wants to be both and neither. He
speaks to his ideological colleagues in the language of
their ideas, yet he transmits across the lines the picture
of himself as a mangled corpse. As a leader of the
Hungarian Writers he is of them, but as fiction he is his
own truth which traverses sides in the dark night of the
soul. Perhaps the triumph of his irony is to show that
they, with their fairy stories by Marteau and Sarret for
Chinese children, are the unrealists, he, not as President
of the Arts and Literary Academy, but as lost soul
inventing his own story, is real. And what is his story?
If only I could invent it, imagine it, and knock a hole
through this newsreel, this Brains' Trust, this farce of
a debate between ideologues, one side of which says
nothing.

IV

At meals, during the first two days of the conference, the French treated the Russians much as the British treat royalty, standing up when they came into the room, earnestly attentive to their lightest dropped remark about the splendours of Venice. By dinner on the third evening, they were taking action to avoid having to sit near them, and they were referring to Pobedin, Korovin, and Pomyalov as *le prêtre athéiste, l'archéologue triste*, and *le bandit*. Sarret had abandoned the theory that it was the ideological gulf which made distinguished Soviet writers, when exported by official organizations, appear inexplicably boring to their Western colleagues, for the one that these were 'the wrong Russians', Grade B intellectuals, or a second Eleven.

On the third evening, at dinner, Olim found himself manœuvred into a place between the solid Russian bloc and Magda, the interpreter, on his left. Beyond Magda sat the cheerful, ruddy, virile-looking Italian novelist, of curly, cherubic appearance, Leonardo Longhi. Next to Longhi, on the farthest side from Olim, was Csongor Botor, talking to his neighbour, Sereno. Their interchanges, though amicable, seemed only interludes in Sereno's long pensive silences—glimpses of the continuous white monastic wall which surrounded his being.

Longhi, besides being vivacious, was informed and had his uses. He did not accept the prescribed diet, the '*menu fixe*' laid down by Bonvolio's secretariat, and he demanded of the waiters, the '*carte*', from which he chose exuberantly, and with erudite speciality. He was not even satisfied always with what was on the '*carte*',

68

and sent waiters worrying to the kitchen to discover whether there were not items unprinted—perhaps unprintable—there. For instance, this evening, he succeeded in wringing from the *Stella* larder a special kind of sand worm, long, white, flat, and narrow. He entertained his neighbours by telling them how when a boy (before he became famous), he had caught (if that is the word) these in his native Calabria, watching for the small borings, heaped round with minced-sand hillocks, which showed where they were hidden.

'Did you have to dig them out?' asked Olim, who visualized Longhi clearly enough, in shorts and with brown knees, a fisher-boy among fishermen, before he did that which Olim more and more clearly identified with the Fall—published his first best-seller. 'What we did was sprinkle salt round their holes.' 'You mean, they feed on salt?' 'Oh, no, certainly not. But the salt causes their little hiding places in the sand to dry out, absorbing its moisture, and then they rise to the surface, so you can easily pick them up.'

Longhi went on talking about his prelapsarian occupations in sun and sand. Then he was the hero of the stories which had made him the hero of his readers. He liked moving conversationally back and forth between the time when he was a character who is 'real' and the time when he became the highly successful creator of this character himself. He still went back to Calabria, slipping in amongst his fishermen to his previous life, but enjoying, amidst the sweat and alcohol and poverty and swearing, a *deus ex machina* status of the idler, the gourmet who is in no way different from the others, except that he is engaged in writing his book.

Not that Longhi didn't enjoy his fame; he insisted on it. He revealed this evening that he was incensed by the idea, put forward by Dunstan Curlew, during the afternoon session, that in the West—at all events, in England, by contrast with China—only bad books were read by the masses, good ones by the élite. At any rate, if this was so in England, it was not the case in the Italy of Leonardo Longhi's village. His books were esteemed by the best critics all over the world, but what he valued even more, he said, was their vast and—as he would call it—'authentic' circulations. As he chatted, one had only to look at him to be aware of his self-appreciation: it lay like a wreath among the curls on the intelligent brow of this chubby Caesar. That on which he insisted most—which might not emerge, he said, from the circulation figures, was that his books had been taken to heart by the peasants of his native Calabria. 'In my own village, for instance, since, naturally, they can't afford books, the circulation has only gone up by one, but everyone reads me. They read me not being able to buy, not even being able to read. They've clubbed together to buy my first and second book—one copy of each. After the day's work, they gather in the village square, and the village school-teacher reads out Leonardo Longhi—whom they know so well—to the peasants, at the rate of a page a day. They are exhausted by their work in the fields— the oppression in that area is perhaps the worst in Italy —so they cannot read more than this. But in all that, you have the basis of a popular culture.' And he went on to talk about the better conditions of a changed society, in which it would be possible for the peasants to have more time to read his books.

Taking them up one by one, and throwing back his head, he popped the white shell fish into his mouth. His naïveté had a melting charm that affected his neighbours. Olim, who since the first evening had been allergic to Magda Karinthy, in the benevolent radiance spread by Leonardo Longhi asked her how she was enjoying her trip. She smiled. 'She is enjoying herself very much indeed,' said Csongor Botor. 'She has even

found an admirer.' 'What is his name?' asked Olim.
'Romito.' 'How did you meet him?' 'He met me. He
came up as I was walking to the hotel after the meeting
and invited me to have an aperitif.' 'Which you did?'
'But of course,' Botor said, wagging a finger humorist-
ically: 'Take care! There are underground caves and
cellars below the canals.'

'Venice! To Venice!' said Pomyalov, raising his glass.
His damaged eye gave him the air of a great mauled
tom-cat. 'We want you to come to our country,' he said
in German. 'We have many faults, there are things you
will not like, and we welcome criticism. We are aware
of our defects, but proud of our achievements. We think
we have made many mistakes but also that we have done
very good things. We are proud to welcome critics
when we are assured that they will understand our point
of view.' He talked about the United States where he had
toured. American culture was decadent but he was en-
thusiastic about one and all of the leaders of industry. He
invited Olim to stay with him in his Moscow apartment.

Olim raised his glass to the toast and asked: 'Do
Russians like Italian wine?' At this, Pomyalov started
talking indignantly to his two colleagues and then asked
Magda to translate their joint protest. It was against
Olim's implication that because propagandists of the
West declared that Russians were excessive drinkers,
therefore all Russians, including themselves, were ad-
dicted to drunkenness. They went on to point out that
there were also heavy drinkers in England, France, and
especially in America, but this did not make them draw
the conclusion that the French and English in this room
were drunkards. Olim explained that he had not made
the implication. His apology was accepted, but the
Russians drank water throughout the rest of the meal.

A few minutes later, he attempted a different approach
with Pobedin. He asked: 'Don't you think it would be a

good thing if the great Russian translator of Shaw,
K—l, were invited to Malvern, to see performances of
the plays he has translated?' Pomyalov caught this suggestion in flight as it were, before Pobedin could answer
it. He then transmitted through the translator the
answer that he thought it would be an extremely bad
thing. 'Why?' asked Olim, astonished. Magda Karinthy
explained that Pomyalov thought Olim had said K—l
should on no account be invited.

Further explanations would have exonerated Olim too
completely. A misunderstanding so difficult to understand showed a will to misunderstand. The meal was
over, and the Russians got up huffily, and, all of them
together, left the room. Olim now assumed his aggressive *persona*, so quite wishing to annoy, he walked over
to the place where Dunstan Curlew remained still
seated at table, a predetermined look on his face, as
though he were where he was as a result of the ratio of
his own trajectory, when he came into the room, to
forces surrounding him. 'What do you think of the things
now admitted by Krushchev to have happened under
Stalin?' he asked. Curlew gave him one glance, and
scooted out of the room.

'May I ask you a question?' asked Magda Karinthy,
following Olim out into the street. 'You can ask me as
many questions as you like. Maybe, at the end, I'll want
to ask you one, and it won't be hard to guess what that
will be.' She ignored the facetious bluster of this and
said: 'Do you mind if we walk on a little further?' 'Oh,
as far as you like.'

They took coffee on the piazza. Just beyond their
table at the outside edge of all the tables set in the
square, tourists walked to and fro, Venetian children,
belonging to a different world from these foreigners,
chased one another, and jumped on to the saddle of the
red granite lion at the side of San Marco.

A great glow from the Square was reflected on Magda's cheeks

She looks—he thought—quite chipper, chippy, chirpy. He felt a motor start up in him that might take them a long way. With a certainty that the answer would lead to bed, he pressed on:

'Well—the question.'

'What political party do you belong to in England?'

'None, but I vote Labour.'

'What party does Mr. Dunstan Curlew belong to?'

He hesitated. Looking at her, he realized a great deal depended on his answer. He said: 'I don't know what party he officially belongs to. But whatever party is really his, isn't my party.'

She sipped her coffee. Then he offered her a liqueur. She had a Benedictine, which she drank as if it were schnapps or vodka, at one gulp. He had several cognacs. Then she said: 'I couldn't help overhearing a question you asked Mr. Curlew just before we left the Luna. Would you be so kind as to tell me his answer to that which you asked?'

Thinking that she put things a bit pedantically—but that might be due to her otherwise almost perfect English—he said: 'You mean the question about Krushchev's speech?' She nodded, almost furtively. 'Well, he didn't answer. He just walked away.'

'Oh.' She gave a sigh, a sigh of determination. Then she said: 'Some of us, Mr. Asphalt, would be very glad to know why you think it is that Mr. Dunstan Curlew, the world-famous scientist, who must be so scrupulous when making experiments on inanimate objects, yet does nothing to denounce the results of an experiment affecting the lives of thousands of human beings, when it has failed?'

'That is just what I went up to ask him.'

The question, coming from her to him was not nearly

so much a question, as a statement of a position with wild implications. Suddenly he appreciated the extent to which during the past few days, he had moved into an atmosphere where everything was 'political', everything had ideological complications. He did not greatly like it. This question was a dramatic assertion: like tearing her Party card up in front of him, and setting light to the bits with a match, in her coffee saucer. For a moment he felt panicky, imagined her crossing frontiers, changing sides, and his being responsible for her when she left the desperate East for the disillusioning West. He would have to take care of Magda Karinthy for the rest of his life. He wondered what Elaine would have to say to that.

He played at considering the question objectively (though heaven knows where 'objectivity' lay between them). Well, he made a show of attempting to answer it dead-pan-wise. 'It might be precisely because he regards society as an object for scientific experiment.' 'All the same, why doesn't he admit the experiment has failed?' 'Perhaps because he doesn't judge the freezing to death of a million contemporary rats as a failure, if he thinks that, as a result, the future will provide for a billion happier, better, eugenically raised ones.' He added, 'I am sure Curlew is perfectly sincere.' He laughed.

'Has he ever lived, do you think, in a country which is the object of such experiments?' 'Visited often, lived never.' She hesitated. 'Do you agree with him then?' 'No.' 'In that case,' she exclaimed, suddenly indignant, 'you must be making fun of me.' 'Not at all. I was trying to be objective.' But his attempt had been, really, to qualify. And he realized that they were where there is black and white, but no shades.

'You were pretty nasty to me two nights ago,' he remarked toughly, riled by her indignation with him. 'Well, you are intelligent. I thought you would know why. I couldn't be nice to your scientific colleague and yourself at the same moment.'

'Couldn't you . . .' he was about to add something much more to the point, when it struck him that she had already come down on his side of the fence. To him this was like throwing a switch. Olim Asphalt, the spasmodically careful LITUNO official, clinging on to his contract, and Olim Asphalt, the post-ex anti-communist, was superseded by Olim Asphalt, satyr, esquire. 'Why don't we go out in a gondola?' he asked, pulling out all the human stops of his vocal chords.

She nodded as though she had just this in mind. They went outside the piazza to the canal that runs near the Ca Giustinian by the Biennale, where he had heard the gondolier last night. The same curling sparkling individual was there. He asked them where they wished to go, and when they said out for an hour nowhere in particular, his attention automatically became a slide rule grooved along varying degrees of privacy.—'The Laguna, the Grand Canal, or *i piccoli canali oscuri.*'

For ideological reasons, they obviously chose the Laguna, where walls would not have eyes and ears. Seeing what? Hearing what? The weather was warmer and finer, though not entirely seasonal. But Venice seemed preparing for the Easter Sunday, due in three days, which would change the interior stones of San Marco to peach colour brushed over with the flickering of massed candle light, while outside the golden statue of the Saint on the campanile would be floodlit. Meanwhile, it was sufficiently cold for the gondola to be provided with a blanket which Olim drew over them both, and then, freeing them from its too broad hint, he moved away from her to his side of the boat. Contiguity remained ideological.

'I've met your friend Csongor Botor,' he said, in a voice which he hoped might appear to conceal some subtly exciting threat. 'I can tell you that he cut a very different figure on Lake Balaton from his appearance at this conference. But I dare say that might be said of my official appearances also.' His defiant, ashamed laugh again.

'I know nothing about him.'

'Don't you? You mean that you happen to be an interpreter from Hungary and you happened to come with him, and you know nothing about him?' He nudged her, causing the gondola to rock.

'He belongs to an older generation. That makes a considerable difference in our country.'

'Well, so do I. And I'm pretty close to you. Getting closer every minute.'

She said nothing. He did not look at her but he thought she might be presenting the cutting profile of his first evening.

'Tell me then, what you think about him—about Csongor Botor?' he asked, really interested.

'We don't like him. We say that he reads and talks Russian.'

'You mean—you don't trust him?'

'We don't trust anyone much—least of all Botor.' They were moving out through the mouth of the Grand Canal, and he was wondering whether he really altogether liked the church of Santa Maria della Salute, with the stone scrolls under the dome, on top of which statues were placed—whether it was not too much like an object that could be picked up and placed on a white table-cloth —a vast silver cruet.

Quite apart from the swaying of the gondola, he had a dizzy feeling, like going rapidly up and down from an elevator which lifted him up to his concerned, moral, social self, then dropped him down to his private satyr one.

Olim sat in up in the gondola and looked down at her. Lying flat on her back, she was reciting in her cold dry voice, which went rather strangely with what ought to have been a thrilling foreign accent, contemporary facts which sounded as remote as some very past history. 'We know a lot about Csongor Botor. Before the war he was leader of the surrealists and right up to the changes he was what they called reactionary. But then he changed or seemed to change at any rate. He wrote several articles in praise of Aragon, in Paris, who had switched then from surrealism to communism. During the war, he did not pretend to be on the side of the Nazis, but nevertheless he was one of those who thought they were "on the side of history". One doesn't have to like history to accept it. One learned that at school,' she added with something that was almost discernible as humour.

She looked up at him with genuine curiosity about his opinion for the first time: 'Do you like Csongor Botor?'

'How can I know that I like someone whom I've only been out with once? We went out to that castle of the writers, and then we went into the vineyards for the wine-tasting. We got so drunk, I can scarcely remember a thing about it.'

'He is the kind of person one would like in spite of *almost* everything. Unfortunately we know too much about him to allow ourselves the luxury of liking him.'

The austerity of this chilled Olim, who felt the need of very relaxed personal standards in which to flourish. He was suddenly struck with horror at the glimpse of a world in which you couldn't escape from moral public values into amoral private ones. The two might be brought so close together that the one would always be a judgment on the other. Even this kind of outing that he was having now would have political implications. He wanted to grab her quickly to reassure himself that seductions had no moral significance.

Now that they were in the Laguna, which for a few moments was a little choppy, Olim even began to feel slightly sick. What impressed him more than Botor's career was Magda Karinthy's use of the pronoun 'We'. Who were these formidable 'We'? They did not like their oppressors, but he felt they would not like him, either. He had the impression of frowning alien free-living young people who were endlessly preoccupied with desperate gossip—not so much personal as socio-logical—the gossip of the younger generation about the reasons why the old had betrayed them.

'You keep on talking about yourself as "we",' he pro-tested. 'Who are these "we"? Are you speaking as a member of a group? Or is it just that you are not a real person?'

'As far as you're concerned, do I have to be a real per-son?'

'Got me there!' He burst out laughing. 'All right, I would like you to be real. I'd like to know about you personally, and after that about this group you call "we".'

'As a matter of fact, I am rather different from the others, though that has nothing to do with my being or not being a person. For one thing, I'm Westernized. Perhaps you've noticed that I can speak English and French! I'm afraid that makes me special. Then I have an uncle who's a famous Marxist historian, an old-style sentimental idealist—very rich, in fact still quite rich.'

'And what about those people you call "we"?'

'They are just the young.'

'What do they have in common?'

'That they have nothing in common with the old: that is, with the people who put them where they find them-selves.'

Like the gondola, his mind seemed floating, some-times near an object, sometimes moving away from it, seeing different structures from different angles. He was nagged at by the idea that he was missing an opportunity: and that this opportunity itself might become something, for the moment, at all events, terrific.

'Look,' he said suddenly. 'Here am I. Here are you. We each have our personal qualities, which are separate from one another. We have bodies and minds, I mean. They aren't shared by anybody else. In spite of Sarret, I don't believe they belong more to an ideology or a society than they do to what we both have in common— that we are human. Wouldn't it be civilized for us to realize this, and act on it?'

'That is all true. But it isn't important.'

'Then what the hell is important?' he said angrily. 'Is this important?' He leaned over and kissed her.

'That's what I thought you meant, and that's what I thought unimportant.'

'Oh, oh, oh,' he groaned. 'What a complicated little piece of stuff you are!'

'The things of which we were speaking were more important,' she said.

'Oh, oh, oh!'

'Sarret is right up to a point, What one thinks important is largely the result of one's situation. For instance, you think it important now to kiss me. I think it important that a representative of LITUNO should know one or two things about "us".'

'All right,' he said ironically. 'I'll use you as an information bureau. Tell me some more then.'

She simply waited in silence until he put more questions to her.

'Why should a person with Botor's record have been made President—or whatever he is?' he asked, sourly. 'Because he is so unreliable that he is thoroughly reliable from their point of view!' She said this triumphantly—it was evidently one of the elucidations her set was most proud of. 'I don't quite follow.' 'He's open to flattery at one end, to threats at the other. The people they don't trust are the trustworthy. The people they trust least are the idealists. All the same, we think that, in the conditions of our kind of society, Botor is one of the people we most like. We like him better than the Party leaders, and we like him better than the idealist communists who've now turned self-righteously against the Party.'

'Do you like him because he's a great poet?' 'All that means nothing to us. Besides, he is no longer. All that doesn't exist.' 'Why, then?' For the first time, she did not have the immediate answer to a question. Then she said: 'I think it's because he's unhappy.' 'What is he unhappy about?' 'Well, most of our intellectuals have betrayed their friends without thinking twice about it. But we have the impression that he's quite unhappy about Premontvian.' 'And who is Premontvian?' 'Premontvian is a poet who was also a monk, and who was the best friend of Csongor Botor before the war. The two of them were known as "the blessed demon and the damned priest". Botor was ordered to denounce Premontvian at a meeting of the Writers' Association. Of course, everyone knew that he only did so because he had to, but all the same Premontvian was arrested. The story goes that after the meeting, when the socialist poet Falus came up to Botor, Botor made a wry smile, and said, "After all, Premontvian was always a bad poet".'

Once started, it was amazing how informed she was about everyone over there—or rather, he suspected, how informed were They, who gossiped endlessly. Pobedin, she said, was notoriously 'finished' and therefore safe for export, Korovin was an innocent, and Pomyalov? Would he like to know what Pomyalov had written in *Pravda* about Rajk when he was on trial?

Still feeling a bit sick, or faint, he nodded. She had it by heart: '*The notorious traitor and Fascist Rajk is not*

*good enough to be hanged. We demand that he should be
burned at the stake like a sorcerer of the Middle Ages.'*

He lay back, not looking at her, but his mind filled
with her. He did not want to look. He preferred thinking, working out for himself what she was like. He
remembered the hard profile she had turned to him at
dinner, the first evening. Were these confidences of a
kind which would soften her appearance? The question
intrigued him sufficiently for him to glance at her lying
side-face there a few inches from him. He expected he
hardly knew what change. Her expression offered nothing to him, seemed scarcely less shut than previously.
Her features were anyway peasant-like as though carved
of wood, and he had the hallucination of two profiles,
like the sides of a box, into which the expressive mouth
and eyes had been nailed. Curious that the most responsive thing about her—it struck him—was her hair.
There was something pathetic and touching about these
little turned over shavings of curls. They reminded him
of dolls in villages, and dancing in the streets.

Now they were moving out of the Grand Canal towards the Laguna. The waters opened and suddenly
seemed darker, a great engraving of serpentine black
lines, framed in by a fantastically carved edge of domes
and towers and statues and palaces, gilded with lights.
Lying there—he locked in his thoughts, she so curiously
rigid and hammered—they were like effigies sunk in a
mirror out of which they stared through crepe gauze.
To their right, the low wall of the *punta della dogana*—
the ancient customs house—seemed the lean silhouetted
bows of a destroyer, with behind it an ornate and
rounded poop—the dome—they were now leaving—of
Santa Maria della Salute.

'Do so many other of the young in Budapest feel as
you do?'

'Of course.' 'You keep on saying "of course", but to

us, none of this is at all obvious.' His use of 'us'—as
against her use of the pronoun—reminded him of a side
he was on, and made him feel faintly hostile, yet more
than ever personally implicated with her. She replied,
on a note of dry aggressiveness: 'The great majority of
us feel the same about things, though not in the way that
M. Sarret condescends to imagine our attitudes.' 'But
aren't the young organized—all of them—into Party
Youth groups and so on?' 'You mean what we call—
The Young Persons' Brothel?'

'By that, you imply that the morals of the young in
the Party are loose?' he asked this eagerly—hopeful
again. 'Not at all. The Party is very puritanical. That is
why the young converted themselves into one large
brothel.' 'I don't understand.' 'Well, perhaps it isn't
very clear. The Party wanted a spiritual brothel. We
provided it with a physical one.' 'You mean—to save
the spirit?' 'Not quite that: to lose it in our own way,
not theirs.' 'To be damned for instance?' 'But that
would be too serious.' 'What do you mean?' 'Besides,
it would be bourgeois. Like an essay on Baudelaire by
M. Sarret.'

'Then you aren't bourgeois?' She paused, and then
said committally: 'No. We aren't serious.' He felt that
perhaps after all Sarret was right. A gulf separated them.
In the guilt-gilt surrounding darkness he envisaged
another darkness—framed by barbed wire, where the
heart, to survive, had to become heartless. There were
perhaps more divisions, more gulfs, more cracks, more
of isolation, in heaven and earth than were dreamed of
in Sarret's philosophy. The body too was an island
which had its language flashing across to other islands,
he said to himself insistently. He took her hand.

Her hand remained in his, and with all the perversity
of his will, he decided to force his demands on her. He
bent over her and—conscious of her being a foreigner

who heard the English words as through a mist—said
embarrassing nonsense: 'You little tease. I know very
well what you want. You're just longing for me.'

He loosened her dress, touched the gulf between her
thighs, punning drunkenly to himself with the idea of
Sarretian gulfs. After what he mentally described to
himself as a 'softening up' process, he looked straight
into her eyes. This was a bad moment. She looked
straight back into his with an expression that said
nothing. Her lips moved slightly without her speaking.

The moon had risen yellow as a pumpkin above the
Doges' Palace and, beyond it, the palazzi converted into
hotels, behind a wide promenade, on their left. It
dwindled rapidly, like an emptying pricked balloon
whizzing up the sky. Moonlight clanged down heavily
on waves, languid as reefed sails, through which the
gondola went pushing on. Then the yellowness drained
away: the moon turned to that silver which segments
crimes against a black backcloth, illustrating distantly
the Paris roof under which Elaine was lying, the bent
profiles in the streets between walls of Eastern Europe.
He rejected the reproach beamed out across several
hundred miles from Paris by his mistress. For in his
private morality, love in an islanded second is beauty
cut off from all other experiences, and would go (he
thought) spinning down corridors of remembering
which he was already beginning to anticipate. This
moment was struck of that minting. He drew the two
sides of her blouse apart, and lifted the cover sufficiently
to see the flesh like a carving, with her rounded breasts,
and below them, the denting and embossment of her
ribs. Her body in its partial nakedness was soft, luxurious, Western, and made a quite different impression
from her Social Realist face. It seemed to belong to
Parisian scented bourgeois poetry which she kept down
there under her dress.

The idea of himself as satyr with ripe lips and ill-
shaven skin, now dominated his consciousness, and saying things that he would not have permitted himself with
a woman whose native language was English, he
attempted this, the gondola gave a squelching heave,
the gondolier nearly fell overboard, and he heard
Magda saying to him, very distinctly—'Please realize
this means nothing to me.'

'Why the hell should it? Did I ask for it to mean anything to you? If you want to know, it doesn't mean a
thing to me either,' he said ferociously, adding more
mildly, 'All I would have hoped is for you to say
nothing.' Then he gave again his shameless laugh.

He rolled away onto his back, physically apart from
her. The whole situation, he thought, using the epithets he
most frequently applied to himself, was 'typically absurd.'

'Go home,' he said, to the gondolier, conscious that
there could be no vehicle in which such an order was
more ludicrous. The moon stared down mercilessly,
drawing attention to the fact that he was fifty. And to fill
the cup of his banality, he was conscious of a wild wish to
take the train to Paris and fall into the arms of Elaine,
who was kind to him. He was, ludicrously, in hell. He
looked up at the stars standing above the figure of the
gondolier erect as a tower, his oar a strut supported by
the quicksilver surface of the water. The idea of Sarret
was in his mind, at the centre of this sky. To do Sarret
justice, perhaps he knew more about all this than was
evident in his logic which made him its victim, for the
torrents, the oceans of words that poured out of him were
not just philosophy, but a world. They contained hotel
bedrooms and beds, cars and bars, boulevards and cine-
mas, drugs, absinthe, cigarettes, contraceptives, lovers
—normal Lesbian and homosexual—partisans, reactionaries, professors, intellectuals, psychologists, ministers;
and young men coming from the provinces to lose their

ideals in the Latin Quarter. For Olim to write his novel, *Littérature Engagée*, he must not think of Sarret as the incarnate mind that spoke in conferences, but as world in language which could do nothing but discover truth, and never lie. He must think of him on his travels, or asleep, or in bed. The truth would be in the fiction. And perhaps this Magda Karinthy, now not translating from and into Russian, was the Magda of fiction that was the truth he would write in *Littérature Engagée*. Now the gondolier had started singing and it was to his chanting *Luna Luna* that Olim fell into a drunken hang-overing sleep.

*   *   *   *

Botor was alone in a small oval room like an *intaglio* of green agate at Florian's. He was seated at a round table which looked out onto the piazza, a huge shop-window. He sat at the edge of his chair into which he had let himself down gently—as if his body were a great sack of pains looted from his bourgeois past, that he, a burglar, was condemned to carry about everywhere with him for the rest of his life. He ordered a glass of *crême de menthe*, having the idea that this was all his stomach could now digest in the way of spirits. Then he leaned his elbows on the table. Then extending his fingers of both hands, he held his face in them. The cheek-bones seemed a kind of handles conveniently provided for such support. In this position, he hoped that his body, with its tremblings, its recent habit of—at one slight move—seeming to jump down an abyss, its terrible emptiness, as though it were some modernist sculpture with holes cut through it—he hoped to fix his body in an iron pose through which his turbulent thoughts might pour—like water frothing in a trough. He could not, of course, control them, but he hoped by containing them to prevent them agitating his bones and flesh. Thoughts were hunting him. But gradually they did become more coherent, and, by keeping very still, he could listen to them. It was a speech they were making, a speech in which the Absolute Truth (for that they claimed to be) addressed Sarret in a hall which was the cavity between the surface of the brain, and the inner side of the skull.

'You are wrong, utterly wrong. There are indeed two worlds, but they are not as you think they are, my dear M. Sarret.' (It was impossible to avoid the vulgar and stupidly pretentious irony with which his thoughts said 'My dear M. Sarret'.) 'They are not literary gentlemen sitting at a café table of the Boulevard Saint Germain des Prés' (cheap again!) 'and explaining that they cannot understand one another's different interpretations of Marxism, decadence, social realism, Proust, Joyce, etc., because each group represents a different ideology. I tell you, gentlemen, it is perfectly clear what the truth of the matter—and that is, the difference—really is. Yet the truth of this truth is that if one knows it, one has extreme difficulty in getting one's words into any sort of order, because one is completely engulfed by each separate instant of reality. Therefore one cannot pursue the words to the end of the sentence. How can I explain that reality is that which, in being lived, cannot be described or explained? You talk of social realism—but things that happen to you can be so real that you can't call them realism—because—and this is what I am trying to say—"reality" is in itself an abstraction—I mean, to call things "reality", gentlemen, is to fit them into a context of other things already thought of, and this makes them unreal. Gentlemen, I have not explained this rightly. What I mean is— things can be so real—they tear you apart—and if you think at all—while you are experiencing them with the horror of a death-bed realization which is perhaps the final truth of life—then all you can think—if you think at all—is that no one can possibly express this because —don't you see, gentlemen—to express the reality of the one who thinks and feels and suffers in our world, implies a reader with calm balanced eyes, a reader sitting in a chair and looking down on a page on which things are printed in lines running parallel, and able to take them in. All this already implies that he is far removed from that reality. Reality of the kind I am trying to talk about cannot be written down, it cannot even be remembered the moment after it has happened, because memory would already have smoothed it over, rounded it into a smooth soothed object like a pebble thrown out of ferocious seas—whereas the real imprisons you in its moment which is totally separated from every other moment. That is your ideological gulf, M. Sarret: the gulf between the single separate horrifying moment of realization, and the recollected moments strung together in a necklace of polished memories. But each real moment claims that there is no other moment apart from its terrible self. It rages at the idea that anything else could be more appallingly real. Horror is envious. In your countries, gentlemen, there is Remembrance of Things Past, in our countries there are moments with gnashing teeth that tear you apart, devour you into themselves. For the sake of the sacred truth, I implore you, gentlemen, to drop talking about realism, engagement, and the rest. No one has the right to talk about reality who does not live night and day on a diet of the irremediable!'

This did not do, it did not do at all. It was his mad dog ego: the one he thought had been shot or tamed or muzzled five years previously. Leaping the loop, leaping through a hoop. Rhetoric of the ego, his greatest weakness. This which could substitute the epithet of his self-description for the substantive of what he was, could bury his vital defects under the flourishing epitaph of supposititious posthumous fame, obscure spiritual failure in the glamour of vocation. The President of the Academy! An honour which he knew to be the sign of his debasement! His immortality! (A buried fire which still insistently burned through the betrayals and surrenders of every hour of his present life!) He who had betrayed——

He did now find Florio's intolerable. He paid his *conto*, and went quickly out into the piazza. Slid out there into a glittering tank of similar forms gliding across a wide dim floor, and darting under columns. The feeling of the anonymity of the living under the shell-like carvings and grottoes of the dead, was a relief. For a moment only. Then his eyes grew accustomed and it all grew lighter and lighter.

He walked under the arcades past shop windows full of lace, filigree jewellery, leather wallets, beads, photogravure reproductions of masterpieces, chandeliers, and frightful Venetian glass knick-knacks. Here, out in the open, the dialectic, the gale of history blew in full force against him again, so that while certain thoughts opened great spaces under his feet, others became like straps, pillars to which he clung or hung.

'It is my painful duty to have to stand here and criticize the most recent volume of poems published last month by our colleague Ladyas Premontvian. They have quite justly been singled out for blame by the Party Press. We have to be grateful for these critics for their guidance.'

The statues on the skyline of the further side of the piazza were frozen witnesses of his speech to the Writers' Association. The room was surrounded by lights, with rows of windows, and he was grateful that he could see only figures standing up, and few faces. The words he was saying were ones they all stonily knew and they all knew that if he didn't say them, someone else would have to. He was a privileged scapegoat selected to attack another scapegoat just because Premontvian had been his best friend. But whereas Premontvian was a martyr, the scapegoat who attacked the scapegoat was the scapegoat condemned by history. He dimly felt that, even then.

The room seemed to darken, with lights showing only in corners. The so-called intellectuals were men stripped of their individuality, their honour, and even the respectable dignity of age and seniority. They all shrivelled back into dim obscure beginnings in unknown classrooms. 'I do not have anything to add to the censure of our comrades, who are today our truest critics. Despite themes of working-class life he ostensibly chooses, evidently comrade Premontvian describes poverty not because he wishes to participate in the common task of abolishing it through socialism, but because he clings to the reactionary concept of Our Lady of Poverty. . . .'

Being artists, there was a horrible curiosity amongst all of them as to how a member would take such a ruinous attack. Reactions varied astonishingly. For instance, Heves had simply bowed his head ironically when he had been accused of separatist nationalist tendencies. Premontvian, who was prodigiously fat, at first panicked. His huge face broke up into planes that seemed all to move in different directions, his eyes seemed to drive out from their sockets in an effort to shed responsibility for his body. Then quite suddenly he recovered, partly at any rate. He said in the comic manner which was half-serious self-parody: 'I don't accept the President's description of my poems. In the first place, I had never been told that we had to write according to prescriptions laid down by the Party. If I had been told, I would have done so——' (this was so much in his comic manner that a few members started tittering)—'in the second place (and now he looked absurdly sincere)

I do sympathize with the poor. I may be fat and self-indulgent, but anyone who read my poems with care would see that I am not a figure of the 1880's who writes about Our Lady of Poverty. There was a deep irony intended in using a cliché with overtones to it.' He suddenly started talking in an adult way about poetry—the way that was most forbidden—defending his poems sincerely against the charge that they were reactionary. 'In terms of the 1950's I was doing what Alexander Blok did with Christ in *The Twelve* in 1917.'

The mention of Blok of course gave his opponents an opening. The socialist story-writer Falus got up and said sarcastically that those who emulated Blok could only expect the fate of Blok. Premontvian suddenly started shouting at him: 'All right, I withdraw my defence. When a poet is not read, but expected to be written into, he should resign. He cannot expect to read other's thoughts into his own writing. Do what you like!' And he sat down suddenly with two distinct streams of tears spouting from the little eyes in his huge face.

After the meeting, the members of the Association (who had, of course, supported Botor's motion unanimously) stood up, without speaking. Botor became aware that Premontvian had left the room, and then (as though the Sacrament had been blessed at Mass, and the moment the core of most sacred silence had passed) he lifted his eyes. For some reason, the socialist poet Falus walked across the room and shook his hand warmly.

And then Botor, who loved to adorn his works with dedications, quotations, references used with a profound irony, amazed and quite pleased himself by quoting aloud that passage in *Julius Caesar* which always seemed to him to contain the seed of mysterious wise political comment: when, after Caesar's murder, the mob tears to pieces Cinna the poet. Looking straight at Falus in that fixed way which holds an auditor's half-embarrassed attention to any kind of spontaneous reciting by heart, Botor spoke the voices as though they were question and answer in a liturgy. His hair stood up, he extended an arm, he declaimed as though in the Roman forum. '*Your name, sir, truly.*' '*Truly, my name is Cinna.*' '*Tear him to pieces, he's a conspirator.*' '*I am Cinna the poet, I am Cinna the poet.*' '*Tear him for his bad verses, tear him for his bad verses.*' '*I am not Cinna the conspirator.*' '*It is no matter, his name's Cinna; pluck but his name out of his heart, and turn him going.*' '*Tear him, tear him. Come brands, ho, firebrands!*' He shouted the last words across the room, with his eyes staring, as they stared now and he started shouting across the piazza at the judging, witnessing statues—'When Falus was arrested a few days later, and interned for some four years in Recsk, I gave money to his wife. I tried to intervene in favour of Heves, the communist poet, tortured to death. I tried to atone for Premontvian's expulsion. Yet I was relieved when I heard that Premontvian was ill in prison. I did not regret the death of Heves. I see in the release of Falus now a threat.'

And yet there was no excuse. When he did that he touched a zero of behaviour where no human feeling could reach and forgive. A climate in which nothing grows. Zero.

He moved along the side of the piazza under the colonnade, as if he were leaning against the side of a cliff in a storm. He came to the plate-glass window of a café across the wide passage which goes alongside San Marco. There, as though in a shop window, he saw Sarret, Marteau, Borès, and Longhi. In the gold light of the interior, above the white top of the table, through the gleaming transparency dividing him from them, they looked like saleable objects in a shop, or an advertising display, wax fruit in a bowl, tailor's dummies. Sarret was jerking his arms and body in animated conversation, occasionally opening and shutting his mouth quickly in a snap of laughter. The way he moved made Botor think of mechanical joints—ah, and that creaking of limbs on wires was not unlike the dry cicada rasp of Sarret's voice. The four of them looked gay yet not joyous, seriously occupied with intense intellectual frivolity, putting down their ideas as if they were cards placed on top of one another in a game, Sarret's lowest trump killing any of their aces. And then he noticed, seated at a table not far off, with an expression of nostalgia and malice, Olim Asphalt, also looking at them, the Englishman who brought back to the outer edge of Botor's mind a scene in a vineyard on the shore of Lake Balaton.

Csongor Botor walked diagonally across the lower half of the Piazza towards the Ca Giustinian. Out there, between the hotel and post office, he heard the voice of the gondolier of their first evening—Carlino, whom he had missed till now—just returned from his trip with Olim Asphalt and Magda. Botor walked up to him. That he felt unafraid with this young man, seemed an immense assuagement. Carlino's cheerful appearance, his curling hair like a cap, his smile, extraordinarily gave him the feeling of the deliciousness of sanity. 'Carlino—where should we go?' he asked, hypothetically. 'The *laguna*, the Grand Canal, or the little obscure canals!' Carlino reeled off. 'How much do you charge?' '1,500 lire for an hour.' 'I call that very expensive—' 'But it is the night—' He leaned forward, extending one hand, a humorous and ardent figure of Mercury. 'I wasn't complaining. But it is too late.' 'The signor can sleep all day. It is I who have to work. The gondola is very restful for the signor.' 'No.' 'Why won't you come?' he said, pleading, but suddenly curious in a personal and friendly way. 'Perhaps because I am afraid,' said Botor, as if quite joyously confessing. 'Afraid? Afraid of me? Me—' he burst out laughing. And Botor laughed too, laughed till he bent double, and tears choked him. 'Afraid. Not just of you. I am afraid of everything,' he laughed. 'Then with me you need not be.' It was true. He felt a wave of unafraidness move over him, delicious as death, so beautiful that he could have said—take me, throw me into the *laguna*, knife me, let me drown, so long as I am not afraid. 'I will really come tomorrow night. I promise.' He turned away, walking through the darkness as the voice 'Gondola! Gondola' with a slight laugh through its rising accent, faded into a distance where there was peace.

V

On Good Friday, in San Marco, Olim Asphalt was one of a great crowd of tourists. Standing at the edge, he watched them all, including himself in the spectacle. In their clothes like photographs in newspapers or fashion magazines, they looked two-dimensional as hoardings. The pavemented floor on which they stood was uneven, imitating the Adriatic seeping under, far beneath, which, through the centuries, had sculpted the flagstones after its wave-curled form.

The tourists formed the two horns of a large crescent shadow closing on the altar, whose encrusted jewels shone with reflections from massed candles. Above their heads, the brassy light entered the pits of arches and the concavities of domes, from whose apices wings and faces bent, looking down on the modern travellers through argus-eyed mosaic.

It seemed as though sheets of gold-foil were slowly, perpetually falling, twisting through the atmosphere of incense, flecking lights on walls and pillars. A gleaming canopy, like the cover of a great dish, enclosed and domed the ghostly crowd.

At the altar, priests in white satin and gold brocade, vestments that removed them from contemporary shadows as if they had been visitors from Mars, stiffly performed their antique ceremony. To Olim, on the edge of things, their masque looked like the play within the play in *Hamlet*. Did it explain the plot of the conference table, the speeches and folly? Priests, attended by their

94

acolytes, made their grave gestures one to another, which communicated nothing to him: he was content for their significance to be as remote as interplanetary signals through space.

Machine run on Holy Spirit. Spirit, *essence*, ghost, multiple meanings. *Bank of the Holy Spirit.* Idle siftings interrupted by his noticing Pobedin on the far side of the altar almost exactly opposite where he, on his side, was standing. Under their tufted eyebrows, the elderly Russian writer's eyes reflected the glow of the candle-blaze as though he were receiving the flutter of dove's wings. That Pobedin should be there looking like a hermit or ascetic standing at the entrance of his cave in some Spanish painting of ecstasy, was perhaps an accident of dim religious light. Or perhaps it in some way explained the mystery of his survival, just as Korovin's might be connected with his pre-adolescent look. At any rate, it was difficult to believe that Pobedin was experiencing a conversion as he gazed at the priest-gyrating altar.

When, at the end of the service, the crowd dispersed, Olim followed Pobedin. They met near the main door under a vast mosaic of the Last Judgement. Their heads were just below the deepest part of hell. They found themselves beneath the damning and the damned, so low in a bottomless pit that the forks of demons jabbed harmlessly above their heads.

On this fringe of the congregation, the crowd talked touristically and unabashed, aware that this was a 'catholic' thing to do, so it was easy, while they were still under the spell of the service, to ask Pobedin how it impressed him. 'I understand such ceremonies very well,' he said gravely, in his professorial German. 'I had a religious upbringing, and my uncle was a priest of the Orthodox Church.' He looked at Olim from the full distance of his gaze across steppes and forests. 'What do you think of it now? Does it make you at all nostalgic?' Pobedin reflected on this, with his air of portentousness. 'What moves me is to think of the tragedy! All this money and effort spent on deceiving the people, when so much good could be done if it were used on constructive tasks.'

Olim wanted to howl: or else put to him some frightful question out of a wild dream, some almost unthinkable blasphemy: 'Has your religion done more for the unfortunate?'

Instead, he pointed out one of his favourite objects in Venice: outside the porch, the fourteenth-century red granite group called 'The meeting of the Moors', of Syrian or Egyptian warriors each with left hand on a bird-headed sheathed sword, who, with his right, embraces another. Pobedin, mild, responsive to beauty, admired the sculpture, and they walked across to the Doges' Palace for their morning meeting.

The conference was now in its fifth day. The table resembled the scene above a shipwreck, afloat with objects thrown up and around: papers, ink-stands, bottles, sticks and spars, oddments of timber. Passing the place where Borès sat, Olim glanced at a proof lying on the table in front of his empty chair.

The lines that caught his eye ran as follows:

September 30. *We were taken to the little town of Kissegesvar on the beautiful Budoske shore. Entertained by peasants, smiling, and strikingly clean (one remembers the days when soap was unobtainable in this corner of Eastern Europe) who, dressed in traditional costumes, danced their traditional folk dances for us. These, which had become almost forgotten under the old régime, have been revived thanks to the efforts of Professor Laubermann (a refugee from Hitler's Germany who has made his home in Pest). The peasants in rediscovering them, have, through revolution, reaffirmed what was most vital to their traditional way of life. Where there was a casino, a factory for making glazed tiles is now . . .*

Just then, Borès himself, last-comer, arrived. They sat down. At the head of the table, Bonvolio, perspiring, looked like the leader of an endurance test, a captain pointing to the survivors a hypothetical shore, one who recites Tennyson: '*Courage,*' *he said, and pointed toward the land.*

None of the intellectuals more resembled survivors who had taken to their little boat and were enduring, on an endless expanse of ocean, the agonies of thirst and their parching rations, than the Russians, after four or five days spent listening to Sarret. They had always made it clear that they did not consider this ideological journey necessary. They thought there was nothing really to discuss. One either disagreed, in which case there was no point in meeting, or one agreed, in which case there was no point in discussing. They longed to reach the island of Bonvolismus, the course which had been charted so eloquently by the chairman in his opening speech. During the past two days, Boris Pomyalov had been repeating ever more urgently his simple message: 'Let us agree about culture, which we all love, and let us forget about politics which we all disagree about.' With his ragged black hair and his look of having a black patch over one eye, he resembled more one of Marteau's Universals, pirating between lines, than one excluded from mutual understandings by Sarretian gulfs.

All the same land could hardly be reached without some attempt by the Russians to work their passage out of the position of ideological untouchability in which Sarret, with excess of zeal, had fixed them. Sarret had, as it were, allotted them all the rowlocks on the port side of a boat which had an insuperable partition built longways all down the middle. Unless they either refused to accept this position or else pulled against the bourgeoisie at starboard, not all Bonvolio's steering would prevent the boat going round in circles.

Conscious of the gravity of the situation, Pobedin, grey and tense, got up to say that he was prepared at last to speak for himself and his colleagues. Within a very few minutes he had demolished the ideological ingenuities of Sarret with his own irrefutable ponder-csities. For what he showed beyond doubt was that the great army of the banal, the dull, the conventional, and the boring, includes all sides. Wherever the ideas laid down by society are accepted without dispute, wherever no convention of communal thinking is challenged, there Pobedin pitched his tent and gazed across dividing plains of warring armies with eyes burning like the two quietest stars in the universe. His the faith of those who know that the conventional is more important than the convention, and the convention than the standard that establishes it. So, however ideologies divide, he was with those who accept unquestioningly the social creed within which on either side the convention-loving live. No frontier could interrupt his profound spiritual kinship with those, of whatever side, time, or place, who accept views laid down by the authorities.

His speech, therefore, appealed to the chosen few who recognize the simple worth of one who repeats what has been said dogmatically already a hundred times. The only awkwardness was that he had to get out of the ideological ditch Sarret had dug for him and his colleagues. This meant that he had to attempt an agreeing-to-disagree agreement with Sarret. He therefore began by expressing his profound regret that he had to disagree when M. Sarret said that there were tremendous divisions between East and West. M. Sarret had spoken as though he believed that the division between the two sides was absolute and it was only by an effort of total self-effacement that a person on one side could enter into the point of view of someone conditioned to the other. That act of self-effacement M. Sarret called Engagement. 'The word Engagement,' said Pobedin, 'simply does not exist in my country, both the concept and the word itself are untranslateable.'

At this Sarret sat up hopefully, exclaiming, 'Ah!' as though to shout: 'Eureka! The gulf!' But Pobedin quickly confused this hope with a great dull fog of making different things the same. 'Instead of engagement,' he said, 'we in Russia have the concept of responsibility, which is the same thing—Russian writers have always been responsible. This has nothing to do with ideology. Russian writers were in the past socially responsible, they are responsible today, they will be responsible tomorrow. Tolstoy was responsible, Dostoyevsky was very responsible, so was Pushkin, and so, in a different way, was Tchekhov. They all felt that each, in his different way, had a duty to observe toward society,' Pobedin went on solemnly.

He then outlined the orthodox view, repeated for twenty years by every Communist literary critic, of the difference between what he called 'Western individualist responsibility' and Russian, 'truly traditionalist responsibility of the individual toward the tasks of society.' Eventually Sarret abandoned the attempt to maintain any longer that there was some mystique making it impossible to enter into Pobedin's ideology. With a resigned shrug of the shoulders, he dully watched the spectacle of Pobedin going flattening on. Pobedin now described what everyone present recognized as the conventional exception to the conventional orthodoxy. 'There was, many years ago,' he said, as though revealing some tremendous schism within the régime, 'difference of opinion as to whether the Soviet writer should be responsible to some particular publishing house, or to some larger organization—the Party or the State.' Having revealed this gigantic controversy, he looked up and across the table as though scanning the ever-opening future, and pronounced: 'After the revolution, and, indeed, until quite recently, the tasks of Soviet literature were to instruct the masses. Today, however, the stage of widespread public instruction has passed, and literature instead of being concerned with spreading wide, has begun to go DEEP!' He stopped dead here for a few seconds, with an expression on his face that recalled a horse brought to the edge of a canyon. He seemed solemnly to be staring down into abysses. There was one other subject which had been brought up in the Conference to which he ought to devote a word, he added, gravely as a bishop or headmaster mentioning sex. 'That is the matter of Social Realism. In the Soviet Union this offers no problem, I am convinced. The Soviet Writer has roots in the lives of the people because he lives in the Socialist Society. Therefore he cannot help being a Social Realist. I am sure that all Russian intellectuals agree about this. Since, even under the Czars, Russian writers have always been very socially conscious, Socialism, in transforming this social consciousness, has also inherited it as a tradition.'

Sarret, after his despair, followed by the moment of hope in which he thought the gulf had been made manifest, was now simply bored. Marteau had an expression which clearly said: '*Quelle blague!*' Dunstan Curlew clasped his hands in front of him and bowed his great head like one who, although himself a bishop, finds listening to pietistic utterances the greatest trial put on him by his faith. Botor stared blankly across the table, grasping a pencil tightly in one hand. Sereno— Sereno had the most surprising reaction. He sat bolt upright and followed Pobedin's words with a flushed, attentive expression.

Any hope the French might still have that their Soviet colleagues were going to contest anything, were now finally quenched by the idealistic, sentimental Korovin. He lifted up his head, thatched with mossy hair, and with shining eyes produced thoughts that might have proceeded from the mouth of some leprechaun brought into an early nineteenth-century drawing-room from the Scottish Highlands or the Irish Fens: one who, untouched by the march of time, watched sheep and drank from pure streams. He had a wide mouth, curved back round his face at the edges, and when he spoke the effect was of a charming carven elf who gushes one pellucid trickle contributing to the whole battery of massed fountains. While Korovin was speaking, Sarret's mouth fell open as if to exclaim—'*Merde!*' Whatever it was, the wordless expression lacked the unsulliedness of Korovin's stream. Korovin was now saying: 'I agree with all my colleague has said about Dostoyevsky, Tolstoy, and Tchekhov. I would like to add to their names those other glorious ones of Goethe, Shakespeare, and Byron: and since we are in Italy, also Dante. The good and the beautiful are means for ever accessible to us all, whereby we can unite ourselves in spirit with the past. There is a sense in which we Russians feel that not only Tolstoy and Dostoyevsky, but also Goethe and Shakespeare are members of our organizations of writers and intellectuals.'

Boris Pomyalov contributed some tough figures about the immense membership of the Soviet writers' organizations and the yet more immense sales of their books.

Sereno turned his head towards Bonvolio and slightly raised one hand. This produced a silence which lasted for some seconds, broken at first only by a slight 'ah!' from Sereno, a kind of uttered pause which took in what had just been said and anticipated what was to come. His delivery, like that of everyone there not French, was influenced by the fact that he had to speak in a language foreign to him. Having spent much of his life in exile in France and Switzerland, his French was fluent, but speaking it had a curious effect on him. He seemed to regard the foreign language as a kind of musical exercise. Speaking, or, more exactly, singing it, he was one of those musicians who go in extensively for 'repeats'. In common also with singers, his face preserved a detached expressionlessness, whilst from his mouth proceeded extremely meaningful sounds. The effect resembled those cartoons in which, from an impassive face, words written in a drawn balloon, sing out of a sketch.

His speech then was more like a great aria than a discourse, or oratory. The more so since, after a few politenesses, ghosts began to appear and fill the room. Sereno began: 'Our Soviet colleagues have come here —have come here, I say—with the evident purpose— the evident purpose—of carrying on a co-operative discussion. The more welcome to me, personally—the more welcome to me—since I have the same intention— the same intention . . .' There was another pause like a musical notation before he went on . . . 'Since de-Stalinization, I have thought a great deal about my friends—my colleagues—my friends whom I knew in Russia twenty-five years ago. During the past days, I have been reading the works of those—those who from out of their prisons—in various countries—Fascist or Communist—or from their places of exile—their islands and ends of the earth—have written the facts which must now surely be made available the world over, all over the world.'

Names now began to strike out of his large, impassive, pear-shaped head, like sounds from a great bronze bell—Karl Liebknecht, Rosa Luxembourg, Léon Trotsky. They sat there in cells with but the smallest narrow

window slitted on the world. Between abstractions they
poured pamphlets on to thin paper defending their
actions, they wrote poems to swallows that wheeled at
dusk around the prison yard. They tapped out messages
from wall to wall. They went into exile in a land of
cactuses.

At this time . . . no, before this, he'd gone to Moscow. . . . He'd known those poets, those story-tellers,
those film-producers who for a few years had turned
cinematography into a most exciting modern art . . .
poets with their visions of an ideal future seemed then
in harmony with political leaders who were also philosophers . . . who were also close to the people.

There were meetings . . . friendships . . . conversations all night in cafés. . . . It was a time, yes, a time
when the visions of artists fertilized the inventions of
scientists. . . . A picture of the city of the future was
opened which was not just Dunstan Curlew's perfected
machine for living in . . . but in which the imagination
was regarded as equally important with utility. . . . There
was good faith . . . and because good faith, therefore
sympathy with the aspirations of the Germans, the
Austrians, the Spanish, who also wanted a better society.

If freedom had not been betrayed by the Russian revolution then almost the whole of the intelligentsia of
Europe would have formed a single movement . . . not
weakened by doubts and poisoned by lies. . . . Such a
movement would certainly have made the tyrannies,
with all the murders in their train, impossible.

All this had been destroyed by the man called Stalin.
. . . Or that is what we were now told by friends of our
colleagues here from the Soviet Union. . . . Or should he
say poisoned by the group of men, the abstraction, now
called Stalinism.

He leaned back in his chair, looked up at the ceiling,
his eyes like balloons that might wander up there, and

said: 'I welcome this meeting. . . this meeting . . . because we have arrived at a time of cancelling out. . . . Against the sum of achievements we balanced the sum of victims and arrived at a kind of zero . . . an end which is a starting point . . . a place where we can let the truth in, as M. Marteau suggested might be done.

The force which gave life to the revolution . . . within the meeting of socialism with science and with imagination . . . was the concept of a single humanity. For that reason I am depressed by Sarret's dividing human beings into two irreconcilable camps.'

'In my heart . . . in my heart . . . I have never broken or quarrelled with my Russian colleagues. Friendship has been interrupted . . . cut off . . . but only with hammers and axes, and these don't really count. . . . I have remained faithful to their warmth in personal relations and their principles, their principles, to them I have remained faithful.'

Another pause, then he pursued: 'And these principles, I am glad to say, are now honoured again, once more honoured. I would like confirmation of this point from the colleagues now sitting here, that those principles and those faces, are now once more honoured. Unfortunately this honouring cannot give them back their lives, bring them back from the dead. Unfortunately.

'With deep emotion, I listened to the very true words that M. Pobedin spoke about Russian literature. Gogol, whom he had not mentioned, Gogol, who wrote *Dead Souls*, did not Gogol, Tolstoy, Tchekhov, have a unique place in the minds of readers all over the world, a unique position which outbalanced the fame of every other novelist, living or dead? Why? Above all, because they voiced the suffering of the oppressed, they wrote the words that were in the mouths of the perhaps silenced victims of tyranny, had even charity for those rejected not only by tyrants, but by liberals as well. They had charity for criminals, murderers, outlaws. Alas, much as one would like to do so, one could not agree altogether, be quite in accordance with the view, that the great Russian tradition is unbroken. Perhaps it is in abeyance, I hope it is only in abeyance, but what recent novelists, what novelists of the twenty-five last years, have given words to the victims of Stalin, the unjustly condemned, the executed, those sent to the slave camps, the deported, the tortured and silenced? Traditionally, Russian literature is not just popular, in the sense of being of the people, folkish, it is also non-conformist, it has always been political not in the sense of taking orders from above, but in that of being on the side of the people against their politicians—politically anti-political, one might say. The tradition was broken when writers began to support the State against society. . . .'

But now, just when he seemed in his stride, he hesitated. The meeting had got to a stage when time no longer counted. Every speech seemed too long or too short. There was no sense of proportion. Those who spoke at any length became lost in the stream of their own words, whilst those listening did not take in words at all, which had become an element, the weather. Somehow they grasped what was being said from the ability of the speaker to press on in a particular direction through the confusion, inertia, resistance, that had accumulated in the air of the room, like static electricity. Perhaps Sereno lost direction and impetus, allowed his ideas to become dissolved in the stream of so many other things already said, as an inevitable 'historic' result of the period of decay into which the meeting, like an isolated segment of history, had fallen.

The speech had come to the place when Sereno ought to clinch the argument, or at least launch out on a massive peroration. But instead of this it was beginning to change into other things—dissolve into the smoke of Sarret's endless Gaulois' cigarettes, disintegrate among stubs of pencils, be fanned away among whispers and by the murmurs of the intellectuals, their gusts of laughter. It still had the power to crystallize into an image . . . 'I also have fought against tyranny . . . I also know the meaning of cunning, anonymity, exile, and prison . . .' and a picture emerged of Sereno as a young man in the hills of his village up in the North, Sereno chalking slogans upon walls, Sereno mourning a cousin murdered on a penal island because he bore the same name: images went wandering up to the Reconciliation on the wall, the brawny young Sereno with his passion for freedom, set among the warriors, the princes, the gods.

The enormous sprawling speech took over Sereno's whole life, matched against these other lives. There was beauty in Sereno sitting at the table watching his youth which had so much courage and dignity, yet the very moment when, like his speech, his life should concentrate all its past into a ball that burst through the confusion of the present into a clear future, he remained content to invoke the lithe tigers of memory of the past and set them running among the conference of intellectuals.

Now, making a show of recovery, yet repeating what he had already said, he returned to the charge against Sarret, as though this were the anchor he must cling to, in order to bring the dirigible of his eloquence down into the room: 'I cannot enter, I find no way to enter into the point of view of M. Sarret, which divides the world into two irreconcilable camps. There is only one humanity, in my view . . . only one humanity . . . and the meeting place of this humanity is the confidence that we are all at some point ultimately the same, in being human. Without faith that human beings are fundamentally the

same everywhere, there is no point of meeting . . .
because if we were not the same in being human, then
we would belong to different species.'

Csongor Botor held his pencil pressed against his
teeth, his mouth rather unpleasantly wide. With a
malicious smile, his quicksilver glance turned from
Sereno back to the Russians, at whom he looked almost
subserviently.

Then a window suddenly blew open. From the courtyard below rose a great drumming, trumpeting, and
shouting. The draught lifted papers from the table,
drowned the murmur of voices, dissolved tobacco smoke.
Pomyalov, grinning, lurched up from the table, and
walked across to the window, out of which he waved
convivially to the crowd of wedding guests visiting
Venice, assembled below. He felt himself to be the
spokesman of the common man. He leaned far out of the
window, gesticulated to the crowd, and then, slamming
the window to, came back into the room, conscious of
shutting out the world from the hermetically canned talk
of the intellectuals.

By the time the window was shut and Pomyalov,
bonhomous, had returned to his seat, Sereno's speech
had faded away like smoke on the horizon of their desert
ocean. And now, since positions had been taken up by
nearly everyone present, nothing could prevent Sereno
being attacked according to the routine of dialectic.
The fact that they knew the answers he would make
made it all the more necessary for Sarret to give them.
Exhausted, disillusioned, betrayed by the failure of his
team to enter into the oppositeness of their ideology, he
assumed the ironic manner of a professor dealing with
an emotional, well-meaning, but confused, pupil: 'It's
just because I sympathize with M. Sereno's wish that
we discuss things frankly, and establish *real* points of
contact, that I don't agree with this talk about a com-

mon humanity,' he began. In a mechanical, business-like
voice he went on: 'It is not to exchange platitudes
about humanity that we meet here, but to discuss
points of difference; and it is in order that we should
examine seriously the possibility of overcoming these
differences, that it is necessary to understand how basic-
ally opposed our attitudes are. Otherwise we should
only arrive at superficial agreements, based on sentimental misinterpretations of a humanity we share.'

Alexander Pobedin gravely, solemnly, thanked Sereno
for what was clearly an important speech. Pobedin said
he could not reply to the many significant things Sereno
had said, until he had had time to study the speech more
closely. He could suggest now, though, that it was not
altogether just to say that Soviet writers had failed to
express the sufferings of humanity. If M. Sereno would
study the books of Russian Communist writers at the
time of the Civil War, he would find they bore witness
to a great deal of suffering. It was an interesting
abstract question which might be debated sometime—
Pobedin went on with the courteous smile of one considering a theoretic problem put to him for the first time
—how far it was the duty of the writer to express
suffering.

Curlew, raising his massive head with its great load
of hair, spoke next.

Dunstan Curlew was a changed man. He no longer
excused himself for being a scientific specialist more or
less gate-crashing a meeting of literary aesthetes. His
attitude now was that of omniscient realist come into his
own, a practical mind packed with projects, an administrator, an incisive analyst of other people's follies, and a
tabulator of deep schemes. His attitude towards the conference was that of some exasperated man of affairs who
has without prejudice tried out the poets and found them
wanting. With a sigh he gets on with the job. Or,

rather, if the Conference had consisted only of Curlew—
he seemed to be thinking—he would do so, but unfortunately there were these others always in his way.

He gave up all pretence of listening, and while others
were talking, confined himself to making out lists and
drawing up programmes for the coming conference,
which, if he had his way, would be a very different
affair. His own *'interventions'*—as the French call such
speeches—consisted of referring points he made to what
appeared to be some master plan placed in front of him
on the table. A terse introductory thesis followed by
headings 1, 2, and 3, sub-headings alpha, beta, and
gamma, was his formula.

He spoke in the relaxed mood of a universal mind
willing to deliver a lecture to the completely ignorant on
almost anything: 'One of the best characteristics of
English civilization,' he began, 'is—or so it has always
seemed to me—the concept of *le fair play*. Another
strongly held English idea—the converse of *le fair play*
—is the idea of what the English hold to be *oonfair*. It
seems to me that Sereno is being *oonfair* in introducing
politics into the discussion. But since politics have been
introduced, one may perhaps point out that if the
Russian team contained members of the calibre of
Sereno and Sarret, they would be able to reply to the
charges that had been made. One of the things the great
Sobolov would say if he had come to Venice was
that it was *oonfair* to attack Stalinism without mentioning Hitlerism. A Russian of Sobolov's calibre
would also probably have something to say about colonialism.'

'Certainly they may talk about colonialism. I shall be
glad to hear, and probably I shall agree with them,' said
Sereno. 'As for Hitlerism, I did not anticipate that I
would be invited to mention every crime going on outside Russia as an excuse for Stalinism. In any case,

many of the things I had in mind, happened before
Hitler came to power.'

Botor, leaning forward, with elbows pushed against
his side, and his clenched fists lying on the table in front
of him, now started speaking—shouting almost—in his
loud, harsh voice. 'I am profoundly shocked and disappointed by what we have just heard M. Sereno say.
What I most deplore is the lack of charity in some of
these remarks. Why does M. Sereno not try to understand the suffering, the real suffering, of the writers of
that time? Then perhaps he will not judge them so
harshly for hiatuses in their work. Then, too, in the
spirit of charity he will try to forget the past—and
welcome what is happening now.'

As he repeated most of what he had said previously—
difficulties he had undergone—his privileged position
despite these—his detachment—the touching love the
people had for him—his proletarian sympathies—nevertheless his frank admission that he was 'bourgeois'—he
stared straight into the eyes of Olim Asphalt sitting
opposite him. His words became meaningless, the room
flooded with light, the whole of Venice outside seemed
pouring in through the windows onto the walls, as
though filling a vacuum, and beyond Venice, figures of
friends, a whole civilization which rushed in to staunch
this barbaric void of the conference table. Memories of
sensible conversation over café tables, were like an ague,
an aching through all the limbs. Suddenly Olim remembered with absolute distinctness his afternoon with
Csongor Botor on the shore of Lake Balaton five years
ago. After the banquet of writers, Csongor Botor,
taking him by the arm, had walked him round the mag-
nificent tree-planted and landscaped grounds, with the
view of the lake beyond them. 'You see what we have
done,' he said. 'Our revolution is a revolution of pure
intelligence, achieved, ultimately, by the surrealists. It

is what you and I have always been wanting, *mon cher*. Surrealism not just of art, but of life around us, surrealism to be discovered within the concept of social equality which releases all the mad forces of the eccentric common people into the midst of the city insanely uninhibited. The war began the process when the streets revealed accidental juxtapositions such as a bidet like a helmet settled upon a dowager's mad wig which was a chandelier. The Party is the midwife bringing forth this crazy birth. I can assure you that the statue of Stalin looking over the Danube is the wildest hallucination which has yet transmogrified itself into bronze. I will tell you a most encouraging story. During the war the most famous sculptor in Budapest—unfortunately a very bad one—was commissioned to do a statue of the airman son of the Fascist dictator Admiral Horthy, who had been shot down. Just at the very moment when he had completed it, the Russians 'liberated' our city. In their enthusiasm for inferior art, they immediately commissioned this sculptor to do a statue in the uniform of the airman son of the invading Russian general, who had been killed in battle. What did our sculptor do? He chopped off the head of Horthy's son, replaced it with that of the Russian pilot, and made a chip or two on the body, transforming the insignia from Horthyist to Soviet. Now bad as this sculptor is, he shows us the permanence, the supremacy of art, over the will and instability of politics. We are the same constant artists, and the material we use remains also constant—words or bronze. The sculptor's example suggests to me the wildest possibilities: poems which if read forwards conform with the will of politicians, if backwards, mean the exact opposite: pictures, which to acquire their true meaning have to be turned upside down, or which, like those puzzle drawings we used to look at in our childhood, concealing dozens of unseen mocking faces within the elaborated leaves of a tree; collapsible works which, the moment there is a change of government, can by the alteration of a word, the taking out of a screw, change their whole aspect—thus representing at the same moment the permanence of their material, and the mocking adaptiveness of their ingenious form.' It was impossible to tell whether he was being serious or facetious, whether his was a programme requiring courage, or a prescription for cowardice. He ended with a burst of his famous central European Homeric godlike laughter.

Olim Asphalt, who was always deadly serious about those public matters in which he was so impeccable a moralist, inquired: 'All the same, aren't you a bit afraid of what may happen in politics? Isn't all this freedom just a temporary phase?' 'Afraid?' roared Botor— 'Why should we be afraid? They've got us where they want us, haven't they? We've got them where we want them, haven't we?'—and he pointed, with a movement of his arm that encircled the landscape, to the castle. 'But you may have to write what they want.' 'Well, isn't that just what I've been saying? They don't know what they want, and they wouldn't know, even if they had it!' 'Why?' '*Why? Why? Why? Mon cher?* Because they are fools, and we are clever.'

The recollection switched off, abruptly, as it had begun. And suddenly, as though his head had been charged from the oratorical accumulators sitting round him, he felt it bursting with a speech that drove out of the window. 'What you fail to realize, is that while I have to live the life I do live, it is impossible for us to marry. I know it's difficult for you but you should think of me as a person committed to his work and vocation, a wanderer. Imagine yourself married to a sailor, for instance; at every port, a conference of LITUNO. If we had children, of course, it would be different. As it is, we do have a tax-free salary.' Across the invisible wires in permanent connection between Elaine and him, her voice came back piercing as an icicle: 'Why do you think I want you to marry me? You seem to count on me a great deal. Or perhaps it is just your guilt—you are afraid I would do something for which you would not forgive yourself if . . .' 'Let's be truthful!' his brain implored. 'By all means!' And she became silent as if a door thick as a mountain of rock had slammed. He cut through this a tunnel where everything was words and every word was meaningless, unpardonable, destructive, and irretrievable.

There was more talk, of course, endless talk, in which Sarret threw Proust into the discussion. Pobedin declared that Proust was for the most part decadent, though sometimes socially significant. Marteau retorted: 'If they consider Proust decadent then let us not discuss Proust, but let us by all means discuss decadence.' Bonvolio said they could all agree to discuss why they agreed to discuss Proust's decadence. After this, they decided to spend the rest of the week being strictly practical: and only to discuss what they might discuss at a future discussion. But really, Olim reflected, they had been discussing this all the time.

VI

So their table, adrift with papers, notebooks, pencils, words, words, words, poured ideologies out over everything they saw, like that white rain-cloud which, on the evening of Olim's arrival, had made the corners of palaces at the ends of canals seem black and white photographs projected upon a screen. Everything was transformed into cerebral terms within ideologic concepts of analysable history. Not marble, nor the gilded monuments could resist being melted down into materialist motives underlying ethereal imaginings. A thick net dragged statues down to dialectical history. And standing above it, there were the grinning, squabbling faces of the modern intellectuals, imprisoned by their own awareness which put them at the centre of past and future historic struggles. The squat, pink-faced analysts asserted their superiority over the superb inventors, by a few tricks of intelligent exposition, which, explaining everything, made somnambulant, creative dreaming impossible, and locked them themselves inside their dull world of chemists, detectives, and policemen. Since all the past was imprisoned within the contemporary cerebral interpretation, there was an ironic sense in which Pobedin's saying that Shakespeare, Dante, and Goethe were contemporaries, was true.

One afternoon they were taken on an excursion arranged in masterly fashion by Bonvolio, admiral of a fleet consisting of three speed boats. The Russians, Borès, Magda Karinthy, and Dunstan Curlew got into one, with Pomyalov at the helm, urging the crew to make as much speed as possible, and waving triumphantly at the other craft, left trailing far behind. Sarret, Sereno, Bonvolio, Longhi, and the venerable Italian poet were in the second boat. Marteau, Alex Merton and Olim Asphalt brought up the rear. Marteau sat in the cabin, the light playing on his curled mouth and prow-like nostrils, the boat below him seeming a masterly illustration of one of his swift, surf-cutting expositions.

The speed boats entered Torcello's minute harbour—mouth, rather—of the single canal that splits the little island like a straight vein through an agate-green flat stone. They moved slowly up the canal, threading through the single bridge arched like a stick caterpillar, to the minute village which is Torcello: an uprooted or superannuated Venetian square containing one of each of everything that symbolizes Venice—a campanile, a cathedral with Byzantine mosaics inside, basilica, museum and monuments going back to Roman times, among dust and grass of the piazza.

They all lunched at a long trestle table in the garden restaurant behind the cathedral. As on the first evening, Olim Asphalt found himself next to Magda Karinthy and Alex Merton. And, as on that occasion, Magda presented him with a profile that seemed to assert a partition, between him and herself-with-Dunstan-Curlew. Again, Olim had the feeling that behind this barrier an understanding, perhaps at his expense, was reached.

He was determined to break up this party. 'Bloody-mindedness' was a weapon he was always gaily prepared to use. 'Not looking my way this afternoon?' he asked Magda. 'Well, it isn't the first time we've been cut by you, is it?' He said this in a way that made it easier for Dunstan Curlew than for her to understand. 'She plays fast and loose with us, doesn't she—but that's the privilege of beauty even over there. But she wasn't like this the other night on the gondola—' he went on, exclusively to Dunstan—'Pretty hot stuff, I can assure you. You try. old boy. She hasn't given you much of a break, I can see that—but just keep on trying.'

He went on with this impossible banter, sheltering behind his reputation for drinking. Magda looked as if this English was too idiomatic for her to follow. Dunstan Curlew, holding his head down, looked as though he were taking refuge on the ideologically correct side of a Sarretian gulf. Bourgeois ebullience was totally incomprehensible to him.

Olim gave up and looked at the scenery. Turning back to them a few moments later, he discerned that the short-term effect of his malice was to warm up the relationship between Dunstan and Curlew—perhaps this was what he wished to do. Magda's cheeks were bright red, and her eyes shone as it were joyfully in Dunstan's direction, spitefully in his. (Her general two-dimensionalness permitted her to appear different on each side, he noted, as he had done before, on the first evening.)

The scientist was in what seemed great unbuttoned mood. His immense head wagged too and fro like a huge wrinkled papier-mâché carnival mask, while from somewhere deep inside it there came gurgling sounds as though his mixed animal and intellectual spirits were warmed up, simmering pleasantly. He entertained his neighbours with amusing, if oddly stereotyped Arabian Nights Science Fiction tales of eccentric colleagues.

There was Gander, eminent biologist, famous for his willingness to expose his own physical person, or parts. of his person, to experiment, as publicly as possible. Newspaper readers were familiar with pictures of Gander entering a Diving Bell, to be plunged squatting among squids in the bottom-most darkness of the ocean bed, or entering a balloon to be jerked up into the stratosphere. They had seen him being roasted in front of blast furnaces, or trussed up like a fowl, with his huge sad moustaches on either side of a nose osseous as a beak.

From an intimacy of scientists that seemed as deep as the interior of a kangaroo's pouch, Dunstan Curlew produced his very special Gander item. Having to undergo an operation on a somewhat intimate part of his body, the biologist insisted on having a local anaesthetic: during the performance he delivered an exposition on the exposed part of him, to his assembled mostly female audience.

Axtable, ichthyologist—Curlew went on—while detached and sceptical in his examination of facts, was helplessly credulous in the face of human beings. He was too innocent to think that anyone lied, and too literal-minded to believe it possible that anyone could imagine anything. Woe to the mariner who, on one of Axtable's trudging seaside holidays, unwound a fisherman's yarn of sea serpent or submarine monster he had had on the end of his line. Axtable carried round a note book entitled RARITIES for such occasions, and whipping it out would have the poor embarrassed mariner draw or describe exactly what he had seen to the accompaniment of murmurs from Axtable: 'Incredible! Quite extraordinary! Sometimes I feel that ichthyology is a science of which we have only scratched the sea-surface! I must write to the keeper of the Naples Aquarium about that!' 'But——' and this shows that belief sometimes does lead to truth, went on Curlew, squinting Jesuit-agnostically, 'Axtable's willingness to believe once led him to a real discovery. A student whom the professor was examining, through nervous dread of Axtable's beetling eyebrows, found himself inventing an entirely new fish, tail and fins assembled from answers he improvised to the examining professor's crescendo of ever more excited questions. A mutation that was! Axtable, after awarding the student a First for his information, went home, ransacked aquaria, dredged the sea almost, to confirm these data. Finally he did discover a fish corresponding to the student's invention. It now bears the name of the student, himself in charge of an aquarium.'

In the excitement of his narration, Dunstan Curlew spilled a drop of wine on the tablecloth. Obedient to science, it docilely spread itself into ragged, roughly concentric rings of different density and coloration. Flattered by its behaving so 'typically', Curlew pointed to the stain, and said: 'You see, the wine is giving us a demonstration by splitting up into its component substances, some darker, some lighter, some denser, some thinner. Wine went on patiently doing this for centuries without anyone appreciating its humble exercise in self-analysis. Then someone noticed that the spilt liquid behaved in this helpful way on a cloth or blotting paper, and, ever since, this has been the recognized way of analysing its components.' Bellowing amiably, he wagged his great gold fleece.

Magda Karinthy's expression was now wholly drawn into single-minded admiration of the narrator. Watching them, Olim noticed a sudden change come over the scientist. Curlew stopped talking, and stared at her, His enormous flaccid face, directed towards the radiance of her cheeks, became absolutely still, while at the same time it changed from pale pink to dead white, as though drained of blood. The effect was unearthly—the strangest conjunction of the earliest most primitive manifestations of attraction, with the most recent scientific idiom. Olim knew that there lurked somewhere under these folds of flesh, as though peering between the fronds of primeral ferns, two eyes, boring into Magda's bright cheeks.

The sheer horror of these Rites of Spring compelled him to break the silence which had frozen the whole table as though some agnostic fallen angel of science were winging above it. With a cry he bellowed out the unsayable: 'I say, prof, what do you think of Krushchev's declarations about Stalin and the cult of personality?'

Curlew, whose reflexes appeared to have slowed down (perhaps as the result of the absence of blood in his perspective areas), retracted his head a few dazed inches, and then conceded: 'Well, it does seem that a good many things happened which one could not have taken into account.'

'Oh, what sort of things?'

'We seem to have made some serious mistakes. I don't know how it happened, but it is bad.'

'Would you now share the point of view of those like myself who decided some time ago that terrible crimes were being committed *over there*, and that the system of dictatorship made these inevitable?'

Curlew tilted his head to one side. It appeared now to have become de-self-hypnotized from its fixed pose— a little blood was flooding back into his cheeks. 'There is not just one system you have to choose from. There are two. And of the two, I prefer the communist.'

'Today! Now! You still prefer it?'

'You have to consider the utter unnecessary misery and waste and lack of opportunity that exists in the world as it is at present. What people fail to realize is that things don't have to be as they are now.'

'And what, after Krushchev's speech, do you imagine it is that prevents their being better than they have been in that part of the world?'

'Well, for one thing, people themselves. Human beings are the trouble. One person who is greedy and dishonest, who gets into a strong position, can undo the good done by hundreds.'

They had got up from the table, and were out there in the little garden in front of the restaurant, on the flagged pavementing among the roses.

'Wonderful! Wonderful!' Olim crowed. 'Doesn't it make one think! You, a scientist, failing to calculate on simple human fallibility, which all the saints and all the poets and most of the historians, are agreed in indicating. Really, you make me superstitious, you make me believe in Sin, and still more in the Last Judgment. Can't you imagine the scene! In front of all the assembled dead of all the centuries—I did not know death could undo so many—when, after perhaps, Rousseau, has spent the first week reading his Confession to the Almighty, the trumpet summons Dunstan Curlew to explain why he ignored the murder and incarceration of tens of thousands by his machine for improving society, and he answers—more briefly than Rousseau, it is true— 'One does not see how these things could have happened!' Going right up to Dunstan Curlew and thrusting his face under the great sea anemone frondes of his hair, he said: 'One has not eyes, one has not ears, one has only a brain!'

Actually Olim Asphalt believed involuntarily and obsessively in the Last Judgment, and this scene probably affected him far more than it did Curlew. To dissolve the image of Elaine pleading her torments before the Throne, after Curlew had reduced the saints and poets to laughter, he walked over to Sereno, who was standing contemplating a small fountain. Producing a camera, Olim photographed Sereno in this pose. 'It has all been as I thought,' said Sereno. 'They have said nothing. After I saw to it that their instructors—the police—those men who had been sent to supervise them—went away—what could they say? As for Sarret, he makes it his business to make discussion impossible. Csongor Botor was more interesting. At least he said the exact opposite of what he thought, and one could deduce what he meant by reading it backwards.'

As he finished saying this, Botor came up to them. Ignoring Olim, he said to Sereno: 'I hope you under-

stand that what I said at the last meeting had no relation
to my private feelings. In my Faustian breast I have
divorced my public figure from my private soul. Everything you said was perfectly true. My only criticism—
your information is not completely up to date. Things
in our countries are worse, far worse, than you said.
And if we try to make them better, they may get worse
still. That is the explanation of my attitude.'

He gave a humiliating smile to Pobedin and Pomyalov,
who were approaching them, arm in arm. 'My friend
Pobedin has been saying that he would like to live here
on this island, in a convent,' said Pomyalov. 'Wouldn't
you?' he addressed his colleague. 'It would be peaceful,'
said Pobedin, with his courteous, lost, old-world smile.
'But he has one condition,' said Pomyalov. 'He will only
do so if he can share his cell with a nun. Ha! ha! ha!'
They wandered off, inseparable, to join Borès, who was
sketching the portico of the cathedral.

Olim Asphalt was now happily established in the role
of manipulator, a puller of strings, with all these
characters who offered up their official roles, jerking to
his behest. In this mood he walked along the towpath
beside the little thread of the canal, to the bridge. On the
far side of this, it framed the flat transparent blade of
the campanile laid against the sky, like an Omega in its
curled calligraphy. Standing apart, in the vineyard, he
saw Bonvolio. It was the Agony in the Garden. He
paced to and fro, clasped his hand to his head, sometimes muttered, and, more strikingly, sometimes opened
his mouth inaudibly uttering a loud top note of some
kind, like opera-singers who, in rehearsing, mouth, but
do not sing, their highest notes. Olim turned back, and
was confronted by Sarret, standing on the side of the
bridge nearest the piazza. He now entered into a Soc-
ratic dialogue with the philosopher which seemed
already all laid out in both their minds.

Olim

M. Sarret, there is a question I would like to put to you.

Sarret

I would be very glad to answer.

Olim

You think that there are two completely opposed attitudes in the world today: the bourgeois, which represents the interest of capitalism; and the communist, which represents that of the proletariat?

Sarret

Yes, with a few qualifying circumstances, that is what I do think.

Olim

You believe that if one has bourgeois attitudes, one supports capitalism?

Sarret

That is so.

Olim

And that in so far as anyone succeeds in identifying himself with the communist attitude, he is on the side of the proletariat?

Sarret

With certain reservations, that is, broadly speaking, what I believe.

Olim

At any rate, you believe that if, even for what may seem good reasons, someone gets into a position which is anti-communist, then he is setting himself against the workers?

Sarret

Yes, with a few qualifying circumstances, that is so. Yes.

Olim

Well: I would like you to consider the following hypothetical situation. You, M. Sarret, have been sentenced to a long term of imprisonment in a communist state for a political crime of which you know yourself to be, in fact, and in thought, completely innocent. You are sitting in a cell alone in a prison of, let us suppose, Budapest. From there, you learn through the rapping on the wall of other prisoners who are also in solitary confinement, but who are in communication with the outside world, that a bourgeois journalist, an official hack, called Olim Asphalt, has written an article saying that you are completely innocent of the crimes of which you have been accused, and setting out authoritatively both the truth of your opinions, and of the unjust trial by which you have been condemned. Would you be pleased or displeased at this news ? Would you welcome the idea that somewhere there was a witness for the truth against those who had wrongfully imprisoned you ?

Sarret

(*turning round on his heel, which he had pressed rather deep into the soil.*) Ah. You may be surprised to hear that that is a question I have often put to myself. It is, indeed, a dramatic question, and not easy to answer. But I have tried to answer it to myself in this way: of course, I do not know what my reaction in such circumstances would be, but that does not matter. I know now, not being in prison, and therefore being at this present moment impartial, what I would wish it to be. I hope that I would consider that if your article helped the cause of those who were opposed to my unjust gaolers, of whom I was convinced that nevertheless they represented the proletariat, then you should not have published it.

Standing at the edge of the canal a few yards from

them, his arms folded Napoleon-wise across his chest, and on his wooden features a wide, sardonic grin, was Botor. He seemed to be enjoying the view of the vineyards. He seemed to take in everything on the island. Sarret nodded to Olim as though to say, 'I have answered your question with the utmost precision. For the time being, you can hardly expect any more,' and walked away to rejoin Marteau.

Botor's presence, disturbing though it was, yet made Olim sensibly aware of the shining, peaceful island. For all he had noticed of it till now, it might have been a disc revolved by all their talk and restless energy, on which they were standing—the only still thing, the hub of the slender, transparent-looking campanile. Now it seemed as quiet as an engraving ; campanile, cathedral, piazza, basilica, vineyards, drawn above the soil flat as the single line of a horizon, one of each of everything.

'Shall we go for a stroll?' Olim asked Csongor Botor. 'There's not very far we can walk on a postage stamp.' Nevertheless, by crossing the bridge, they got to the vineyards on the other side of the canal, and found themselves separated from the rest of the party by a hedge of vines. The vine leaves were beginning to shoot their transparent flint spearheads, thin and green, very clean and pale, out of the black stems. A man, his shirt stripped off, was tending them. Botor was still grinning. The light caught his aureole of standing-up white hair. 'Do you remember?' Olim asked. Suddenly, the thought crossed his mind that perhaps Botor had never really recognized him. He might easily have thought he was some other visitor from England. 'Oh, yes, I do remember. I would like you to know that.' 'How long ago was it—the wine-tasting in the vineyards, when we drove out from the castle—you do remember, surely, you can't possibly not do so.' 'A century ago. Two centuries ago.' He laughed, a little foolishly.

'But, after all, already then, before the coup, you had a communist government?' 'That was the year of the changes—since then there have been a lot more changes: every month there are changes.' He said 'changes' in the first half of this sentence as though it committed him. In the second half it established the gulf between them. Botor turned back towards the bridge.

Had they not returned just at this moment, Bonvolio, an irascible shepherd, would certainly have called out to them to come at once and get on board. Their two motor-boats were waiting to take them to Murano where, half an hour later, they saw the glass-making. In a burning, glowing workshop, men, naked to the waist, thrust tubes into a brazier of molten glass, raised them to their lips with the gesture of followers of Pan trumpeting through goathorns, and blew marvellous glass bubbles. These they twisted, rotating in the air, altering their shapes from circles to oblong, or oval. Then with hammers, tongs, pincers, they worked these forms on anvils, adding a knob or a handle, nipping off an end or a bulge. The muscles of the forearm of a youth twisting a balloon of glass seemed a ripple that communicated its turns into spirals of the glass. When an error was detected in an object finished or half-complete, the workman would throw it on the ground with the extravagance of a perruqued aristocrat on the stage, hurling his wine-glass at the wall, after he had drunk a toast.

Here were foreman and workers, like Bacchus and his pards. But the glass-making was a show-window of Venice, and perhaps these workmen were not the real proletariat, perhaps they were largely putting on their act of craftsmanship, and resembled ballet dancers rather than 'real' workers. (The intellectuals always had doubts of this kind when confronted by workers. Perhaps, in some way, they were not 'real'.)

They were taken to see the finished products of the workmen, in a large gallery which was a showroom. There they were: covering the floor, heaped on tables and on shelves, reaching up to the ceiling, objects of such hideousness—thick, twisted, convolvulus-like, lumpy, bubbled, and coloured, Venetian glass, with its barley sugar and acid-drop textures.

Amidst this endless array of shapes of twisted toffee, under candelabra of pink and blue roses and dropping beads, surrounded by a small army of pierrots, harlequins, and columbines, one show-case of plain glass stood there like a reproach. It was the factory museum, and contained specimens of work going back two hundred years: a few wine-glasses on very long stems, a plate engraved with signs of the Zodiac, bowls like calyxes, some bottles, jars, vases, and carafes, of transparent, slender, petal-thin transparency.

Alex Merton and Olim had got together like a chorus, in the display gallery. Their sneers, which had begun already at school and at Oxford, were sufficiently private to go unnoticed by the Russians, deeply impressed by the results of the glass industry (though Pobedin said he regretted so much beauty being lavished on capitalist purchasers).

'This does make one realize, all the same, that the bourgeoisie is decayed,' said Olim. 'Not just the bourgeoisie,' said Alex, 'this is what the proletariat adore.' And he pointed to a wall on which hung the most hideous object in the factory. It was a glass crèche, made the previous Christmas by the workers for their own delectation. 'Besides,' he added, pointing to the Russians, 'this is their first glimpse since they've been abroad, of social realism. For the first time they find something contemporary to admire. And hasn't Sarret been telling us that they are the proletariat?'

They were on the pavement at the grey canal edge

at the factory quayside where the motor launch was
waiting. It was suddenly quite hot. The others were
still wandering among glass monstrosities. Alex leaned
against the wall, his elbow pressing it, and his hand
touching the back of his head. Olim looked at him,
taking him in and not taking him for granted, seeing
him for—it seemed—the first time in years. With his
soft, smooth hair in which the comb seemed to have left
lines like an engraving, his grey eyes, his features of a
family mould, rather strong, but which left some mystery about himself within this handsome casing—he was
Englishly distinguished. Whatever their faults, Olim
and Alex had never surrendered a single joke shared
between them.

'You see,' Olim said—'Sereno was right about Sarret. Do you know what he said to me just now?' and he
recounted the conversation which had taken place between them. 'And he said he hoped *I would not publish
the truth if doing so would discredit unjust gaolers.* Didn't
I tell you his philosophy was a stick he used to beat his
true perceptions with? There it all is, in a nut-shell! The
truth observed, the particular experience, has to be sub-
mitted to the doctrinal propaganda of the side supposed
to be inevitably, unalterably, eternally right, automatically benefiting humanity!'

'Well, ever since this Conference started, I haven't
turned one stone that doesn't seem impregnated with
ideology!'

'And then there's Dunstan Curlew who, when I
asked him what he thought of the Kruschev report, said:
"*Mistakes that no one could have anticipated seem to have
occurred!*"'

Olim was hooting with his loud self-mocking laughter.

'But you're surely wrong,' said Alex Merton, a bit
testily.

'Why?'

'In fact, now I come to think of it, I don't see why you don't confess that it is I who have been proved right. Didn't I say they wouldn't change?'

'Well, you're being right doesn't make it any the less funny.'

'I remember you're saying that when things change people should change with them. But should they really do so? It may be logical to control and adapt oneself by circumstances, but what do you expect? That they all come here and say "We were wrong"?'

'As a matter of fact,' said Olim, 'that's just what I do expect.'

'But would it really be helpful? Isn't there a lot to be said for the attitude—my country right or wrong? After all, if the moment intelligent people realized their country was wrong about something they joined the opposing side, they might be saving their own souls in some way, but they would be confusing issues dreadfully. Surely the real reason why one resents the "ex's" and "anti's" thrown up by ideologies is that they resemble over-squeamish lawyers who suddenly defend the prisoner they are prosecuting because they discover that he is innocent. This might be "honest" but it would destroy the law. Someone who turns against the cause he has belonged to was either irresponsible when he joined it or he's an anarchist who's also a puritan when he leaves it.'

'Politics aren't the law.'

'Also, your theory that if one changes with changing circumstances then one becomes a person who develops is wrong. The trouble with people who go into opposition against their own side is that finally they become more stuck than anyone else. Their side may develop, but they stay as the persons who proved themselves right in leaving it. Surely that explains the position of Sereno.'

'But what if you discover the laws of the State are anti-laws? That's really the position of Sereno. He discovered that the Soviet constitution was simply an instrument of oppression at home, a trap for liberals abroad.'

'All the same, isn't it more useful to realize that Curwen is clever and wrong than to have to cope with the awful complexity of his confessing that he has been stupid, and is right?'

'It isn't a matter of being persuaded that an argument is wrong, but of acting because thousands of people have been murdered.'

'Acting . . . acting . . . acting . . . how?' Alex seemed to be on tiptoe, his eyes shining.

'Well, then, you force me to be idiotic. I have no basis for believing in penitence, and I am a pretty good example of an impenitent myself. But what I really mean is—repenting!'

'You're in all probability perfectly right. Repenting —yes—but how?'

'In some quite unsophisticated way. Going on a pilgrimage or crusade perhaps. Wearing sackcloth and ashes,' he laughed, self-parodying. 'Anyway, by taking some sort of action. Not talking and eating banquets.' A moment later he added: 'For Christ's sake, don't tell them I said that. The food and drink are the only tolerable things about this. And as for repenting, I . . .' he laughed again. 'I have my own little private concentration camp I can't give up.'

'And Magda Karinthy?' asked Alex, hurriedly, before the others could overhear them.

'We went out in a gondola.'

'How are you getting on? Are you seeing her again? Will you be able to make her?'

'We haven't spoken since.'

'Why not?'

'The Party has its reasons that do not know the heart.' Olim spluttered, very pleased with himself once again.

The others joined them and they poured into the two large speed-boats which raced to the landing nearest the piazza.

Back at Venice, one more treat awaited: a special showing of an Italian anti-Fascist film. The action took place in Florence—a Florence no tourist had ever seen or heard of, without the Arno, without the Medici chapel, without Michelangelo's David—just tall, barrack-like tenements, along wide streets, in a bare landscape like a deserted strip of beach. Everywhere was concrete and sand. Everything happened either in these streets, or in bedrooms, one of them that of a nice young man who had a nicer, at first ugly, but later—the camera saw—pretty, fiancée. The Fascists gained control, and the unpleasant youth who was a Fascist leader tried to get all the people in the tenement to become Fascists. The nice young man, who had not thought about politics till then, realized through their faces and their uniforms and their actions that the Fascists were bad, so he refused to join them. Meeting some very good communists, he became an anti-Fascist. After this, his life was battles in which he was always on the right side. He did much anti-Fascist activity on his bicycle.

This film all took place in these grey rooms and grey streets, with workers, and uniforms, and speeches, and violence. The whole mythology was so familiar, in a language difficult to follow, that after a time Olim wearied, and started looking at his neighbour, Dunstan Curlew. Curlew was watching intently, leaning forward in his seat frowning at the screen, and breathing heavily. Whenever the anti-Fascist hero was bullied or beaten, he heaved a sigh. At moments, he was so overcome that he had to look away from the screen, holding his head in his hands. The Fascists threw the anti-Fascist youth's bicycle into a bonfire which they had lit by burning books of good literature. At this, the anguish of Olim's neighbour seemed intolerable. He covered his face with his hands. He did not look any more at the screen. Tears streamed from his eyes.

As they came out of the cinema, Olim, shadow-dark, with his mop of black hair and his silhouetted leanness, rushed over to Alex Merton and asked: 'Did you see Curlew?'

Alex smiled at him—a bit forbearingly—and said: 'No. I was glued. My eyes were glued to that imbecile film.'

'When he saw the anti-Fascist's bicycle thrown on the bonfire, he groaned, he howled, he buried his face in his hands, he could not bear to look at the screen!'

'I don't believe you! You're inventing the whole thing! You make up everything!'

'How is it that a person who reproaches Sereno for mentioning tens of thousands of real victims, can be so moved by fictitious suffering?'

'He cares for what he sees enacted in front of his eyes. What he hears spoken about, remains an abstraction.'

'But he accepts the crimes of Stalin in the name of an abstraction—progress, the hypothetical happiness of people who are unborn.'

'All the same, the real acted out incident causes him to suffer profoundly. It might be just that which is so dangerous. The dictator doesn't lose his power to weep over a worker's dead child, and as long as he retains this power, everything he does seems justified to him. Hitler wouldn't personally put a Jewish child in an incinerator. Anyway, after all, who cares for what happens to thousands of people one has never seen? Who cares? Do you care? Does anyone? Really! Admit the truth!

VII

The final session was to decide on that culminating piece of meaninglessness—which all participants at conferences know to be meaningless, but to which nevertheless they attach the utmost importance—the communiqué. No one would act as a result of having read this, in fact, it is doubtful whether anyone ever would read it, and even if he did, it could not possibly communicate any message that would affect him in the least. Yet just because it was a verbal formula and those responsible for phrasing it were intellectuals who—most of them—lived by writing, their professional honour seemed at stake. There was a feeling that although the communiqué must inevitably convey nothing, this nothing should combine the inspiration of a prose ballad by Sereno with the exactness of an experiment written up by Dunstan Curlew. It was regarded as a literary exercise in an accepted form, and each member of the Conference, even while sneering at the very idea of it, nevertheless considered that this very pure example of hermetic art should be an improvement on the content, form, and style of all other communiqués.

Bonvolio was the only one there who wanted the communiqué to communicate anything. And for him, it had a supremely important meaning: it was to be the manifesto of Bonvolian Thought and Teaching.

The communiqué was the expression of what Bonvolio had resolved to accomplish through the meeting of intellectuals drawn from the two sides of the opposing world-factions. That meeting existed, was palpable, was here, in this room in the Doges' Palace. And that is precisely what the communiqué had to say.

But first of all the intellectuals had to be made to see, and to admit in public, that when they met under Bonvolio's aegis, they shed all their national and party political loyalties, and had become international intellectuals, members of EUROPLUME, re-born within the Thought of Bonvolio. They had to be made to see what was so obvious to him—that they represented nothing except their will to meet. Beyond the Bonvolio doctrine there lay, of course, in the future, a kind of Transcendent Marxism, a politics based on the fact that through meeting, and through accepting Bonvolismus, the intellectuals had acquired a material interest in bridging gulfs.

EUROPLUME eventually would become a kind of Class Interest of the Mind within the Class Struggle. It was, in fact, the Synthesis of all other struggles on the plane of the Intelligence.

As far as he himself was concerned, Bonvolio could say that, from the bottom of his heart, he represented no one but himself; he who was EUROPLUME, the synthetic man, the new unity of East and West. He was the Bridge incarnate. All the diverse interests of the different individuals meeting here, were fused in him. He was the first world-political, international, intellectual man, a kind of missing link between nationalists and the world patriots of UNO and LITUNO.

Knowing as he did that this meeting had spent a week discussing nothing, and that it had no programme beyond the proposal to call another meeting, he calculated that the contents of the communiqué would be a vacuum to be filled by their chairman.

Bonvolio still clung to the idea that criticism could be overcome by arming his propositions at defensive points with words such as 'precisely', 'concretely', and 'exactly'. As a second line of defence, he decided that it would be strategically wise to accompany his manifesto with appeals for help in drafting it to those better equipped with gifts of clear exposition. Bonvolio regarded logic as something that could be added to new-born, naked confusion, like a fig-leaf or a napkin.

He was extremely nervous. All day, during the excursion, he had tended to walk apart from the others. At luncheon, at Torcello, he had eaten in silence, brandishing his knife and fork over his food, as though they were weapons guarding him from interruption, while he concentrated on his Thought. From time to time he had crushed his handkerchief against the high, bare dome of his head, as though to stop steam escaping from it, with a corresponding loss of energy.

When they left the cinema after the anti-Fascist film, he announced rather tersely that in half an hour's time they would continue their meetings at the Doges' Palace. There were a few protests, but since there were no women to be considered—apart from Magda, who was only an interpreter—these were not taken seriously. He brushed them aside.

As soon as they were seated, Bonvolio plunged into his discourse. He was very agitated, and it was understandable that his opening words produced an effect of utter confusion. Phrases such as *'society is the same as culture but culture is not the same as society'*, and *'we in this room pass out of society and through culture into politics, and hence back to society again at a social-cultural level'* puzzled Borès, who was trying hard to make notes.

Then, Bonvolio referred to the communiqué, the object of this session: 'In my view, which is always subject to correction, the communiqué that we shall give to the press is of world-historical importance in the future of intellectual life.'

Until he said *communiqué*, the attention he had been attracting was about as much as that given by an audience to a tuning-up orchestra.

At mention of this sacred word, there was a stiffening of backs and an alerting of pens and pencils.

'I have outlined here my own sketch—which I submit to you, subject to all sorts of corrections—my own sketch of the communiqué.' He produced a sheet of paper. 'I implore you to give this your most precise attention. This is, if I may say so, the fruit of ten years labour, the heart of my philosophy. It would scarcely be an exaggeration to say that, on and off, I have devoted those ten years to formulating these few lines. They may not have that exactitude and precision that some of you here can infuse into a thesis, though I do think that they are expressed with the utmost concreteness of which I am capable. What, precisely, I feel is that we ought, at this meeting, to affirm the fundamental bases and principles of our society, incarnated (if I may say so, at this time of Easter, without blasphemy) in the physical presence of those who are here, coming from such opposed places of origin.'

This, and a good deal more than this, left him a bit breathless and there was time for Dunstan Curlew to suggest with weight of practicality, that perhaps the chairman might now read the proposed communiqué. Borès interrupted to raise a technical objection to its being read without having been 'issued'. Bonvolio, far too excited to hear this, proceeded to read what he had written, viz.:

'*We intellectuals from countries in Eastern and Western Europe having met here together for this week in Venice, are in agreement that our meeting manifests our sense that in meeting, we represent, not the opposed factions of politics, but the unity of culture which transcends political divisions.*

'*Accordingly, we are decided to call a larger meeting*

of intellectuals coming from different parts of Europe, East and West, to discuss matters in which they may appear to disagree, within the wider agreement that they represent not the opposing forces of politics, but the cultural unity signified by the very fact of their meeting.

'*We wish to record our conviction that as the result of this meeting and the one that is to follow, a new force has come into intellectual life, a force traversing all national political frontiers. This is* EUROPLUME. *The defence of this force, in which we participate, we call the* POLITICS OF CULTURE.'

There was complete silence for a few moments. Bonvolio was unnerved. He said: 'Although this is the core of my thought, I do not regard it, considered as exposition, as complete. There are precisions and, let me say, concretizations, which require to be added. I do not claim for it that logic in which M. Sarret excels. But then, why should I? This is a co-operative organization, and our results come from all of us giving what we have to offer. Give me now your logic to add to what I dare call my inspiration. All I implore is that you remain true to the spirit of what I have just read, because this is simply a summary of the aims and ideals of EUROPLUME which have brought us here.' Staring round the room with a menacing expression, he added: 'Unless you already agreed with me and with this you would not have agreed to meet.'

There was a slightly longer silence. Then Borès, who had chewed well the end of his pencil, said: 'I fail to see how we can comply to a statement which seems to commit us to so much without having a text before us which we can examine *line by line, word by word, letter by letter.*'

Everyone agreed that a communiqué required a written text which might be examined *line by line, word by word, letter by letter.*

Accordingly, secretaries were sent forth to type out in multiplicate Bonvolio's heart laid bare. Meanwhile, the Conference, suddenly business-like, discussed who should attend the next meeting. Dunstan Curlew had a list of young scientists, all from Cambridge or London, who, he thought, should be invited. (*'Culture,'* he said, *'is not just literature.'*)

When the text was in front of them they tore into it like a pack of hounds. Marteau was first. Leaning forward with his hands clasped in front of him on the table, he said in sentences occasionally broken off by fits of laughter: 'I really have to protest that there is an assumption in this document which I fail to understand.' He looked at Sarret, and had to put his hand over his mouth before he could proceed. 'What I fail to see is any connection between the fact that we have real differences and that we have agreed to come into this room to discuss them. When we arrived here a few days ago, we did not leave our opinions in the cloakroom with our overcoats, and agree to belong to nothing except EUROPLUME which in some way overrides the differences we had before we came here. When we go back tomorrow to Moscow, or London, or Paris, or Budapest, we are, in the most important respects, the same people as those who came here a week ago, from those places. It is chic that we have met, but we ought not to nurse too many illusions . . .' his words trailed off, drowned by his amusement.

Sereno's contribution was an enormous, helpless, amused shrug, and an indicating movement of his eyes, first to Marteau, then to Bonvolio.

'Surely,' said Alex Merton, 'there docs not have to be a communiqué? A simple test: can any one of us here remember a single communiqué from a single meeting of intellectuals? We are just wasting our time. Let us by all means issue an announcement that we have met, discussed things, agreed to meet again. That is all that is necessary. That says everything essential.'

'Order! Order!' shouted Bonvolio, infuriated. 'You are speaking on a matter that has nothing to do with the agenda!'

'I was speaking about the communiqué. Surely that is what we are discussing,' said Alex urbanely.

'We were not discussing *having no communiqué*. We are discussing *having* a communiqué,' yelled Bonovolio, beside himself. 'We were not discussing making an announcement. You speak out of turn, before the chairman has called upon you. As chairman, I call you to order. You ruin everything! You are opposing the spirit of EUROPLUME in which we are all agreed!' And he burst into tears.

'I apologize,' said Alex Merton.

Then the Russians rallied to Bonvolio. Pobedin said, slowly and solemnly, that he thought the communiqué expressed a beautiful ideal, and although the formulation might be slightly altered, this ideal should be retained. Pomyalov said toughly that as long as they agreed about culture there was no need to quarrel about anything. No one could disagree about culture. He agreed with the communiqué because it excluded politics. The important thing was not to bring in politics.

After that, Bonvolismus was like a bull in the arena. It had to be killed according to the rules. Borès proposed that a sub-committee be set up to re-draft the communiqué, taking into account the wishes that had been expressed by the meeting. Curlew, who saluted in Borès the screws of efficiency, seconded the proposal, and suggested that Borès should be the chairman of the sub-committee. Borès returned the compliment by proposing a programme-planning sub-committee with Curlew as chairman. Sereno, benevolent, said that the

communiqué-drafting committee must be sure to incor-
porate as much as possible of the Thought of Bonvolio.

Then, since the sub-committee required separate
tables, and the others were glad of a little relaxation,
they all adjourned to that café, into which Botor had
peered at midnight when he saw there Sarret convivially surrounded by his colleagues.

Olim Asphalt rejected the Chairman (Bonvolio)'s
proposal that, as representative of LITUNO, he ought
to sit with Dunstan Curlew on the Programme committee
responsible for drawing up the Themes of the next
agreeing-to-disagree meeting. Instead, he volunteered
for Marteau and Sarret's communiqué drafting, which
he, rightly, supposed would be more amusing.

Marteau and Sarret took over the business of drafting a communiqué which would reconcile a discussion
between irreconcilable Easterners and Westerners with
the Bonvolio Doctrine.

'*C'est idiot, mais quand-même, il faut le faire!*' They
were bursting with ideas, bursting with nonsense, delighted with the absurdity of it all. 'Why do you try and
make Bonvolio unhappy?' Marteau asked Olim. 'He
was perfectly content till you English came here.' 'All
the same,' said Sarret, 'it is difficult to include within
our manifesto something that makes nonsense of any
manifesto, and that is what we have been asked by the
meeting to do.' They experimented with several ways
of calling upon a meeting of intellectuals to exchange
ideas, while, at the same time, declaring that, in meeting,
their agreement to meet was more important than whatever they might disagree about. After two hours of
discussion, Sarret read out a draft. '*Mais c'est du pur
blah-blah,*' said Marteau. 'What,' he asked, 'is our communiqué? It is the zero of the intellect, it is the figure
0, it is the pure circle that surrounds nothing. Multiply
anything by our communiqué and it becomes nothing.'

'That strikes me as interesting, and true,' said Sarret. 'Let us admit, then, that the communiqué does have a certain attraction. You have hit on a striking idea there.' —He always found Nothing irresistibly attractive.— 'The manifesto itself is pure undiluted vacuum. It postulates its own position as an abstraction (the idea of meeting) deduced from other abstractions (namely, the divergent points of view of those who meet).' 'The famous bridge is not even successful for one-way traffic,' said Marteau, 'it is an abyss down which all who meet agree to fall and become nothing. That is why we have spent a whole week of our lives here having everything we said converted into nonsense.' 'But perhaps it was nonsense already,' Sarret laughed. 'Ah!'

While certain soldiers of culture lounged and laughed and made jokes, while others tore to shreds the garment of his Thought, Bonvolio sat alone at a table, staring straight ahead of him, perspiration pouring down his cheeks. Marteau found it difficult to look at the *pauvre type* without beginning to laugh until the tears threatened also to pour down his own cheeks. Every time he looked at Bonvolio he turned to Alex, at the table adjoining theirs, and said: 'You're very, very cruel. Look at poor Bonvolio, look what you have done!'

The final meeting took place after dinner. The communiqué, which had been so much discussed before, and which now bore no resemblance to Bonvolio's ideas, was accepted without discussion, as was the programme and also the list of those to be invited to the next meeting. Suddenly, it seemed pointless to add any more words to the mountain that had piled up during a week. All that was left now was for Bonvolio to remind them that they had with them Olim Asphalt, representative of LITUNO, which so generously had given some material aid to the present meeting. He hoped that Mr. Asphalt would be able to explain to them the conditions in which LITUNO would be able to assist the proposed extended conference.

Olim Asphalt spoke in a voice violent with scarcely repressed emotion. Dipping deep into the bran-tub of a past which seemed stuffed with different personalities marking different stages of his career, he adopted the manner he had used when most of those present had been in their revolutionary prime, and he was President of the Cambridge Union, and leader of his cell at Downing College. 'I'm going to be pretty frank about LITUNO,' be began, 'probably franker than anyone so far has been about anything here. This is my last speech as representative of that organization, because after this I'm going to go back to my hotel—that is, after I've had a few drinks—and send in my letter of RESIGNATION. You may be surprised to learn that what finally decided me to take this step is the present meeting. Just for the reason that this conference is so much more interesting than most projects supported by the Maison de LITUNO, it helped me to see the futility of myself being in my present job. This meeting has provided me with a clue to the failure of all such meetings, gentlemen. The root of the failure is that in order to meet, we have to put the idea of meeting before that of saying anything which might make any future, or even the continuance of the present, meeting, impossible. M. Bonvolio expresses his awareness of this when he constructs his whole philosophy on the idea of meeting, until the meeting itself is supposed to express and represent nothing else except the idea of meeting, in a vacuum. If M. Bonvolio carries the idea to the point of *reductio ad absurdum*, then M. Sarret carries the idea of the impossibility of meeting to the same point. M. Sarret likes meeting people in order to tell them why he thinks it is impossible for them to meet.

'The fact is, that if we were really truthful, this

meeting would rapidly resolve itself into fighting one another. If I were to say, for example, that three of our colleagues here are accessories to one of the most extensive acts of political murder in history and that one of my English colleagues is *their* accessory, then they would want to knock me down. Besides, they might tell me some very unpleasant things about the society and the beliefs to which I adhere. Still, if we could seriously exchange lists of murders, I believe we might be getting somewhere.'

Bonvolio shouted: 'No one here represents anything. Except for you, and you are supposed to represent LITUNO. I call upon you to fulfil the task for which your Director-General sent you here.'

'Exactly,' said Olim Asphalt. 'In just the same way as EUROPLUME represents EUROPLUME, so LITUNO represents LITUNO. The first demand made on a writer who joins the latter organization is that at a meeting like the present—a meeting of writers—he shouldn't, *qua* writer, say anything. For if he did, he would soon find himself saying that some writers were better than other writers, and, worse, some worse. And if once he started saying that, he would risk wrecking the whole organization.

'But now, it is my task to explain to you my own role and the role of LITUNO at this meeting. I am an administrator pure and simple. I would like those of you to understand this who may still have some lingering regard for me as a writer of a novel. Speaking then purely and simply as LITUNO'S representative, I have to point out to you that the only parts of your deliberations which concern me are those which suggest channels through which LITUNO'S funds may legitimately be directed without there being any possibility of such expenditure being challenged in two years' time at the next international gathering of the national representatives. I want to make it absolutely clear that I am here not as a person, or a writer even, but as an official. . . .' He really over-emphasized all this, even going so far as to say that officials like himself, who happened once to have been writers, no longer held any interest in literature as such, and he hinted that nothing cured a writer so readily of his love of literature than belonging to an organization devoted to promoting 'international literary relations'. He looked persistently at Botor, as though the whole of this shaming discourse were for some reason meant for the Hungarian.—'Let no one here imagine that I am in any way a free agent, or that I am in the least to be relied upon, or that, if I offered advice to LITUNO, it was at all likely to be followed. My own feelings and wishes do not come into the matter. I resign, as a gesture, an example. For I think one of us here ought to mark this meeting by humiliating, debasing, devaluing himself in some way. Of course,' he ended, 'I know this is silly.' And he gave his laugh.

'We may all agree with Mr. Asphalt's conclusion,' said Bonvolio, with surprising sharpness. 'And, since he has resigned, we do not take his views as representing LITUNO, nor this organization. In fact, he is nothing but himself, a private person.'

After he had finished, there were sympathetic murmurs—'*Après tout, c'est triste cette histoire de LITUNO*,' '*ce pauvre type, Asphalt*,' '*embêtant*,' etc. Strangely enough, this gave him a ferocious satisfaction. He was staging, in a miniature, symbolic way, the instructive spectacle of Olim Asphalt, a literary reputation, committing *hara-kiri* in front of their eyes. On this strange note, the Conference ended, with very few good-byes. Olim left the room quickly. Downstairs, he waited a moment, wondering whether Alex would follow him out to offer a kind word, or whether he had disgraced himself too deeply. Alex did not appear. Through the dark he saw Dunstan Curlew, well wrapped in his greatcoat, hands deep in pockets, head bowed, moving as though through a tunnel out of which he would emerge on the other side of the Alps at a meeting of scientists, 'genuinely progressive' and constructive. Csongor Botor came out of the portico. Then Marteau came up to him, smiled, shook his hand warmly, and said merely ' *Mes félicitations.*'

It was not late—an hour till midnight, and Botor went straight to the place where he had first sighted Carlino. Like magic, the boy was waiting for him. The moment he saw Botor his face brightened with the promise fulfilled and he started off his cheerful chirping, 'Gondola! Gondola!' 'Gondola! Gondola!' Botor repeated, and then said simply—'Carlino!' The naming of the name was a release from so much. 'You come out in the gondola with me?' asked Carlino. Botor noted that the 'with me' sounded like a special service provided by this particular gondola. This was just what he himself thought it. 'Certainly.' 'Where do you want to go, Signor?' At that he gave his shrug that read—'Anywhere—it isn't important.' 'The Grand Canal, the Laguna, or the little dark canals?' 'All of them. It is my last night.'

For the first few moments that he lay in the gondola, his immediate sensation was of nostalgia so strong that he felt he might faint. For some minutes he was overwhelmed by the sensation of this most luxurious of forms of propulsion, this seat in a box in a theatre that looks beyond a foreground of roofs on to the stage of the sky. The relaxedness exhausted him, the ease disturbed him, and this was scarcely astonishing, since comfort—the coiled, unnoticed spring even the poorest have when they drink a cup of tea, the cushion without which life is exposed at every moment to the terrible—had become impossible to him as sleep. All he was left with was thoughts acting upon his mind.

He had to fight his way beyond sensations to a sustained awareness of what was going on around him—the palaces of the Grand Canal, that hung balconies and ornaments over his eyes like heavy fruit, and which concealed humming behind windows like a tune or a dynamo—conversation, love, intercourse. The windows were laced over with spidery stonework, and against walls and balustrades, spears of reflected light darted up from the canal—the canal that was Grand because, as one approached the Laguna, it opened out a throat acknowledging the open sea.

With the thrusting forward movement of the gondola, buildings seen from below showed innumerable facets twisting and turning round, like sculpture revolving on a pediment, or like cubist painting.

Venice was an artefact which lay open to destruction with the other remnants of civilization, and Nature would survive, Nature even if there were no life left on the world, and taking one of their frightful plunges his ferocious thoughts confronted him with the sneering observation—you have lived now to see that it wasn't Nature that you ever wanted and needed. If you had wanted mountains, plains, trees, fields, and all living creatures, men and beasts to become the same and single grey herd, then why aren't you happy now?

This was confused, and now he seemed to recover a nagging need to clarify his thought, even to himself. Governments had discovered a means of constructing a drain down which the quality of living flowed out of the streets into subterranean cellars, leaving above it nothing but the mass-produced, identical patterns of social men living among utilitarian walls. The rhythms were drained out of language, the colour from the houses, the age from wine, the taste from food, the variety from dress, the salt from converse, the daily magic out of things despised like listening to jazz or shop-window gazing. And after all this had been drained out, what was pumped in was social purpose, will, instructions, propaganda, fear, and suspicion.

'Is the signor comfortable? Shall I put over him another blanket?' '*Va bene, va bene!*' But Carlino must have noticed that he had started his twisting and writhing. Now a thought leapt into his mind like a cry—'I am not bourgeois!' He had to think back to what it was answering. Sarret, of course, Sarret who stood over him with a lecturer's wand, pointing the thesis of which he was the illustration—the bourgeois with bohemian background tormented on the rack of dialectic.

But he was not bourgeois. This was a revelation, a certainty! Whatever else he might be he was a changed man. He did not want to go back to that. He did not want to be comfortable. He had, at last, in his own mind found the way out of the slavery of his former freedom. Crammed, stuffed, deluded, accepted, and accepting, surrounded by his own circle within the wider circle of all those spiritual and aesthetic wheels revolving inside economic wheels, was what his bourgeois life had been. He hated this, but he did not want that. The fatherland of the bourgeois was comfort, his goddess success. What was his nostalgia? Not for Paris, not for New York, not for Olim Asphalt's London. His unhappiness was of today. To be modern, he must cling to this. If he was told he was reactionary—he could answer, 'I am unhappy.'

I have had my home turned into a house where every brick is a flame that can burn my hand, every love rests on a scale where it weighs itself against a fear. I can claim to be nothing except my own uprooted thoughts. He started laughing—a seizure which sometimes overtook him. I am a spirit. It has taken materialism to prove it. I am a spirit. The only question is, am I a ghost, or am I some eternal existence, driven out

of cities and bodies for a period, waiting to be re-
born?

No. Dead and damned for what he had betrayed. He
had been struck down by being publicly forced to act
according to the weakness of his private nature, and he
had delivered the irretrievable sentence against himself.

The palaces began to fade. Carlino interrupted.
'Would you like now to go into the little dark canals?'
He said 'yes' with absurd gravity of consent. The affec-
tion, the confidence he felt for Carlino did not prevent
him toying—fondly almost—with the idea that he was
a policeman also a criminal who might murder him. In
a society ruled by murder as the law, there would be
happiness in finding a murderer whom one could trust
like a doctor who puts you under the anaesthetic.

The gondoliers were secret police and the little dark
canals led underground to what passages, what cellars,
what . . . He searched for the third image that would
be a climax. That he could do so proved how easily
reality could turn back into literature again, into
journalism even. He was withdrawing from the real
into realism, he would soon be able to give a lecture
about the writer divided between his social and his
aesthetic conscience, at a literary session, with Borès in
the audience. He would be able to argue about Engagement. Yet now he had touched the burning core of
reality, he despised the literature which transformed
what acted upon you into what was thinkable. He
wanted the word to be the object from which you could
not get away. The fire that freezes the hand that feeds it.

They did now arrive at a canal so dark it seemed
like the bottom of a trench. There was no illumination
at all the whole length of it; only at the end, where
another canal crossed, a lamp shone, hanging between
houses, like a great planet with a bluish blaze.

Carlino had stopped the gondola, which he pulled up

against the side of the canal, resting his hand against the wall. Unspeaking, he seemed to be awaiting further orders. Botor, very arrogant with his colleagues, was now entirely preoccupied with humbly considering Carlino's feelings. 'Why don't you sit down?' he asked. 'Where?' 'Sit down here, beside me.' He moved to one side, and made room for him. The boy climbed into the seat from his sentinel position at the back of the gondola, and sat down about six inches away from Botor, his head slightly bent in a way that, through the darkness, Botor found simple and touching. The boy had a curious, attentive awareness, not servile, yet docile, respectful in a way that verged on sympathy. He was simply waiting, Botor realized, not expecting anything, not noting or judging, objecting or sneering. He had perhaps a great discretion, as though he regarded every situation that arose with every passenger in his gondola as unique. Botor smiled. They were alone. He knew himself to be a very special case. That, at any rate.

'Are there many gondolas at night?' he inquired. 'Not at this time of year. Only five or six going from near the piazza. A great many in the summer.' 'How many trips do you expect to do on a night such as this?' 'Three, four, perhaps five.' 'What hours do you work?' 'From ten till five in the morning.'

'Are you a Catholic?' 'Yes.' 'Have you been to Mass today?' 'When I got home last night, I went to bed for two hours. Then I went to Mass.' He added: 'After that, I slept for the rest of the day.'

'And do you belong to a political party?' The boy hesitated. Botor said ironically: 'You do not have to answer me. I am not a policeman.' 'I belong to no party, but I vote communist,' said Carlino. Having said this, he became a less poetic character. He talked rapidly. The city was over-populated. Thousands had to sleep in condemned rooms, on the level of the canal, where they contracted tuberculosis. The communist party said that it was necessary to build a great new industrial town on the mainland, adjacent to Venice, where the workers could lead lives of health and dignity. The new motor-boats of the touristic capitalist enterprises set up waves that made cracks in the foundations of the city. Venice would fall into the sea and become a few ruins, like Torcello. *I Americani*.

Botor listened to all this, and then said: 'Perhaps we should go on.' 'To the Laguna?' 'Yes, to the open water.'

The questions he might have asked, he thought, as he lay back again, were about what happened in the little obscure canals, altogether what was Carlino's commerce in the dark of his gondola. By not asking, he had answered some question.

Carlino asked, 'Weren't you with those two I took out last night?' He had little difficulty in making Botor understand he meant Olim Asphalt and Magda Karinthy, Botor had another of his terrific fits of laughter, a series of guttural exclamations that seemed almost to tear him in pieces.

'What is your party? Are you Easter pilgrims?' It might have been simpler to say 'yes'. The next best answer was perhaps '*poeti*', so Botor said that. 'Oh, *poeti*,' said Carlino, with his air of judging nothing. 'Have you written poems about Venice?'

'That would be difficult, there are so many already.' Carlino did not follow this up. He remarked, almost at random: 'The signor is extremely serious.'

As they emerged from under the Bridge of Sighs, into the Laguna, Botor, to show he was not altogether this, clambered up to the stern of the gondola and offered to propel it. Carlino accepted this gaily enough: giving him the oar to hold, and placing his hands over those of Botor to guide him. He sang *Luna Luna* to set the rhythm of the movement. They went out further into the Laguna. Then suddenly Botor felt Carlino grip his body with both arms while he fell over towards the water which rose up to meet him like black thongs.

Carlino had caught him, and settled him down again in the middle of the gondola. For a few moments he had fainted. When he revived the boy was much concerned, as though their friendship had gone on a very long time. Indeed, it did seem an eternity since the last meeting of the Conference. Now Carlino kept on asking how he was, and whether he wanted to return. But Botor told him to stay just as they were.

He had recovered from his faint in a strange state of mind, a kind of delirium of happiness. Venice and the Laguna seemed extremely beautiful, the water was as restful as a bed or as strata of stone and soil weaving skeletons under the earth. His mind filled like a cistern with words, not as when he was composing, in his past infinitely fruitful period, but as when, sometimes, in the night, he had half-woken and had the impression that the sides of his body were the banks of a river through which a powerful current flowed, rustling and whispering, bending reeds over, swarming with images and phrases. Now he seemed to lie comfortably at the bottom of a pit with a rectangular opening that looked up at black sky of stars. His grave. Above him, Carlino's towering form seemed a statue, beyond which, in the distance, like a little model at his feet, the two Byzantine columns which supported the statues of St. Teodoro and the lion of St. Mark, with, behind them, the outline of the campanile, and the squat, crowded bulbs of San Marco's domes, were all spread neatly on a tray. On the summit of the campanile, the statue suddenly broke into gold. Someone had pressed a switch. Drowsily, he asked Carlino whether the flood-lighting was for Easter. 'Yes. Always at this time.'

Although Botor had lost his faith—all his faiths—
Carlino's answer gave him a sensation of his own innocence, as though he were a child again, in church. He
started thinking of the incidents of the past day. While
Carlino had slept after Mass, Botor had been standing
in the vineyard on the island of Torcello. He realized
now why he had had the impulse to wander off there
among the vines, and why for a moment, when confronted by him, his hostility to the Englishman from
LITUNO had melted.

The Englishman, Olim Asphalt, was right in putting
into his mind the idea that their meeting would remind
him of another meeting, in another vineyard. Yes!
Was it two, three, four years ago? They had driven
out that afternoon into the caves where, on the shore
of Lake Balaton, there was the wine-tasting. The wine
was Badacsony. He doubted whether the damned
Englishman knew that. Moaschkovitz and Pomgracz
were with them . . . alive then. It was true the English
man had been there, but he flattered himself if this afternoon, on Torcello, he thought it was the memory of
his presence that had caused Botor's emotion. The
cause was unknown to anyone, unknown even to Pomgracz. It was that he had seen—seen! How seen!—the
labourer in the vineyard. It was a glimpse only. They
were drunk as they drove past him in the car. The
terrace of the vines in which he stood stepped down
the slope. Through torn spaces between spear-shaped
leaves, the lake glowed with waters combed sideways,
and, climbing up to meet the vine-spire vanes, distant
mountains painted rocks and trees and snow into a sky
of burning glass. Lake below, mountains above, and
between the lane of turreted leaves, the human form—
the labourer in the vineyard. His dark-tanned trousers
formed a pedestal of bark, split, stripped at the navel,
peeled to reveal the bare torso of burned sun-god,

Apollo carved in wood, breast of lyre, mouth coining song. Through his mere physical existence, he seemed all the eloquence of that day, writing the poem of his silence, his absence, his distance. He focused on to one point the meeting inspirations of remote times. He made the picture of a future without him intolerable as a desert blown up from a dust-bowl. Wanded gods descended into the vineyards, their hands loose-clenched against the wrinkling blue sail of the distant lake. His flesh was filled with statue, as the grapes he tended with wine.

There the poem was, so clear, so complete, simple as a single line, luminous as that day. It was perfect in his mind, he saw it clear and whole. He knew it as though he had been born with it silver in his mouth, and it would be scrolled within his hollow bones when he died. And yet it was at this exact moment that he realized that the virtue which could enable him to write it had gone out of him. There was no form, no rhythm, only the perfectly clear idea. The rhythm that can no more be defined than the unstated revelation in the shaping of a single letter of handwriting, had gone.

Statues. Statues. Another idea, thought of, never realized, recurred to him. His essay on Statues. It was a meditation, 'amusing' in his style which now seemed to have too much about it of the café, on the fact that statues have no internal organs. The clarified surfaces of Michelangelo's David conceal nothing inside that contradicts. The inner is primarily unspeakingly consistent with the outside. Within, it contains the forever unawakened, untouched stone of Carrara, without sin or malice, thought or digestion. In myth, of course, it was common to fall in love with statues, and—his essay suggested—perhaps this was not only because they were more beautiful than real beings, but because they

were intrinsically self-consistent. What they stated
could never betray. Their virtue was all marble. Joke.
Now, looking up at Carlino, he remembered how an
instant ago he had seemed a statue standing there at
the end of the gondola, and he saw that his mind had
really been led to this thought by the conversation about
going to church: the idea of the boy's qualities being
of an external virtue that decided his innerliness. When
Carlino had said he went to Mass, and that afterwards
he slept, this was the speech of the marble sleeping
within the outward-facing surface. And there was another thought he could add now about statues. People
had been murdered by them—*statua del commendatore*—
such a murder was the revenge of daylight marble truth
upon the blood-filled intestinal dreaming of malice and
vice. The light had its revenge.

Poetry, the essay, how they were reasserting themselves! It was the first time for months that they had
been allowed to do so by the hunting thoughts. Furies.
And now in the darkness of the gondola, on the black,
shining water, and with the statue Carlino guarding
him, he felt woven so deeply into a tissue of unreality
that the real emerged at the back of his mind as an
action on a stage utterly removed and distant—through
the wrong end of a telescope. He saw very clearly what
he had been afraid of. He saw he was right to have been
afraid. A future exactly certain! It was the daylight
truth. He looked down at it now from a height, without
being troubled by the image of his fear.

Here it was, then. Premontvian and Cuertan. They
would come back from their prisons. Received with
flowers and cheers. Greeted in the cafés, the streets,
the Writers' meetings. He would not dare look at them.
They would dispose of him. In his heart, he must thank
them. Praise them also. He would have to resign. This
would end, for him, he did not know how.

Yet this fear which he had been afraid to look at, he saw now was not the real fear. Saw now what this was. They would not stop at him. They would turn on their gaolers, the powers behind the police. Or if it was not they who turned, then the flowers and cheers would be found to conceal bombs. Others would rise up. The students in the streets would tear down statues. A short, deceiving victory, and then the tanks roll back. Everyone suffer. None help. The prisons be worse. Fools!

Yet, beyond this there was worse, the ultimate fear. Was it the ultimate? He peeled off his fears layer by layer, always thinking this must be the centre of the onion. The last, or the last but one. This. Everything that happened to him for the rest of his life would only uncover his utter desolation, his absolute solitude. He sighed. Rolled over in the gondola. Am I unhappy? Until now he had been alone because of the absence of friends. The friend he had betrayed. But now was worse. Now he would be alone because the friend returned. Ladyas Premontvian. He came, they came back, out of their prisons: they would show he had no friends.

Csongor Botor was breathing extremely heavily, twisting and turning as though some beast inside his body were trying to bite its way out. Carlino Morandi (that was the gondolier's full name) became exceedingly alarmed. He began thrusting forward his gondola furiously, as though sweeping the waves to one side and behind him. The gondola tilted up and down as if in a storm. Carlino Morandi brought it in near the quayside in front of the little piazza before San Marco. On the pavement, looking down at the gondola, stood Olim Asphalt, dressed in tuxedo, a flower in his coat lapel, his hands in his pockets, and a wide sarcastic chortling grin spread over his face. Seeing him, Csongor Botor managed half to sit up. His jaw dropped and he uttered an exclamation which might have been 'Hullo!'

At that Olim lifted a great hammy hand above his head, waved idiotically, and looking from Carlino to Csongor Botor, and then back again to Carlo, said in his loud tolerant humanist voice—with that absurd smile like a cut melon—'Je constate, c'est tout.' Then tactfully uninterfering, he turned away, walked two unsteady paces, looked back again, and shouted over his shoulder at them, at the top of his voice: 'RESIGN! RESIGN! RESIGN!'

When Carlino Morandi, stooping down over his cargo, kicked it to ascertain whether it had resigned, only Csongor Botor's eyes seemed conscious.

Then the sky rocked with bells that filled the universe for Easter. Csongor Botor had an absurd ludicrous vision which caused him for the last and final time really to break and crack on that rack of laughter, roar of tears which had been tearing his body. He was in a prison, under the crumbling ruins of a city. Was it the dungeon of the Doges' Palace? Out there, up there in the centre of the sky, through falling walls, he beheld Sarret, naked, bespectacled, cherub, bearing a flag, just above the tower of the campanile. Round him unfurled scroll on scroll of the endless writings which wound out of his intestines, words that complained he had been deceived for twenty-five years, words denouncing his deceivers, words even upholding his colleague, Csongor Botor, under the rubble down there, words declaring his support of the victims of the tyrants, words for ever endlessly explaining, complaining, declaiming, dissecting, deriding, sneering, while little jokes broke in the sky all round him like bursts of flame from rockets. But never once finally, simply, did he say: 'Excuse me, gentlemen. I was wrong.'

1956 and 1957

THE FOOL AND THE PRINCESS

TO

CHRISTOPHER ISHERWOOD

THE FOOL AND THE PRINCESS

'I was happy.'

The living-room window looked out on to a narrow garden at end of summer packed with faded leaves and petals. Between this garden and the road, a low iron balustrading surmounted a narrow base of blackened bricks. On the further side of the road beyond the tarmac was another row of houses, connected, semi-detached, like Siamese twins. Each bistre-coloured house had a peaked gable surmounted by a dilapidated iron feather.

Mr. and Mrs. Harvey Granville sat on the sofa of their living-room in front of the window facing the view. Both had that staring expression which faces have when they look at themselves in a mirror: as with a vague hope of looking beyond the flesh into the mind.

Indeed, they might have been looking at the mirror of their own house on the other side of the road, for it was the same. The sensation that he was staring at his own image at the centre of wife and home had come to Harvey Granville often since his return from Germany.

His saying, 'I was happy' was the end of five days in which he had said no word about the year spent away. He had said nothing and she had noticed his silence. Wasn't it odd that he didn't seem even to notice Home? He behaved in the way which was the opposite of what Kate had expected. She'd thought there'd be too much to say, too much to look at. True, he did play a bit with little Dunky, but even this he did as though his own boy were a child he'd just met and grown fond of, somehow, not their child.

Kate was frightened. Most of all she was just tired. If she had spoken to Mrs. Barnard, who lived next door, about it, she wouldn't have complained of his being unkind but of something worse; of his being uncanny. She didn't know what she'd be telling. By now the evasion had become overwhelming. Even the most painful truth would hurt less than the silence of the past few days. As they sat on the sofa gazing, out at the road, in this house which would be theirs when they had paid another five instalments, each noticed a whiteness in the other, a glassiness, a physical intensity as of flesh waiting for the knife or the disease.

'I suppose you mean that you've never really been happy with me,' said Kate, in her recent dull, flat, realistic voice. 'I suppose you find me boring. Well, I'm not surprised. But it isn't really fair if we have no happiness to look back on. It isn't fair, Harvey, really it isn't. We've never had the chance to give each other a good time, have we, Harvey? First of all there was the war, then there was Dunky being born, and then you went away and now everything seems finished.'

'But we have been happy, Kate, honestly, we've been happy, as happy as I'd ever been in my life until this happened. Everything isn't over either. We shall be happy again.'

'Then what's the matter?'

'It's just that everything's different. It takes getting used to. Germany gave me a kind of shock.'

'But what's different, Harvey? You haven't told me yet what happened.'

'Well, to put it very crudely, and I suppose I can't put it any other way, I met another woman, at the D.P. camp. It sounds an ordinary thing to happen, but she isn't ordinary and she isn't extraordinary only because she happens to be a princess!'

'Oh, Harvey, a princess! You with a princess!'

Suddenly she burst out laughing. It was a grave crisis of laughter. She fell off the sofa, kneeling on the floor, clinging to one leg of the sofa beside him. He seriously watched the top of her head with the hair parted in the middle, coiling in two waves over her ears and drawn into a 'bun' at the back of her head. It was the kind of hair, auburn, frothy at the edges, which is always a little untidy: the two waves foamed, each with a little spray of disordered ends which caught the light. While she was laughing like this, these two waves of hair made him think of things weeping, drowning: a weeping willow, a picture in the Tate Gallery, which he had seen with Duncan Ballard once, of Ophelia floating, drowning on a transparent stream under which were the washed pebbles. She was piteous, and yet looking down on the two dividing, meeting streams of her hair, he was conscious of choice: whether to pity her as part of himself, or whether to feel quite outside her grief.

He touched her shoulder. Then he drew a photograph from his wallet. She looked. Within a grey mist-like bubble of light in a muddy pond, drifted the head and shoulders of a young woman. Her black hair framed her oval face. The features were symmetrical, with large clear eyes and round-looking lips which showed black in this photograph. The expression was calm, possibly intellectual. But everything seemed undecided in this prison photograph, taken in a hard light to emphasize the physical proportions and to ignore what could least accept to be ignored—the expression.

'Well, your princess is certainly a beauty,' said Kate. She might have been intending irony.

'Do you want me to tell you about her?' he asked, putting on his calm.

'It's certainly better to know what's coming to you than know nothing. You do at least know where you are when you know what's coming to you. I can't expect you to tell me everything. I don't think I'd even want to know everything but if you do tell me something, do let it be the truth. Then I can make out the rest for myself. Harvey, after the last few days I could bear to hear anything.'

'What's been so special about the last few days?'

'You know it's not been the nice home-coming I expected.'

'You're right. I'm very sorry. I'm really very sorry. I'm ashamed of myself.'

'Go on with what you were going to tell me.'

'Her christian name is Moura. She's got an unpronounceable other name, but I won't bother you with that. At the camp, they call her the princess, because she's supposed to be descended from nobility or something. She hasn't ever spoken to me about this herself, but she hasn't contradicted it to me either. She lives with her mother and her sister in a hut of the D.P. camp where I worked. Kate, I've never been with her more than a quarter of an hour alone.'

He stopped, flushed, bewildered, conscious (as she was also) of his honesty and his dishonesty. His lips had spoken the literal truth, his eyes knew that what he had just said was true—and yet it was so irrelevant. With an expression of sharpened pain he plunged to a deeper layer of truth: 'Well, I'm just telling you that, though it doesn't make any difference to my feeling for her. She and her mother and her sister were deported by the Germans from their town and made to work in an arms factory near Munich all through the war. Then, later, she acted as interpreter. She knows several languages. She was an interpreter in the camp.'

'I don't see what all this has to do with *us*, Harvey.

Was it in connection with translating that you got to
meet her? or what?'

'The first time I saw her was the first day I joined
the camp. I noticed her at once. I didn't make any
attempt to meet her for a long time; it's difficult to
explain why, but it was partly just because she made
such an impression on me. At that time, before the new
Director of the camp—Wingfield, who's there now—
arrived, the camp was very rough, in some ways it was
a downright brothel, and to meet a woman only meant
one thing. So for that reason I didn't ask to meet her.
But I think that I always *knew* her, from the very first
moment, almost as well as I do now. Sometimes I feel
that I knew her before we met. I used to think about
her all the time, as one sometimes does think of people.
When I was alone, especially in the darkness, I would
think of her expression. You can see her soul even in
the photograph. Thinking about her and imagining
being with her became such a joy that it was another
reason for not trying to meet her. I felt that I could
wait. I wanted to wait. I even felt I knew her better
through just waiting.'

'But all the same, you did meet her.'

'I never tried to do so. I just met her inevitably.
I didn't try perhaps partly also for a bad reason.
Because, after all, I was a kind of gaoler. I knew that
she couldn't get away from the camp. Still, it wasn't
only that. I truly believe that if I had never met her,
but just seen her and known that she existed in the
world, I would have felt the same as I do now. I would
have been completely happy in a way that I never have
been before. That is what I have to tell you. I am trying
to be completely honest, Kate. You must realize that it
would be just the same if I had never met her and only
seen her. When I saw her something happened to me
which can't be altered.'

'But in spite of all you say, you did meet her.'

'Yes. One day I was present when a Russian official came to arrange about their being returned to the East. She accompanied as interpreter. Then, finally, I ended the day with interviewing her mother and sister. So I was with all three of them in their hut. This was just like any other of the other compartments in a shed which the families there lived in, except that they had done something to make their part of it in better taste. They hadn't got much, but with a few shawls and bits of cloth they had made the place seem civilized somehow. As soon as I got Moura to explain to them what I had come for, the old woman was terrified. She started trying to explain something to me by signs, as though she didn't trust Moura to tell me what it was. She kept on opening her mouth—which looked like a gaping fish, as she hadn't any teeth—and pointing down her throat. It was quite ludicrous really. I thought she wanted me to get her some false teeth, so I kept on saying *Zaehner . . .*'

'What does *Zaehner* mean?'

With a faintly superior embarrassed, handsome smile Granville said: 'It's the German for *teeth*. And then I said *Zahnarzt*, which means *dentist*, in a questioning voice. Those are two of the German words I've managed to pick up at the camp. Then Moura said in her almost perfect English, "No, it isn't that she wants. Please understand. It's something quite different. But don't take any notice. She's being hysterical and absurd." When the old girl saw Moura talking with me, she got still more excited. She started grabbing at Moura's shawl with her hands and wailing. Then she suddenly turned to me and shouted in German, *Gift*.'

'What does *Gift* mean?'

'It's the German for *poison*.'

'Why should she want poison?

'She thought she was going to be sent back to the East.'

'But why should that make her want poison?'

'Moura explained to me then. You see, they had been sent home to their village once before, and then they'd escaped back again to us with false papers.'

'But why did they have to come back?'

A tired, almost persecuted look came on Granville's face. 'I only know what they told me, but I myself believe it. It's one of a great many similar stories which are about as hard to believe as not to believe. A lot of things happen in Europe today which are as difficult to judge as the kind of stories mediums tell at spiritualist seances. But all the same, when they happen to someone you trust, one believes them, especially if there seems no reason for their having been invented. Anyway, this is their story. After the victory they were one of a number of families which asked to be repatriated. They thought that after all they should return to their home, and they had loved their work before the war there. At all events Moura had loved teaching. They had many friends in their village. They imagined that there would be some kind of acceptance of them, some kind of welcome, a band, a bundle of clothes perhaps, something, however shabby, as there is for the French prisoners and even the prisoners of the defeated countries when they return home. But there wasn't anything like that. The guards to whom they were handed over treated them like prisoners. They were put into a train with soldiers, also being repatriated, who assaulted them. When they arrived at the frontier, they were sent to a camp where conditions were worse than they had ever been in Germany. She said that the whole experience was like being deported to Germany in the first instance, only in reverse. After two days in the camp they managed to bribe the guards with a few things

they had saved during all these years. They found that
there was quite a traffic in bribery for deportees who
wanted to be re-deported. They got to Poland, where
they were arrested once more, but again managed to
escape. Then they walked half across Europe—these
two young women and their mother—back to our
camp.'

'Did you give them the poison?'

'Of course not. It would have been quite impossible.'

'Then will they go back?'

'That is part of what I have to tell you, Kate. I
wangled for them not to be sent back. I can't tell even
you how I did that. It all depends, though, on my
keeping an eye on their situation.'

'Are you sure, though, that their story is true?'

'I have no evidence for it except their own words.
But then we obtained evidence of about twenty families
with similar experience in the camp. None of the stories
can be proved individually, but, put together, they add
up to something. There is no other evidence. All I do
know is that they had a genuine desire to return to their
country and in fact they did return. Then what they saw
frightened them so much that they ran away again. It is
difficult to think of any other explanation of their actions
than the one they gave.'

There was a silence at the end of which she said:
'All the same, I still don't understand.'

'What don't you understand?'

'I don't understand why it has to make such an
enormous difference to us, Harvey. I don't blame you
for taking an interest in this family at all. If I had been
in your place, I hope I would have done the same,
honestly I do. But I don't understand why you have
taken no notice of me and why you have to treat Dunky
as though he were a stranger when you get home.'

'I sometimes think that meeting them,' he said, 'was

like a meeting on top of a mountain, hidden in a cloud. And then the cloud cleared away and revealed us to each other more vividly than if there had been never any cloud, cloud of Germany, there before. Now I feel that she has been gathered back away from me into her cloud of misery, cloud of the East.'

They were silent after this. She seemed to be searching in her mind for the origin of the metaphor. Then, as if accepting it, she said:

'And I suppose you mean that you have gone back also into your cloud of misery.'

'No, I didn't mean that at all: you mustn't put the words into my mouth, Kate, or we'll never understand each other. It's difficult and painful enough to work things out as it is. What I do mean,' he continued with difficulty, taking up the metaphor again, 'is that I am the only person who has the power to dispel the cloud for them. Yes, that's it, owing to the luck of my situation, I can bring some light into their lives.'

'I see. You imagine you're a sort of fairy prince who slips the glass slipper or something on the foot of the princess who's a beggar-maid.'

He looked at her quickly and then went on: 'And the fact that I can do so for someone else, means that I become much clearer, much lighter, to myself also . . . I hope I'm not hurting you too much, Kate.'

'Oh no, my shoes fit,' she said, a bit aciduously. 'After all, it hurts me less than when you're shifty or tell me lies or don't take notice of anybody in the house.'

'I think I've told you everything.'

'But—oh, what do you want to do about it, Harvey? What do you want me to do with Dunky? It's you who have to decide, I suppose.'

'Even if I did want to do anything, it would be useless . . . You see she has to stay at the camp. And I'm here. She can't get away. And in any case, she would never leave her sister and mother.'

'So she won't ever be sent back?'

He flushed. 'No, I think I fixed that.'

'Now I suppose you're going to tell me that, after all, you'll leave here and take another job at the camp?'

'No I can't. I've left now and they're cutting down on the staff. I don't mean anything like that, Kate. I'm not thinking of our separating. All I might be able to do would be go and see her every six months. That would mean, of course, arranging my work here so as to be able to get away.'

'Yes, it does make a difference, Harvey. I see.'

He looked straight into her eyes for the first time since his return home. He noticed now that they were red around the edges and that red veins showed in them. His gaze, concentrated mostly on her eyes, occasionally wandered to the rest of her face. He noticed the texture of the skin reminding him of her youth and yet coming out in signs of care and age developed as on a photographic plate. There were three lines on her forehead of which he was often conscious. There were occasions (with friends, for example) when the insistent rawness of these lines made him ashamed, but now they made him feel compassionate. They were a faintly reddish colour emphasized by exposure and by work. He gently touched one of them now with his finger as though he still might find the love which would erase it.

'I hope that I don't make you feel too miserable.'

'I don't mind so much now you've told me the truth. It's what I imagined that makes me so miserable. When you don't say anything or when you seem to be making excuses the whole time I mind.'

'Everything is better now we both know the truth. It is more wonderful than it has ever been before, Kate. It's as beautiful as . . .'

'Oh, don't say that it is beautiful as what you told me, Harvey. I couldn't bear your saying that.' She got up calmly, reminding them both that she had to go and look to little Duncan upstairs. Her calm made him feel frightened, and somehow as if everything he had told her was unnecessary. 'Let's always tell the truth in the future, Harvey.'

They looked at each other as they seemed never to have looked before. The strangeness, the sense of pallor surrounding everything they saw, which they had felt during the past few days, now included themselves, melted them into each other in its white, pure light. He looked at her and he saw beyond approaching age and nagging care, the girl whom he had courted seven years ago with added to her young beauty the inexplicable miraculous generosity which had loved him, cared for him, forgiven him and borne their son little Duncan to him.

Everything he had told her, seemed unnecessary.

During the next few weeks he discovered, though, that their relationship had separated, as it were, on two different levels which now ran parallel. One path was their reaffirmed and strengthened trust in each other which, when they were on it, seemed the final truth of their love. The other path was their day-to-day life in the suburban house built during an epoch when all the houses in that part of London seemed of stucco poured into a single mould: their life with little Duncan, now three years old. On this day-to-day level their lack of understanding of each other seemed to increase; and the path to lead directly to a place where life together would become intolerable.

The very existence of the deeper level where everything was forgiven, mind and body fused, made them the more impatient on the level where everything was wearisome, mechanical and unforgivable. Yet they could not live always on the deeper level, of dreams, tears, acceptance and finality, a life so strange and unfamiliar that it seemed a postscript to their waking lives.

A crisis of anger, of tenderness, or of happiness in the course of their everyday life would enable them suddenly to discover themselves once more on that path where the superficial things did not count. They could make these abrupt, violent transitions. What they could not do was keep the new life steadily in contact with the old, melt down the new differences which divided, in the heat of the new intensity.

One evening, when they had cleared away the supper

things and long after little Duncan had been put to bed, they sat side by side again on the sofa. Kate was knitting and Harvey was smoking his pipe. She said: 'It's nice to sit side by side like this again, isn't it, Harvey?'

This affected him like an accusation.

'Why "again"? It isn't so often that I go out.'

'I know you don't go out during the day for a job but you're out often in the evening.'

'Well, I don't need a job, do I? I've saved quite a bit of money. Whatever you may say about me, I've done pretty well for myself if you consider what I was earning before the war. In 1938, I was earning five pounds a week as a clerk, and now I've lately been getting close on £1,000 a year as an official.'

He was very smug, she thought.

'But you're not earning that now.'

'I prefer to do a bit of free-lancing while I wait.'

'I'd like very much to know what you're waiting for.'

He flushed.

'I've told you, haven't I? Need we go into all that again? We've agreed, haven't we? Anyway, I don't know that I ever really want another regular job. I haven't any ambitions so long as I can get just along supporting you and giving Duncan the chance of a better education than I had. I'm going on with my writing—'

'How will you afford all this? How will you afford the travelling you plan to do, for one thing?'

This got him on the raw. The whole point of his not getting a job was—as he supposed she realized—to keep himself free for what she called his travelling.

Yet he was not impractical. He had plans for what he called 'getting in on the ground floor' of post-war planning, through connections he had made with certain members of the Civilian Military forces in Germany. From the war and post-war years he had acquired confidence in his own power for 'fiddling' through. He was slightly exasperated by her failure to 'believe' in his capacity for making deals.

He looked round the room restlessly. 'Couldn't we change those curtains?'

She looked at the curtains, which were of a dark orange colour: 'Why?'

'I don't think the colour goes very well with the walls and the carpet. . . . And now that I'm on the subject of changing things, I thought if you don't object I'd get a pot of paint and repaint the bathroom. I can't stand that lemon-coloured woodwork with those tiles.'

She put down her knitting and said very quietly:

'You've changed a great deal, Harvey, but you don't seem to realize that I haven't changed. I've been here all the time, while you've been away improving yourself.'

'It isn't that I've bettered myself at all,' he said, but with the same irrepressible flare of satisfaction that made the room seem suddenly too small to hold such triumph. 'I'm different, that's all. I can't help being different any more than you can help being the same.'

She looked again at the curtains. They were certainly faded, though she liked their colour. All confidence seemed drained out of her life. Harvey and she might just as well never have met as be such strangers to each other as they had become. Yet nothing had happened except that he had said some words.

He had meant to explain that he had had a conversion to an entirely different way of life. There was an ambiguity in this conversion. It was real and yet it made him be false.

'After all, it wasn't just Germany. I know you think everything's due to that. But I'd changed long before I went to Germany.'

She looked hard at him. 'When did you change?'

'It was the war, I suppose. In the hospital, when I met Duncan Ballard. I suppose you might say I began to educate myself. I started off reading modern books and then I worked backwards through Dickens and Shakespeare. I began to have what you might call cultural values, and to spend my money not on gadgets but on a little library.' He looked across at some book-shelves built into a niche in one corner of the room.

Then he made an effort to shake off once more this deadly self-satisfaction which parodied a change which he felt really an improvement in himself, parodied even his love. 'I realize how you feel, Kate, and I know it's dreadfully hard on you. I know that I'm selfish, that I'm a prig, that I don't make you happy. All the same, I'm not just a materialist. I don't exploit what I've gained intellectually by trying to make more and more money. I want to go on improving myself and I want to live according to better standards and I want Dunky to be brought up different from what I was.'

'But I try my best to bring up little Duncan well, Harvey.'

'I know you do, darling. It isn't the way you bring him up that I criticize. It's his being brought up in the same atmosphere as Mrs. Barnard's Geoffrey. I'll give you an example of what I mean. This morning I went into the garden with Dunky and he was playing round with me when Geoff came out of Mrs. Barnard's back door. When Geoff saw Dunky he let out a kind of yell, a blood-curdling D-o-n-k! threw himself on to the ground in a horrible way and started rolling about, shouting "Donkee!" And Dunky became transformed at the same moment into Geoff's utterly base and vulgar world. It wasn't important, but I saw very clearly then what I am afraid of—I am afraid of little Duncan being sucked down into that world.'

'Oh, but boys must be boys! Do have some sense,

Harvey! It's all so unreal,' she went· on. 'Duncan Ballard can write novels and earn good money from them. He may have taught you to read but he can't teach you to write and be clever like he is. Yet you talk like him and try to write. But Duncan Ballard won't make you into a J. B. Priestley. All he can do is teach you not to work. I wish you'd never met him in the first place. And then you meet the princess or whatever she calls herself.'

'It doesn't matter, but according to our information at the camp, she has the right to be called a princess, though of course that's only a technicality.'

'Well, what does matter is that she's a Displaced Person. It's absurd for a Displaced Person to be a Princess. I'm very sorry for her, but the fact is that she's a beggar and she's nothing more. As far as rank goes she's not even as high as I am now. She can't make you a prince but she may make you and all of us beggars.'

When she spoke like this, he saw that the level of ordinary things—just as much as the finest depths— could become an abyss. All one could do was pretend to be willing to give up.

'All right. I'll take a job and I'll give up all idea of ever going back to the camp.'

'No. Go back! And don't ever come here again afterwards!'

She burst into tears. There was nothing he could say. He sat watching her, knowing that to touch or comfort her would be a lie, a lie beyond a lie. She left the room. He did not follow.

An hour later he made some tea in the kitchen, took it upstairs and knocked timidly at the bedroom door:

'Would you like a cup of tea, Kate?'

She did not reply. He went into the room. She was sitting up in bed, wide-eyed with dark rings under her eyes. He noticed how tired she looked and once more he was grieved by the three lines almost like scars growing across her forehead. The grief at the centre of their life: this was the tangible truth, shown in those scars.

She smiled slowly, timidly, with her smile of the young girl he had met years ago, strangely purified of intervening time. 'Harvey, come here. I have a little present for you.'

He walked towards her, rather apprehensively. He put the tray with the two teacups on it down on the little table beside the bed. 'What?'

She held a watch in her hand. He recognized the watch but not the wrist-bracelet attached to it. This wrist-bracelet was of small sections. Now that it was not stretched, they half-closed over each other in glittering nickel snake scales.

Harvey Granville looked down at the watch and said 'Thank you.' He felt suddenly faint.

'Do you like it?' Kate asked.

'Yes. Thank you very much, darling.'

'You never told me where you got the watch! You haven't told me much about Germany, you know.'

'Oh, in Germany you can get an awful lot of nice things for a few dozen cigarettes.'

'I didn't know you went in for the Black Market.'

'Well, it wasn't exactly the Black Market. Someone wanted me to get rid of a revolver for him. The best way was to change the revolver for something else. And then . . . he . . . insisted on my keeping this watch as a present.'

She looked steadily at him with wide eyes in which there was an expression which terrified him. It was as though her eyes were fixed on some point where they comprehended all this and then they saw to a point beyond his own comprehension.

Her body seemed almost rigid. He was aware of her flesh, waxy and sagging, as one is aware of the flesh of a dying person. Without her knowing what she was doing, her hand crumpled over the watch, picked it up and then dropped it again on to the white sheet. This gesture filled him with a sense of awe. Then, without saying another word, she got out of bed and left the room.

He heard her walk downstairs feeling her way heavily, with her hand evidently following the line of the banisters. Left alone, he knelt down and laid his head against the sheet and then against the rough texture of the blanket. He groaned. Yet although it seemed to him that he was really suffering, his suffering lacked purity. It proved to him that he was sensitive. All the purity was hers, hers moving downstairs, hers moving out into the darkness, hers if perhaps, she drowned herself in some river. For himself, by comparison with the grief he caused her, his own agony seemed slightly absurd, unreal. He remained like a sinner, who, conscious that he clings to the fruits of his ill-doing, cannot pray. Like the King in *Hamlet*, he thought, and this thought gave him the faint satisfaction in his recently acquired culture which, while making him more conscious of his situation, at the same time strangely robbed it of authenticity.

She did not come back. At last he stood up and listened in the empty room. There was the silence of the early hours of the morning which filled the town with an emptiness dropped from the furthest distances of the universe. There was the sense of streets outside washed by cold dark winds, of London faintly brushed by the reflected lights of the stars. And caged in all the little boxes of the road, human beings seemed to fill the whole night with their obscure misshapen passions which could never be moulded into a street or a prison camp.

He sighed and his sigh seemed to fill the whole house, mingling with the tears of his wife.

He walked downstairs to the little kitchen. The light was on but he could not see her. The naked bulb glared with a white fury which shone on the walls of the small room and glittered on saucepans and crockery. On the mantelshelf a clock ticked.

Then he saw her where she was crouched under the kitchen sink, her knees drawn up, her head bent over them. She was in a sleep which was a kind of trance. He put his arms round her body and drew her gently towards him. She opened her eyes and smiled faintly at him with a smile which was on the further side of these events.

'Come to bed, darling,' he whispered.

She looked at him without understanding. Her mind seemed filled with the ticking of the clock. 'Time,' she said, 'time. It goes through me like a needle through a cloth.'

'Sweetheart, you're very tired. Come now to bed.'

At this she understood. She said in the voice—almost a complaining voice—she always put on when she was worried. 'I'm perfectly all right. Leave me here. You worry too much, Harvey.' She put out her hand and stroked his face. 'That's what's wrong with you, Harvey, you worry too much.'

'Come to bed, darling. I'll look after you.'

Her waking voice merged into her trance-like voice: 'Time . . . the watch, Harvey. Your watch, poor darling, your watch like a cross . . .'

'Why like a cross?' he asked. His voice was tired. He knew now that he was absorbed into a centre of his experience, the drama which he did not want, which he had created himself but which now took him completely to itself and thrust him beyond mere literary self-dramatization into its own truth, the truth of what they were and what they suffered.

'What cross, silly? Why, me and she, the cross on which you're crucified.'

At this point everything might have ended. He would have died with this cross which she had named against his breast.

But the perception of the truth is not always the end. So he took a sponge, dipped it into some cold water and cooled her forehead with it.

She awoke as the dawn filled the streets with faint milky light. They were quite alone in this new day and as though they had never known each other. It was as though they had shed themselves, by a painful and wearisome process of everything except their awareness of each others needs. They did the ordinary things. They put on a kettle and made some tea, then they ate a little bread and jam with it, as though they were picnicking. Yes, it was a beanfeast in the middle of the night. They were happy. Then they went to bed and slept until the usual morning.

III

'Loot, I suppose,' said Duncan Ballard with a glance at the wrist-watch when, at Solario's, just off Soho Square, Harvey Granville stretched his hand across the table to reach for a bread roll.

'No. Not exactly. Though, I suppose, in a way it was.'

Their relationship at that particular stage of its development was registered in this brief dialogue. They could each have taken the same reading of it like a needle on a dial. For both of them, it showed that Harvey was a member of the occupying forces who used the Black Market like members of the occupying forces. That Duncan Ballard took this reading showed how far Harvey had stepped down. That Harvey himself took it showed his curious passivity before Duncan's judgement—result of a saving sensitivity which Duncan Ballard recognized. Without it the relationship, which had undergone so many changes, simply would have ceased to exist. Harvey's modesty, twin with his conceit, was offspring of that sensitivity.

The remark registered—for both of them—the ascendancy the well-known literary critic Duncan Ballard now had over the younger man. Perhaps he had always really had it, but there had been a time when they both pretended that Harvey Granville was on top.

Their relationship was as much part of the war as any war-time relation. Duncan Ballard's war had been a combination of several conscientious compromises which almost added up to his being much younger than forty-one and actually fighting. He was in a branch of

179

Political Intelligence which largely used his 'languages' for broadcast freedom messages to the intellectuals of occupied Central Europe. To several thousand Central European underground workers, who took the idea of being an 'intellectual' more seriously than he had ever succeeded in taking the idea of being Duncan Ballard, his name uttered over the B.B.C. at the end of talks seemed the English accent of liberation.

In addition to Political Intelligence, he was also a part-time Air-Raid Warden, and, during the gap between 1941 and 1944 when there were few raids on London, he had done a lot of talking on a variety of subjects—all tending to link up with the tired citizen's idea of a Post-War Progressive Utopia of endless security, rest and culture, in a rebuilt, perfectly planned London.

Ballard became quite famous as a part-time Civil Defence Workers' Educator, and in addition to the encouragement he provided, he laid the foundations of his own future career in the more lucid intervals of Television.

During the war he frequently got invitations to speak at rest homes, mental asylums, hospitals and prisons— at all of which the post-war vision was held to be therapeutic. It was at a hospital for tuberculosis that he met Harvey Granville, then a patient there.

Very pale and thin Harvey gazed glitteringly at Duncan, all through his talk on the art and architecture of the post-war London. Duncan was faintly thrilled by the stare of those large eyes, blue-black, in the creamy yet bony face. His words did not seem quite worthy of all the aspiration this spiritual animal extended between them. What he said seemed too officious for this almost mystic attention.

At the end of the discourse, Harvey asked a question of a general kind, which yet led the attention directly and certainly to his own 'case'. What would the government do after the war to help young writers and artists participate in reconstruction, so that the New London would not just be the idea of tired old pre-war designers ? There was no difficulty in answering this. In his talks Duncan disposed of millions of imaginary money easily raised for cultural purposes. But the point was that the words were a string which led him—after another one or two questions—to Harvey Granville's unique bed. Almost at once, Harvey started talking about the Hampstead of Keats and his circle. Next, he asked Duncan whether he would be so kind as to 'look over his things'. Duncan took these away. He was pleasantly surprised to discover that they were not Keatsian. They had the virtue of being not even poems. They were slight essays resembling extracts from a journal, comments on characters, incidents drawn from Harvey Granville's experience.

When he had read these crudely written yet authentic observations, Duncan Ballard felt that they corresponded to an experience of his own, something he had always wanted to say. He had the ability, perhaps to write it, but was too uncreative. Harvey had no inhibitions, perhaps because he did not see the difficulty of writing, which existed and was not resolved. Yet with Duncan's help, he might perhaps really do something— if he could be made to see difficulties the critical mind appreciated.

In an essay called *This Ward*, Harvey described the hospital from the point of view of its whiteness: a whiteness which, he suggested, had bleached the nurses, and in some way whitened the souls of the patients, so that their swearing, their dirty jokes, appeared grains and blotches which had not yet been washed out by the blanching conspiracy of cure with illness.

This was very close to something which Duncan

himself had felt when he went into the ward, illuminated, it seemed, by reflections from disinfected haloes. Duncan would never have recognized confidently that others shared or could share this perception. His sensibility seemed to him too isolated for communication. But Harvey, who apparently saw things truthfully, also had the confidence which derived from his being rooted in ordinary people. Meeting Harvey seemed therefore to offer him an extraordinary opportunity of understanding others (of 'entering into life', he would have put it) through identification with this sensitive yet sanely ordinary patient.

Not that Harvey was a patient for long. He recovered rapidly, and rather lost his famished look, his spirituality toning down to a focused glow of sharpness and brightness.

If Duncan never succeeded in cultivating the inspiration at the centre of Harvey, he did find peripheral ways of helping him. Soon after he had left the hospital, Harvey applied for a county scholarship. He wished, he said, to teach, and needed a degree. Then a difficulty arose. His application was turned down by the authorities on the grounds that he was a health risk. Public money could not be spent on training teachers who might break down and become candidates for pensions before they had entered schoolrooms.

Duncan did not share this view of the public interest. His private feeling for Granville now became allied with public indignation about the treatment of those who led 'ordinary' lives and he built up in his mind a huge edifice—'the Granville case'. He wrote to his M.P. He discovered names of borough councillors, and got introductions to education authorities. With astonishing ease and without his ever being quite certain that he had actually effected a universal change in the law, he did find that the objections to Harvey Granville taking a scholarship appeared to have been waived.

As soon as this happened Harvey ceased to wish to teach. The reason surprised Duncan. It was that he had discovered himself to be too good for education. At the same time that Harvey let Duncan's expectations down, he also took him deeper into his confidence, by trying to key them up. He spoke now of a secret he shared with Glen and Ed: they all knew from certain extra-ordinary conversations they had had that they were 'geniuses'. They had talked with a brilliance and confidence that no one today shared and that was greater even than the exchanges of Keats, Shelley, Leigh Hunt and their circle. Glen was an artist who had conceded to becoming a commercial draughtsman, Ed was a writer who kept going with reporting on a suburban weekly. It was Ed who had warned Harvey off teaching. Ed himself had been given a scholarship. In his three months at Oxford, before he withdrew, he saw that the dons had nothing to teach him. One could learn more about literature working for the *Finchley Road Gazette*.

These views were parodies of ones which Duncan himself had once held. In his own case they had not— he now saw—at all helped him, in that of Glen, Ed and Harvey, they made him positively uneasy. At the same time Glen, Ed and Harvey shared transports and ecstasies which he could sometimes envy. They had conversation far into the night in which names were dismissed, lines cited, jokes blown like iridescent bubbles, following a day's outing in Metroland. Just because this was something to laugh at, it was the last thing that Duncan Ballard, in his heart, despised. Keats' sonnet 'There are great spirits living at this hour'—exactly expressed their kind of insight. In moments of excitement they felt the god move through their fingers into the pencil or along the keys of the typewriter. And the god always whispered that he loved them alone, accompanying the announcement with a crack at the established, the praised, the paid for and published. The difference between Harvey Granville's friends and 'the Duncan Ballards' (this phrase inadvertently slipped into one of Harvey's animadversions about the state of letters)—was that Ed, Glen and Harvey never doubted their inspirations and cared little about results, whereas Duncan was made miserable by both.

Duncan's passion for identification of some purer more devoted side of him with an unsullied inner Harvey was so great that it could even follow Harvey to the point where he himself stood dismissed. Success was suspect and unsuccess was pure. He enjoyed in his vision of Harvey the fusion of a livingness he imagined with experience he had not had.

All the same, the relationship had changed from being an alleviation—a window opened on to vitalizing scenes with which he had never previously had contact —to a burden which he willingly carried. The fact that it had begun to weigh made welcome a development which might otherwise have been upsetting—Harvey's marriage. Kate was a more than sensible choice. She was remarkable, had something almost French—he thought—about her, and reaffirmed Duncan's faith in Harvey's intuitive rightness, at a moment when this was rather shaken. What had shaken it was the breaking in of an irony which had the immediate effect of turning what had seemed most serious overnight into jokes—like cream overnight gone sour. The jokes were in the correspondence between Duncan Ballard and George Wurlitzer, a G.I. and poet from New York, lingering, beyond war and peace, in London. Wurlitzer had been more, and more quickly, attracted by Harvey than had any of Duncan's English friends, most of whom remained aloof spectators. George Wurlitzer rushed in whooping that Harvey Granville was his own discovery. Duncan he reproached, though knowing about him, had not recognized his greatness; he had merely used Harvey, and tried to bury him. Everything Duncan had ever wishfully imagined about Harvey's gifts, George Wurlitzer megaphone-magnified. Harvey's writings might be crude—George agreed—but they were the future. Duncan proved he was the past precisely in trying to bury Harvey under patronizing faint approval.

This lasted about a week. Harvey himself could not live up to it, and, just as he had declined the educational system, he deliberately set out to disappoint the acclaiming Wurlitzer. He refused to fulfil the promise of his genius. So within a fortnight of meeting Harvey, George Wurlitzer was writing letters to Duncan about 'the Keats of Finchley and Golders Green'. It was a gathering together of the sophisticates against the naïves.

Duncan joined in the joke about Harvey. Perhaps it affected him, perhaps it acted as a safety valve and in letting out a little credulity, enabled the relationship, transformed, to survive. At any rate, Harvey no longer considered a genius, now preoccupied Duncan as having his place as a character in literature—in a book that a critic could never write. Duncan was disappointed, but also triumphant: thrown back on to his own resources, carrying the Pen Man's Burden of the inferior races who can only be the characters in fiction, which Harvey had failed to take up. Having failed to be the Absolute of art or life, Harvey now demonstrated the qualities of Original Sin, and, this being accepted, was neither good nor bad but, in his case, rather complicated.

In the new dispensation of the luncheons once a week at the Solario Restaurant, Duncan acted the friend of the family, a role sealed by his being the godfather of little Duncan. His attitude to Kate was to account her 'very brave'. At the same time, he sided with Harvey about things like the orange curtains. The whole involvement with the Princess could be taken by Duncan Ballard as an extended exercise of Harvey's taste against the virtues of Kathleen (he insistently called her Kathleen). The essential one-sidedness of his relationship with Harvey, against the hospital, against the educational system, against the world, had found a new, more realistic, detached, almost cynical level. And now Harvey told Duncan everything—perhaps it was the price he paid.

Looking down at the watch strap again with a faintly priggish smile, Harvey said: 'It's funny your noticing the watch. Kate was looking at it this morning too, though it upset her because she deduced different conclusions.'

Graham winced.

'What conclusions?'

'I mean, she didn't conclude it was loot. She thought it had been given to me by someone. And as a matter of fact she was right. Though it was loot also.'

'You mean, the person who gave it you had looted it?'

'No. I myself bartered it, in exchange for something of hers. And then she gave it to me.'

Duncan looked across the table, rather wearily. 'I've never met anyone like you for fascinating complications, Harvey.'

'Well,' said Harvey, taking up the thread of a narrative with which he fed Duncan at these sessions, 'I went into the hut one day, the hut I've told you about, in part of which lived Moura, her mother and her sister. She was alone that morning—at any rate alone in the little aisle formed by their sleeping bunks. We've never been alone for more than a few minutes at a time. She told me that now her mother besides trying to take poison, had also got hold of a revolver. She pulled the revolver out from under her pillow. When I saw it, I said: "If this were found by the camp authorities, that would be one sure way of getting you sent back to the East." To tell you the truth, seeing it made me feel rather nervous. I wasn't sure whether I oughtn't to report the matter. "That's why I want to ask you a great favour," Moura said. "I want you to get rid of it for me." I said I'd do my best. I took it from her, and later I bartered it, on the Black Market, for this watch. The next day, when I brought the watch to her, I explained that it was in exchange for the revolver, Moura handed it back to me and said: "Will you keep it as a gift from me? There isn't any opportunity for us to go out and buy you any memento." '

'So you took it?'

'I just said—Thank you. She said: "I do not tell my mother"'—Harvey repeated this in an imitation of Moura's accent which, in the restaurant, Duncan found embarrassing—'"She would be upset," Moura said. "But it is from all of us." In her heart, she too would wish it.'

'The strap was rather worn,' Harvey went on, reverting to the present, and to London. 'So Kate got this new one—without telling me. She gave it to me this morning. And there was a scene—'

'Why?'

'I think my expression when I looked down at the watch showed her something,' he said, not without a note of pride.

'Did she ask where you got it?'

'Yes. I told her, the Black Market. That was true, as a matter of fact.'

True, as a matter of fact, like so many of Harvey's truths, like Harvey himself, as a matter of fact, Duncan reflected.

Duncan looked at the watch. Then he said brightly, 'I get it. It's your cross—representing Kate and Moura.'

'How extraordinary! That's exactly what Kate said!'

'Well, haven't I always said that that unfortunate woman is not stupid!'

Harvey was delighted, really delighted. This was a big moment between them. It was as if Duncan had handed Harvey his authenticated life back, a medal on a silver plate—an embellished, cruciform symbol, a recognized, respected piece of reality made up of love and suffering.

Things really became easier. Harvey pulled out two more pieces of documentary evidence in the moral case-book which he obsessively kept for Duncan. One was a letter written in a firm handwriting with slanting letters, each of them sensitively formed—very un-English however, as though they might break into another alphabet or a splutter of accentuation marks. The other was a photograph of Moura. The letter ran:

Dear Friend,
Thank you for the parcel. In this cloud which we inhabit it was beautiful to have light shine from outside.

My mother, my sister and myself are happy thinking of you at your home in London with your beautiful wife and child.

You must not think for my sake to break up the happiness which you have in your own house. So I am not sure about your plan to come back here. You must not allow the misfortunes of those who have lost their families, to draw into the destruction those who are united. So consider closely your wife. I can understand how she must love you.

To meet someone who resembles a human being and who greets me as human, creates already for me the idea beyond this prison. Your kindness, your humanity are with us for ever.
                                                    Moura.

After he had finished reading this letter, Duncan looked more intently at the photograph. Then he laid it on the letter and pushed both back across the table.

Harvey took a long deep breath: 'She speaks of my
letter being a sign of light to her from the world outside.
But her letter is just as much a sign of light to me. She
lives in her cloud of Eastern Europe, but I also live in
my kind of cloud I have made for myself . . .' He went
on to elaborate this metaphor as he had done to Kate,
but in Duncan's presence he did not feel quite the same
confidence. He stumbled out of literature again to say:
'I owe everything I have to her (apart from a great
deal of education which I've received from you, Duncan). But before I went to Germany I was divided
between having a shot at selling cars and the idea of
getting in on the ground floor of the new education
scheme, as a result of my Civilian Military experience
which also incidentally gave me one or two contacts at
the Home Office. One side of me wanted to do public
good and the other wanted to make money: I think the
good would have won, especially as I think there is also
a solid future in the education scheme. My only wish
now is to make myself a civilized person. My communist friends think I'm a prig and a snob, naturally
enough, and I dare say they're right: I *am* a bit of both.'

'Perhaps it's rather more to the point to know what
Kathleen thinks.'

Duncan sipped his coffee, holding the cup high over
his mouth between sips, and looking at Harvey over the
rim, with shining eyes. Suddenly, he felt happy. Duncan
asked: 'You consider returning to the camp?'

'Well, I'm not going to take a job there, but I intend
to pay the camp a visit for a few days every six months.
That means I shall have to order my whole life round
those few days.'

Still not really concerned, Duncan said: 'How long
can this go on for, Harvey?'

Harvey did not answer this. Instead, he said:

'I've had an idea. It is that when I next come back

from Germany, you and she and I should all meet for a few days in Paris.'

'Well, some time we might discuss that,' said Ballard, as though he had been given very short notice indeed. Then he said: 'It's more important to know why you think your going to Germany will succeed?'

'I dare say it won't succeed. But don't you see that either it works or nothing works? Whether or not I see Moura, something final has already happened. I've discovered a new personality in myself just as if I had died and were born again.'

'Oh God!' exclaimed Duncan.

The idea that Harvey had authentic spiritual experiences, isolated from those of every one else, experiences of the universe, of love, of death, sickened him. Quite truthfully he said: 'I felt very sick for a moment, that's all. I'm sorry. Go on.'

Granville looked up at him, timidly, humbly, affectionately. 'Have the things I've been saying sounded very naïve?'

'Oh dear, no, not in the least, Harvey,' he answered, meaning that they had and meaning Harvey to understand very definitely that he meant they had.

Harvey did not reply. Relenting a little, Duncan who had been staring at the coarse fur wrapped like a horse's collar around the neck of a lady just leaving her table, looked at him. Then he looked again, with amazement. For Granville was on the verge of tears. His face was flushed, his eyelids drooped over his eyes to hide the emotion which Duncan certainly did not wish to see. With his fork in his right hand he fumbled vaguely at his plate. But in spite of himself Duncan saw the emotion: 'Yes, he is at the centre of things. He's out in the night, in the cold, among the wounded multitudes, in the starving huts, and he has found his heart.'

Granville broke the silence once more. Looking

timidly at Duncan he said: 'I am glad that you take Kate's side. Of course, I realize that I am behaving badly to her.'

'Not at all, Harvey. If there is a question of sides, I'm sure Kathleen does not need defending by me. She is, in her own right, a beautiful woman. Kathleen is a beautiful woman.'

Harvey flushed once more: 'I know.'

They were silent again. But the sensitive recording instrument was a needle fluctuating wildly and quite unreliably now inside Harvey. Duncan had a vague dread of what was coming. Harvey looked at him with intolerable irritating innocence and said with grace:

'Oh, I'm so glad you think that. Of course, I've always thought that Kate was very beautiful but I've never dared to say so in front of you.'

Duncan was so startled that all he could think of was to say: 'I hadn't noticed that you ever hesitated to say what you wanted to me, Harvey.'

'You see, owing, I suppose, to my sense of inferiority, I never imagined that you thought anything of us. I have always been very grateful to you for your kindness and for all that I have learned from you, and I've hoped that perhaps you've got something back from us, if only in the way of copy for your writing.'

Duncan felt in a false, unreal position, as though the whole relationship with Harvey had been exposed as worth only so much paper on which it might be written. He had an impatient wish to scrap it, brush it aside, be done with it at once, rid himself of Harvey as of any other disturbing phantom. What was unforgivable was that it was Harvey who had revealed this arbitrariness of their friendship, not he himself in his own good time. But all he said for the moment was quite pompously:

'On the contrary, I admire your wife greatly and I am devoted to my godson.' He hoped that Harvey was at least vulnerable enough still to notice that he had been omitted.

'Perhaps while I'm away, then, you'll occasionally go and see Kate and little Duncan,' Harvey said timidly, aware that he might be asking too much. He hesitated, then he added: 'I hope I haven't offended you by assuming that you weren't interested in Kate. But (you know what women are) she's always rather taken the line that you were more interested in me.'

'Waiter, the bill please,' said Duncan, really angry now. When he had paid the bill, getting up, he said: 'Perhaps when you're away I'll have the opportunity of showing Kathleen that I am interested in her.'

Harvey looked inquiringly at him. Then gripping the sides of the table, and getting up also, he said: 'Tell me truthfully, Dunk, what would you do if you were in my place?'

Duncan got up and stood on the other side of the table where his face was in the light. He stood there in complete silence staring, across the table he had just left, out of the window. On the other side of the road was a tall grey concrete building—incongruous for Soho —which was a hospital. Then Duncan turned back into the room as though to address the whole restaurant. The light from the window shone on one side of his face, golden on his moustache, transparent green on one eye; it showed very clearly the bitter line from nostril to edge of mouth. He was turning over in his mind a great many ideas as though on his tongue in his mouth which left him with a sour not altogether unpleasing (because his own) taste. There was a malign movement of his mouth, after which he said very quietly and calmly (with a pomposity now consciously and maliciously intended to embarrass), 'I think you should follow your own heart.'

IV

Granville flew back to the country whose cities, from the centre of the air, seemed exposed cells of a beehive whose roof had been torn off, the honey robbed, and the walls shattered. Mere destruction was an industry and the people miners, wandering amongst the slag heaps formed from ruins of their destroyed homes and digging for a little warmth in tunnels and cellars. Trees and fields and surviving villages, farms and animals shocked the eye with their rich innocent colours, like a reproach.

This was the country where the whips had been torn from the hands of the tyrants, where the prisoners had been liberated into camps and sheds to be herded there like animals; where the tyrants were arbitrarily hanged, or else let mingle indiscriminately with the inhabitants who had been their slaves, and where the new masters, the occupiers, were embarrassed warders in a hospital for patients afflicted with disease—warders living a different life on a different diet, yet secretly afraid of the surrounding infection, and furtively playing the games which they knew to be symptoms of the disease itself. Here the most valued pleasure was to fill the lungs with a few breaths of tobacco smoke, and ten minutes of this pleasure, in its little paper wrapping, became the basis of currency with which everything could be bought or sold—office, love, drink, property.

Granville had his moment in the light-filled air where the sun lay like a stone of fire, revolving and shooting arrows of gold upon the flat wings of the aeroplane, and below upon the sparkling cloud-pavement, when he

193

seemed at the apex of his own life. He looked down each side of a triangle. One great line reached back to London and the other forward to the camp where the princess lived in a crowded hut. There, in London, stood Kate, with her flame-like auburn hair and the little veins spread through her body. The house where they lived— one of a hundred such on an out-of-date building estate —was rich and dear and warm, lived in and breathed over. And there was a sense of young life all round her, of Dunky and of other children yet unborn. His high-flying eyes hovered round the pillar of her neck, chose their resting place in the nape just beneath where the hair begins. His mind, suddenly eloquent, as though his whole chest swarmed with words, broke forth into a warm flow of language like words heard in a dream, serene elucidations, passionate explanations, renewed declarations. Yet when he woke for an instant from this trance and tried to shape these words into sentences which he might put into a letter, he could not remember them.

At the foot of the other earthwards-dropping line of the triangle was Moura in the hut amongst the ruins. His whole being flew in and out of hers, she understood the burden of his knowledge. He laid down a great sack of unutterable realization of terrible things at her door.

The pictures disappeared and only a thought was left: that in human relationships, there are no simple solutions of black and white. What is selfish may have an aspect where it is unselfish and unselfishness may be selfish. The sacrifice which Kate required of him was natural and inevitable, and from this point of view it was selfish of him to refuse to be selfish. The unselfishness of his knowledge of the agony of the world was a form of selfishness in his life . . . But words like 'selfish', 'duty', and so on, dispersed the vision.

An hour later, as he stood outside the door of the

Camp Director's office, his thoughts had become far more practical. They were that he mustn't let the Director know his one obsessive wish to see Moura.

The Director was a tall New Englander, with a deal of greying hair, an aquiline nose and the intense eyes of an English Victorian statesman. When Granville entered his office he was standing over his table-desk with hands leaning slightly on it. His head was drooped, he was a little round-shouldered, and he had the appearance of a great grey eagle who had descended amongst these ruins, having seen all things, in order to be kind and stern.

He had a slow, sententious way of talking, more English in accent than that of the English. 'Glad to see you, Harvey,' he said. 'We've all missed you here. I'm sorry you're not staying longer. It's a damned nuisance, in fact, that we aren't in a position to persuade you to take a job here. We need people like you.'

Harvey sighed.

Then the telephone bell rang. Wingfield took up the receiver and Granville heard a conversation about a concert which was to be held at the camp that evening. So at all events he would see Moura then. 'There's a concert this evening in the barn,' said Wingfield, putting down the receiver. 'All the staff hope that you'll be coming to it.'

'I'd like to very much. But meanwhile, can I do anything this afternoon to help?'

'There's nothing much that you can do. Things are pretty well organized just at present. But if it interests you to do so, you can come along with me to Munich. I have a parcel to give to someone there.' He walked across to a cupboard from which he took a parcel. 'Recently I've been having these things posted out to me from the States and I've been distributing them amongst some of the worst cases here.' As they left the hut and walked across a yard of flattened mud to the car, he went on: 'At first, I couldn't make up my mind whether to distribute my parcels amongst a great many people, giving them only one or two each, or whether to concentrate on a few people and try really to improve their conditions efficaciously.'

'And what did you decide?'

'I decided to be unjust, and favour a few. I find that social inequality always produces a certain number of results, whereas if there is complete justice every one almost starves. I dare say that is why I'm not a Communist,' he said slowly with a curious sententiousness which underlined both his seriousness and his grey flat humour.

They drove through the haggard remnants of Munich or rather the remnants of an anonymous, expressionless large town. For everything which made Munich Munich and gave it a unique personal character had disappeared. All that was left were just remains of buildings and a few buildings without character which now had acquired prominence simply by survival. There were many streets turned into discarded shattered boxes with a few beams, columns and girders standing, like gallows. Harvey was familiar with all this, as one knows a story which has been told again and again. He had never understood the destruction. The thoughts and the lives of the people living among these ruins were a mystery to him; and yet they were a mystery which he knew very well, a mystery at the back of his mind always, whether he was awake or asleep. There was a moment now when these streets of broken houses seemed realer to him than the memory of the bright, complacent street where he lived at home with its dismal yet cocky houses. He seemed to press his eyes into this scene, as though the shattered town were part of his own flesh, as a hand caresses secretly a scar.

They came to the cross-roads where there was a wide space beyond them as all the buildings had been destroyed. There were only very low jagged tooth-edges of walls, heaps of rubble, blowing dust in the hard white photographic sunlight. Men and women, drably but neatly dressed, with flesh and in clothes which seemed to have no colour, were threading their ways along paths amongst the ruins. They trickled from ruined block to ruined block over the cross-roads, completely absorbed in their journeyings, taking no notice of the traffic, as though they belonged to a different world from that of the requisitioned cars and the jeeps, an insect world, an ant-world, occupied in carrying small bits of wood from place to place.

From their car, Wingfield and Granville watched these people as though they were removed from them by a great distance. When they nearly ran a man over and he stood a yard from the windscreen, it still seemed as though his proximity were an illusion produced perhaps by looking at him from a mile away through field-glasses. Without seeming to notice them, he just managed to move across their vision without being thrust under their wheels.

'The Krauts have no traffic sense,' said Granville.

He made this remark as one might say: 'It's a fine day.' It was a safe, banal observation of the Occupation Forces which a hundred officers made to each other every day when driving through their particular Zone, just as in Nuremberg, the Occupying Forces greeted each other with the question: 'How many people have you hanged today?'

'I wonder why that is?'

'I don't know.'

'I have an idea it might be because they don't care a damn whether they're run over or not,' said Wingfield dryly.

Now they left the town and drove through poignant green countryside where trees insistently were un-damaged trees and grass was grass. There were villages where fruit trees with over-arching laden boughs, wisteria and roses, seemed to hang over and between the over-sweet houses, filtering the sunlight with their nets of branches. The cream-coloured houses were intensely intact. The very old beams and the gabled roofs shocked Granville as though with a vulgar newness in comparison with the destroyed town of Munich which, in a few hours, had been transformed into a place infinitely ancient, receding into abysses, flying backwards through time to join the craters of the moon.

Granville was very tired after the journey. His mind seemed driven along parallel lines of thought, as the car drove along the parallels of the road. 'They could all be knocked down with a feather,' he thought, looking at the houses. 'I have to keep them up with my will.' Paris would fall, London would fall, his home in London with Kate and little Duncan would be destroyed if he did not sustain them with his will, as Wingfield with his wakeful, watchful mind kept the car from running off the road.

Why had he come to Germany? To see Moura, of course. But this reason now seemed an abstraction, a formula. It was a transparent, vague blur unfocused a hundred yards beyond the windscreen and never getting nearer.

Now Harvey felt absolutely at the end of something, at a point of utter exhaustion, like death itself. Whether he saw the princess meant nothing to him. He repeated to himself over and over again: 'I am going to see her in an hour's time.' The sentence produced no sensation in him whatever. He was quite free, he thought idly, vacantly, not to see her. Simply to go away, to go back home, at most to ask Wingfield to explain that he had

never been. But this course was equally unattractive to
him. He knew that he was acting in a vacuum of his own
inertia. He had not the will to go on, and he had still
less will to go back. The impulse which had brought
him here would work itself out. The whole situation no
longer seemed to have anything to do with what he
wanted. They drove to a narrow street on the outskirts
of a village and stopped at a house. 'The parcel is for
Dr. Grosche who lives here,' said Wingfield. 'Would
you like to wait here, or would you care to come in?
I warn you it's not very pleasant.'

'I'd like to come in with you.'

Directly they went inside the entrance of the stairway
of the house, they were oppressed by a sweet, sickly
smell of decay, damp, bugs and illness. As they climbed
up the staircase, Harvey noticed that all its walls were
severely cracked. Damp spread through the cracks, and
in places the walls were stained with patches of green
fungus. On each floor there was a little window which
looked out on to a garden filled with fruit trees. They
climbed up to the fourth floor, where Wingfield knocked
at a narrow door. There was no reply. He knocked
again and waited. There was still no reply. Wingfield
said: 'There must be someone in, because I know Dr.
Grosche isn't fit to go out.'

Five minutes later, they heard a shuffling in the
corridor of the flat. Then the door was opened by a
man wearing a long white night-dress and night-cap.
In this garb he looked as though he did not belong to
this century at all, but to another time, an age of
eighteenth-century prints of the decrepit husband in
night-shirt and with candle in hand stumbling into the
bedroom where the young wife lies sprawling on the
bed with a satin-attired young beau. He was very thin
and his stomach protruded from out this long slab-like
thinness so that it jutted like a ledge, making his night-

dress protrude abruptly. His face was pale and lined with long, mostly vertical lines which fixed it in one final expression from which it did not now trouble to alter.

He said in a voice which showed not the slightest interest, 'My mother is out. That is why I did not answer. I have been sleeping.'

He made a deprecatory gesture, pointing with his arm wooden as a signpost into the flat: 'You may come in if you like, but you see there is only my mother's room and my room here, and my mother has been out all day trying to get one or two things, and she has not had time to tidy my room, I cannot do so myself either, so it is all in a terrible mess.'

'We should like to come in for a few minutes only, Dr. Grosche. We certainly don't want to bother you in any way,' said Wingfield, 'but we would like to see how you are.'

Doctor Grosche led them into a small room where there was a bed, a table, two chairs and a wicker contraption in front of the window, devised to hold a flower-pot containing a plant. He walked over to the bed and half-reclined on it. They sat on the two chairs. His face seemed almost the same soiled texture as the sheets. The room was filled with an asphyxiating odour, the same mixture of sweet sickliness as had penetrated even to the front door of the house, but here it was much stronger.

'Won't you lie down properly, Dr. Grosche?' Wingfield asked. 'I'm sure you can't be comfortable lying that way?'

Without saying anything, Dr. Grosche pushed back the sheets and got into the bed.

Wingfield put the parcel which he held in his hands on the table, and said: 'A few things for you, Herr Doktor.'

Doctor Grosche looked across the room at the table with the parcel. His face did not change its expression.

Nor did Wingfield seem to expect any thanks. 'Do you get insulin?' he asked.

'I get some, but it is only 30 per cent of what I require for my condition. The Occupation Forces explain that they do not have insulin for the use of German civilians.'

'And what about food?'

'We get our rations, but of course it isn't possible to get the kind of bread required for *diabetiker*, or any of the other foods which are specially required.'

Doctor Grosche answered all these questions in a flat, tired, expressionless voice. There was not the slightest note of criticism or irony in his remarks about the two Occupying Forces, there was not the least self-pity. If his tone suggested anything it was that the situation was as he described it, he knew quite well that nothing whatever could be done, and he would rather not tire himself.

After ten minutes, Wingfield got up and they left the flat. On their way downstairs, he mentioned that Dr. Grosche had once been a brilliant lawyer, that he had never been a member of the Nazi Party and that there was nothing against him. He seemed pleased to say all this. As they descended the stairs the odour of the flat became less penetrating, and then at last they were in the bright sunlit street again, with the fruit trees showing in the gardens and the birds singing.

On the pavement, Wingfield stood still for a moment breathing in the air. His fine profile showed against the background of the street, his eyes looked away, into the distance. In this still posture, he looked a very distinguished photograph of a very distinguished citizen.

'Well,' he said, 'we might just have a cup of tea at

the local Officers' Mess and then we should be getting
back, or we shall be late for the concert.'

Tea was excellent. There was butter and cakes and
fruit salad with cream. At the next table some officers
were agreeing very loudly that despite all the disadvan-
tages of being in Germany you could make more for
yourself on the European Black Market than at home.

It was getting dark as they drove back along the wide
motor road. Wingfield drove steadily, altering his speed
little between thirty-five and forty kilometres an hour,
registered on the dial of their requisitioned German
Opel. Apart from the road billowing up like dirty snow
in their headlights nothing showed except large signs
posted every hundred yards or so along the side of the
road stating that the speed limit was not to be exceeded.
These brusque announcements alternated with a terse,
one-line poem squeezed out of the soul of American
civilization:

DRIVE SLOWLY—DEATH IS SO PERMANENT

The road was one of Hitler's Autobahner. It seemed
to invade the countryside in a wide grey column of
concrete which blotted out the landscape, replacing it
simply with an abstraction—the means of getting
quickly from place to place. Now that it was darkening,
the greyness seemed to flood up from the road surface
at them, like a fog. This colourlessness seemed to suit
Wingfield's mood. He began telling one story after
another about the occupation, all illustrating the same
corruption. He had visited the mess of British Headquarters, to meet there an important economist sent out
for consultations about the condition of the Western
Zone. After dinner, the economist had taken him aside,
and said to Wingfield, 'Do you want to trade any of
these?' producing a dozen German army watches from
his coat pocket. Wingfield related this so sombrely, that

Harvey did not know whether to laugh. But no comment was required. The Camp Director was off now on a truly horrible story. He had seen a French jeep run over a German boy at a crossing. The driver of the jeep got out and kicked the injured youth to the side of the road. Stories of this kind followed one another out of Wingfield's grey, grave face, like a procession of victims with bowed heads and shuffling feet.

Wingfield was explaining now that to the American occupiers, the British and the French were gradually, in Frankfurt, taking the place of Jews. Harvey felt alarmed: the Director's stories, if true, were beyond what he could believe without witnessing the examples offered. The need to interrupt, almost for the sake of sanity, made him bold, and he heard his own voice ask—'How is the princess?'

Wingfield turned round slowly from the driving wheel, and said: 'She is a remarkable woman, an excellent interpreter and devoted to her mother and sister. Whether she is a princess is another matter. There is a good deal of evidence being accumulated by psychologists which seems to show that when dispossessed people are deprived of every motive for existing, they sometimes console themselves with strongly held views about their position in a past society, of which the whole structure is fantasy. There have been remarkable geographical, even historical constructions.'

This portentous tact woven doubtless into monumental cogitations of Wingfield's own brooding isolation, roused Harvey. He said, smarting: 'I don't care a damn whether she's a princess or what she is. The fact that you speak well of her is worth much more to me. I only used that silly name because it's the one all the camp call her by. Outside here, I always call her Moura. When can I see her?'

'Well, I had anticipated your interest in this rather

involved family, so I considered it desirable to separate them at what seemed the best time for a meeting. I'm afraid Moura can't be at the concert, but in any case that may not be the time and occasion which would strike you as the best for a reunion.'

'When shall I see her, then?'

'After the concert.' Her mother is going for treatment to the hospital ward. I thought you might like to see Moura, so I arranged that she should take her mother to the hospital this afternoon during the concert, and that her sister should fetch her back later tonight.'

They returned to the camp, and the Director took Granville to his own lodgings, in a workman's house, at the edge of the camp. There were two barely furnished bedrooms, a bathroom with geyser, and a sitting-room with chocolate-coloured carpet, leather-covered armchair, two tables and a bookcase.

Wingfield stood by the window, looking out over the muddy waste of the camp in which the bored, scarecrow figures of a few inmates were moving, fetching and carrying. 'One of the officers who took over Belsen,' he said, meditatively, 'told me that after a week or ten days of living among these victims reduced to a state of complete inhumanity, he came to sympathize with the S.S. Guards. He wanted nothing more than to finish off the task of annihilating people who had been reduced to something uglier and smellier than death.'

'I can understand that, sir,' said Harvey, using the 'sir' for the first time, 'but all the same.'

Wingfield turned round and looked at him. 'You don't realize how good it is to see you—to be able to talk. The most difficult part of this life is that there is no one to talk to.' His eye caught two cylindrical-shaped objects made of cable on the table. He took them up. 'Do you know what these are?' he asked. 'No, sir.' 'Those are cables with which the guards at Belsen used to lash their prisoners.' He held them like handles, one in each fist, and as he did so, looked over them, straight into Harvey's eyes.

'I will come back again, sir, in a few weeks time,' said Harvey. 'Then we shall be able to talk a lot more.'

'Why should you come back?'

'For the same reason that I have come now.'

'You seem to imagine that nothing changes. We are a very fluctuating population. In six months' time we may all be gone. As for the person who brings you here, that person will probably be abroad in two weeks' time.'

'Why . . .'

'I tried to look after what I thought the best interests of her family, and also of you,' he said. 'They have permits to go abroad where no one will be able to reach them against their will. But she will explain to you herself.'

Suddenly Granville felt extremely homesick. This was a place where madness approached you with thongs. He said: 'Perhaps we should go to the concert.'

They went. When Granville came with Wingfield into the bare empty, reeking barn, which had no floor but the mud, and a few benches on which the sickest members of the audience sat down, while the rest stood in silence, a few of the staff who remembered him came and shook him warmly by the hand. Some of the D.P.'s made a vague lunging movement towards him, like animals that recollect a keeper.

The curtain went up on an opening chorus of girls dressed in clothes that looked like sacking, while they sang a chorus with a political message, to the accompaniment of an orchestra of combs. Then there was a knock-about play dominated by a clown with large red false nose, and torn baggy trousers. Then two gentlemen who appeared to have been, in some former incarnation, ballad singers, sang a burlesque epic caricaturing the progress of Hitler's generals through Europe. Six male Russian dancers now kicked and squatted their peasant dances.

Until now, the whole performance consisted of variations on themes of crude Communist propaganda which appeared to have absorbed every impulse here of anti-Nazism. But now a tall languid lady in a ballroom dress, crumpled and worn, as though it had been preserved in many trunks through many campaigns, advanced to the front of the stage, and clutching the skirt of her dress, revolved in the circles of a Viennese waltz. Her fan, held in the other hand, was of the Austrian court, it seemed. She was every inch a great lady, a countess or princess perhaps, surviving with her one wish: to return to court, and curtsey to the Emperor. Then, slamming down on this, the concert ended with a raucous hymn to Stalin.

V

The so-called hut was really a large long shed, in which twenty women lived. Inside, it was divided by partitions, against which were constructed berths. Standing in the corridor out of which these small enclosures, each containing four bunks, led, Harvey had the impression of being in some penitentiary, or dormitory for convicts. Just as the smell of a bad egg can put one off the very thought of eggs for days, so the smell of the diabetic Doctor Grosche's flat, had either infected everything or made him conscious everywhere of smells that disgusted.

He stood there for a short time, wishing he had not come, almost overwhelmed by nostalgia for cleanliness and comfort. This wooden hut clumsily constructed above the damp mud, supported by its upright struts of splintering wood, and with its shuffling inhabitants, was like a disgusting copse he wanted to cut down. He thought of the clean bright model kitchen at home looking out on to the little spotted apron of a back garden.

There seemed to be people on every bed and behind every partition. It was like a fetid, grotesque Bank Holiday tent. Women were lying in their berths, or standing by the beds they shared with their children, or tending the old and the weary, or sewing, talking and silent. Some of them were reading: there was a kind of desperation about the effort, as though they were straining the words on the printed page which, if they clung fast, would make a ladder up to a world outside.

He walked down the corridor, and then, through the open space between partitions, he saw Moura, the princess. She was sitting on her bed—gawkily, because she had to lean forward on account of the very low ceiling formed by the bed above hers. The pose was ugly. She did not see him and, for a few moments, he stood there in utter detachment watching her, his face expressionless. What he deeply thought was—'At any rate, she's cleaner than the rest of them.' He gradually reconstructed his memorized image of her around this presence, in the light of this naked thought.

She was wearing a white smock-like blouse embroidered round the collar and tucked, at the waist, into her skirt. The long sleeves of the blouse were tied around the wrists.

She looked up and saw him. Her dark hair was soberly parted, brushed back from the high almost box-like forehead, which was as uncreased now as if nothing had ever happened to her to wrinkle it. She was well-formed and she was assuredly someone, but she was not pretty. Looked at whole and steadily, she was perhaps beautiful in a way that would last all her life.

The moment that she caught sight of him lines wrinkled her eyes and forehead. For some reason, he was immensely touched by the fact that her smile and her greeting made her look older. He went up to her, simply shook her hand, and sat down on the bunk opposite. Each of them was forced to lean forward in these cramped quarters, and when they talked their heads were almost touching. It was absurd.

To respect someone else, not to make advances, to take nothing for granted, were signs of distinction in this place, where love could only perhaps be demonstrated by an adoring refusal to touch the loved one, and, given the continuation of such circumstances, there might even be a revival of the medieval conception of

courtly love. In some amazing way, Harvey Granville
understood this, and observed rules of an unwritten
tact. He sat there almost as if he had reverted to his
rôle of an unexceptional civilian military officer visiting
the camp.

'Thank you for the parcels. It was very kind of you
to remember us.'

'Did you imagine that I could ever forget you?'

Both allowed this first exchange to fall away into
silence. Then he asked whether her mother was really
in a bad way. Should he be worried about her? She
answered a bit impatiently:

'She is not really ill. She will be better as soon as we
get away from here.'

He rested his face in his hand and leaned his elbow
on one knee. Like this, with his hand almost hiding his
mouth, he said: 'The Director of the Camp told me. It
must be wonderful news for all three of you. When
will you be free?'

'Almost at once, within a week perhaps, he said. It
is difficult to believe that. To me it's quite unreal. I
haven't understood it yet at all.'

'Where will you be going?'

'I don't think about it,' she insisted, looking away
from him. 'But he says Australia. They have made a
law or something, to admit people like us—people who
are afraid of being sent back where we came from.'

She laid her hands together in her lap, looked rather
helpless, and smiled, in an almost frightened way.

By crouching down, and then spreading out his hands,
with his head leaning against the partition, he almost
lay back on the narrow bunk opposite hers, and he half
closed his eyes. 'I heard that they had increased the
quota, to let in a great many D.P.'s from Europe.
A remarkable thing, really, for the Australians to have
done.'

She made no comment. 'I am very glad,' he said, 'that you will be able to get away from all this.'

'I don't know what I want. But there are all three of us. My mother says she does not want to die here.'

He sat up suddenly, and said in a different voice: 'Can't your sister look after her?'

'No, Harvey, I don't think my mother would like that. You see, she has always depended on me.'

'But don't you have yourself to look after?'

She did not reply. He saw it was a fearful cliché. Yet he had a panicky fear that the conversation was going to continue on lines which quietly fixed the gulf between them forever, without even a word of recognition of what had gone before. Nothing had, in fact, ever 'happened'. It was all simply an idea, and if neither of them referred to it, it would become less than a dream.

She looked up, her mouth opened, and he realized she was about to ask him, in the same quiet tone, how was his wife and little Duncan.

Before she could speak, he interrupted rather wildly: 'There is one thing that makes me sad.'

'Why sad?'

'When I tell you what it is, you will realize the full extent of my selfishness.'

For the first time, she looked at him in a way that he knew very well: with an absorption so complete that it left him very free to look at her. Her eyes opened rather wide under the lashes, her forehead puckered slightly, she was attentive, as though holding her breath. She seemed to be making a great estimate of him, and to have a charity which saw through the faults to what she alone knew and judged to be the best. Her look made him see that some of his remarks were really sincere, that there was a true element of generosity in his gifts of parcels, that he was capable of surprising sacrifices, and that beyond his afflicting self-consciousness, there were unspent mines of goodness and spontaneity. And when she attended like this she was quite unaware of herself, so that he was able to see her loving him, without her even knowing that he did so.

She had seemed so beautiful at such moments—he remembered, though he was not quite certain that this was one of them—that he felt stupefied. It troubled him that she seemed perfect—because this meant that by too great admiration he was losing touch with her reality. Or so, at all events, Duncan Ballard would have insisted. Yet he could not see any faults in her. Her face with the high forehead, the deep-set eyes, the soft mouth—edged by the hair like a wave that approaches the shore—he looked down on this face as on the map in which he vainly tried to detect some indefensible weakness, as though the one he loved were enemy territory.

'I didn't think you are at all selfish, Harvey. At least you have never been so to us.'

'My idea seems very selfish now, even though it was planned in your interest. I had planned out my future with the idea that I should come here to visit you for a few days, every six months.'

She took this in. Her look said that it was not exactly selfish, but she was too concerned with a dozen other answers, to speak this. Then she said, with a movement of her hands, as if laying down two quite separate propositions for him to consider. 'In some ways, I might also have been happier even with that. But there is also my mother and my sister, and your wife and your child.'

The unbearable disturbances of the population all round them in the hut, made silence their only privacy. They spoke so quietly that their voices were murmurings and whispers. Every movement had a concentrated significance. He took her hand in his, and said: 'I came back for selfish reasons, because I can't do without you. With you, I am quite different from what I am with anyone else. You just said that you have never known me selfish: that is because you have only known me as I am with you. When I'm away from you, I'm someone quite different. Obviously I'm selfish to my own family, in my life I'm just as dishonest as everyone else I know.'

She seemed about to say something, and then did not. He was carried along by the rhetoric of his sincerity. What he said now was for an audience that included more than her. 'As far as I'm concerned, the war, and the Occupation and this camp, were things that made it possible for me to meet you. That's all there is to it, honestly. Without them, I could never have had in my life anyone who understood me as you do. My whole world didn't contain such a person with whom I was my best, and who knew the best in me. So now that I've had the chance I can't let it go.'

She looked gravely at him, and smiled: 'That is true also for me, Harvey. I don't intend that we let one another go.'

He took this in the most literal sense and shifting from idealism to managing, said: 'At this moment, it is not easy to see how it can be arranged, but I am sure I shall be able to fix it. You may have to stay some-where quietly for the first few weeks away from here, but while I am exploring the possibilities, I'll see that you get enough money out of what I've saved . . .' His whispering made it sound all the more frenetically practical.

His head, which was close to hers, was like a jar or vase, rotated in the light. With his waxen consumptive complexion, his over-red lips, his hair brushed back flat, his gleaming dark-blue eyes, there was something doll-like, of the tailor's dummy almost, about his head.

To her, this was simply strange, out of another world,
a world of England. It contrasted movingly with his
simplicity and sincerity, with his quivering when he
spoke. He was simply good and beautiful to her, and
the fact that there was some deep lack of decisive control was like a disturbance in herself of which he made
her aware. But now suddenly she leaned forward, put
her head in both her hands, and shook with repressed
violent sobbing. Terrified, he felt it was loyalty for him
which enabled her to keep an uncontrollable grief so
quiet. If he had not been there, she might have howled
the place down. Uttering no sound, her hands and face
were gleaming with her tears.

With her face still wet, she lifted her head again, and
with a secretive yet exaggerated gesture struck her
chest with her clenched hand. A few moments later she
was sufficiently in control of herself to ask a question
which seemed to take up everything he had said, and
give it back to him, as in a tightly clutched, tear-soaked
handkerchief: 'Don't you realize that I have thought of
things too?'

He stayed humbly silent. Then she said: 'But we
don't really know one another. Harvey, we don't know
one another—'

He could only protest, idiotically: 'But haven't I just
been saying that I do know you?'

'You know me as I am here, and you've been saying
that I know you as you are here. But that's different.
Until now, you haven't even known me as I am at this
very moment. You are very surprised . . .' She broke off.
Then she smiled again and said: 'Here you don't know
what it is that we come from different worlds. Here
you don't know what it is that I am ten years older
than you.'

'That hasn't mattered!'

'What does matter is that you wanted to see me here

—and we can't stay here for ever, not even if we really wanted to. Outside, it will all be different. Outside, you know nothing about me, and I know nothing about you. That's all I thought of when I heard we were to go away.'

He saw that to deny this was to deny the truth that they had found together. Almost despairingly, he said: 'But we can be friends.'

She considered this as though it were an object he had given to her, to be handled very carefully. Then she said: 'I shall always be grateful to you.'

He looked at her quite humbly, and asked: 'Do you think that what we had is lost, then?'

'No. I don't think it is lost because it was real.'

This observation quite took on the tone of their hour-long conversations of the past, when he had told her so much about his life, and she had spoken so little of hers, when they had discussed books and ideas, and discovered this strange thing—difference of background and environment are shadows that can be dissolved in an instant of communicating human feeling.

She seemed to look back now over a very long journey over a great many years when she said: 'One thing at least I have learned in my life. The past stays with you if you allow it simply to exist as the past.'

'I don't quite follow,' he said, in the questing voice of their serious objective discussions.

'I mean that what one really had one doesn't lose. What one really was, one is. It is difficult to explain. But it's part of oneself, in one's bones and mind, like the village where we were children. It's only if you're like my mother and, to some extent, my sister, and you insist on dragging the past into the present, that you lose both past and present.' There was a resentment in her voice which seemed completely new.

He was off on an idea of his own which he tremendously wanted to put before her. 'My friend Duncan Ballard says that sometimes there's such a thing between people as what he calls the "invisible menage".'

'The "invisible menage"?' It was her turn to be puzzled.

'Yes. That without knowing it, perhaps even, certain people are bound together, married, always present with one another. The "invisible menage" falls perhaps quite outside all their conscious arrangements. It is always there.'

'Does he think that you and he have an invisible menage?'

'No, I'm sure he doesn't.'

'It is the kind of thing that I don't think exists in our part of the world,' she said.

'All the same,' he said, 'we're talking now like we did in the past.'

'And as we shall in the future, Harvey,' she said, as if quite lost.

'One of the things perhaps they didn't tell you is how far away Australia is,' he laughed.

Utterly dissatisfied, he stood up and said: 'Now we both go back to our separate worlds.'

She did not answer, and he took her hand again.

As he was about to leave, he turned round at the opening which formed the entrance from the corridor, and said quite gaily: 'By the way, what shall I say if anyone ever asks me if you were really the princess?'

She turned on him. 'Fairy stories of that crazy old woman!' she exclaimed.

'What old woman?'

'My mother!'

'Did she invent it?'

'I don't know! I haven't the faintest idea! She lives on dragging the past into the present! She does just what I want you to swear never to do.' But he had never heard her speak before with this fury. Until now, she said nothing of her mother except to show her the utmost consideration. A door on to a wide world had been thrust open, and he realized that once outside it, Moura would be an extremely different person.

'All right then, I swear,' he said, turning away, 'and I'll never ask you about it again.'

And as he left, the aggressive, boney form of Moura's sister, and the toothless, vague wandering old shadow who was her mother, pushed by him in the corridor.

VI

When Harvey suggested in Solario's that they should all meet, after his German visit, in Paris, Duncan Ballard had received the idea as though it were a typical 'Harvey gaffe', if not an insult. In the event, his behaviour turned out to be more characteristic of him than of Harvey. He took over the plan as if it came from him and no one else. Kate wrote to Harvey while he was still in Germany that Duncan had kindly offered to take her to Paris for a few days before they all met there. She did not have to explain that Duncan was like a brother to Kate. The only problem was what would happen, for nearly three weeks, to little Dunky. This was solved by allowing his standards temporarily to be absorbed into those of the next-door neighbours, Mrs. Barnard and her Geoff.

So before Harvey arrived in Paris, Duncan had spent a week educating Kate. She was a good pupil: 'Infinitely more advanced than the Keats of the Displaced Persons' Camp,' he wrote to Wurlitzer. There was still an obscure satisfaction to be got out of discrediting Harvey.

Duncan was really elated. A chaperon indulging the feeling that both he and Kate shared a grievance against her husband, he had a sense of being virtuous which satisfied some quite childish desire in him to be good and kind and amusing. With Kate he was the opposite of his usual competitive snubbing self. He was simple, affectionate and tireless. He took her to modest restaurants, discoveries of his. He showed her buildings and paintings, and kept up his surprise at her intelligence and enthusiasm. She could make nothing of the Monna Lisa, but she liked his chosen Corots and Géricaults. All sorts of small things seemed to illustrate what he regarded as her natural taste and sensibility: qualities which—Duncan thought—Harvey, obsessed with his romance and his princess, ambitious with his 'fiddling' and his writing, had kept down.

His most successful stroke was introducing her to Jules Alain. Jules Alain, when he was little more than an adolescent, had been a contact of the Resistance with the British. Within a week of the fall of Paris, Ballard had met him in an atmosphere of Franco-British honeymoon, Champs Elysées delirious with flags and hymns of Liberation. Ballard's relationship with Jules, had for a few weeks something of the lyrical burning yet dusty quality of that time. The young Frenchman attributed to the broadcaster, and to the B.B.C. as a whole, incredible ideals which seemed to have been brought out of old cupboards containing lilies and Jeanne d'Arc, and hung up as good as new, illuminated by an extraordinary ever-burning flame of French youth. Duncan discovered in Jules the generosity, ardour and faith which are the exact opposite of the qualities usually attributed to the French by foreigners, but which when they are there, seem French and nothing else.

Not that Jules' idealism did not go hand in hand with a hard-baked, resigned scepticism, Duncan was gradually to discover. The idealism and the cynical streak operated smoothly together in Jules' relations with Kate. Her Englishness, the fact that she was not a 'lady', appealed to the political idealist in him, for he atoned for what he felt to be his cowardice in not having joined the Resistance until late 1944, by joining the communists during the Peace. The cynic in Jules immediately grasped facts made very accessible to him by Duncan about 'the husband', the princess, the Germans, the occupation forces, and even shrewder things that Duncan did not tell about his own feelings for Harvey. Jules was loyal to Duncan's unexpressed wish that he should 'interest himself' in Kate.

When Harvey arrived in Paris, ten days after Kate and Duncan, he found Duncan in control of her visit. Kate and Duncan met his train at the Gare de l'Est. In the Metro, on the way from the station, Kate was already explaining to Harvey how Duncan had found for them the top-storey room in the little hotel in the Rue Jacob. At the hotel, Kate took him straight upstairs. Their room had one window facing over a courtyard, another over the narrow street, a large old-fashioned double bed with gilded iron bed-posts, and a lace bed-cover. The wall-paper was of pale pink flowers in vertical parallels. A glass-panelled door led into a wash-room, from which there came a curious smell.

Harvey sat on the bed watching Kate while she unpacked for him. She was completely absorbed in the task, very self-possessed, and seemed protected by a glow of independence, an invisible shirt of flame. 'How do you like Paris, Kate?'

'I love it.' She looked up at him brightly and added: 'One learns all sorts of things here.'

He laughed: 'It's famous for that.'

'Oh, I didn't mean it that way, Harvey. I mean, it gets you out of a groove. I realize now how narrowed down I was getting. Duncan has shown me all sorts of things. I'm grateful to him, really I am. I've been to the Louvre, and Notre Dame, and to all sorts of funny little restaurants. I enjoy it all very much. I do really. I won't be so narrow in my views in future, at least I hope I won't. Do you know, I've even learned some French, what with what I started when I knew we were coming here?' She spoke rather fast.

He said: 'I'm proud of you,' and kissed her. Then he

walked to the window looking out over the Rue Jacob,
and said: 'Shall we go out?'

'Why don't you go to a café, or somewhere, with
Duncan? I'm sure you and he will want to talk. I can
be tidying these things.'

Harvey still stood by the window, looking across the
street.

'Why do you keep standing there, Harvey?'

'I was thinking how extraordinary it was to be in a
town where the walls stay up,' he said, a bit affectedly.
He was really thinking how easily, at the press of a
button, the fall of a hand, they would collapse and dissolve. He was wondering whether he wanted them to
do so. 'How's little Dunky?' he asked.

She told him how he was, and then began again:
'Do go down. I'm sure Duncan's waiting for you.
He's been so nice. You shouldn't keep him waiting.
Really you shouldn't.'

'All right.' He went over, and, once again kissed her.
'Good-bye,' he said. 'I'm glad I've found you again.'

'Have you found me?' she laughed. 'Well, I'm glad
I've found you too.'

There was Duncan Ballard downstairs, waiting for
him in the hall. They went into the street. 'Where shall
we go now?' asked Harvey. Duncan said it depended
what Harvey would like. And then, in his prim, matter-
of-fact voice, like Kate, talking a bit too fast, he explained the situation of the cafés. 'Well, coming from
the country of the dead, I suppose I should go where
there's the most life,' said Harvey.

'In that case, we should decidedly go to the Flore.
Mind you, I wouldn't have said that in 1939. Then
the Deux Magots was the most interesting place. But
the Quartier changed when the Existentialists took over
the Flore and the bar of the Pont Royal, when Sarret and
Marteau and Éloise Bienvue started meeting there . . .'

He rattled on, without Duncan understanding more than half what he was referring to. Harvey was amazed at his confidence. This was Duncan Ballard's hour of triumph. It showed how exalted he was by his idea that others were dependent on him.

The café had plush-covered seats on one side of marble-top tables, and chairs opposite. It was not luxurious and yet it seemed absolutely the centre of a civilization. There was some indefinable right mixture of comfort and discomfort, glory and misery about it, so that, like Hell, it was equipped to receive every kind of sinner—the shabby and the respectable, the poor and the rich, the naked and the bejewelled, the criminal and the intellectual. The only person who would have looked out of place here would have been a saint.

In a corner there was a poet actually having some kind of convulsions, at another, a philosopher was writing an enormous manuscript, and Duncan pointed out a notorious thief conversing with a famous male prostitute. Their names were all known and therefore everything they did in the café had a sublime correcti-tude which it achieved there and could not achieve anywhere else.

The only people a bit out of place were foreigners like themselves. But for the time being the prestige of the war-time B.B.C. carried them through. Duncan nodded in several directions, then seated himself on the red plush 'banc' opposite the chair he indicated to Duncan. 'Well,' he said.

Harvey knew from this that they were taking up their conversation exactly at the point where they had left it off in Solario's. But, he saw that today Duncan was not just the passive listener. He held cards in his hand.

For a moment Harvey hesitated. Then the docility he had acquired as a habit with Duncan, reasserted itself. With a curious feeling of betrayal, he said:

'It's all over as far as Moura and I are concerned.'

'Your princess? You mean that princess?'

'The question of the title isn't really very relevant to the matter at issue.'

Duncan winced, quite ecstatically. 'Yes, I do see that. Nevertheless, she and you have agreed not to try to make a go of it together?'

'She's going to Australia. I can hardly go there.'

Duncan actually looked as if he were going to ask: 'Pray, why not?'

Harvey answered such a possible inquiry: 'I have thought it over very carefully. I can't leave my family.'

'I dare say you are very wise. All the same, perhaps it's my duty to tell you that the situation has changed here also. You won't find Kate the same. She is different, too.'

'No. She isn't the same. I've noticed that,' he said rather dully.

Duncan was annoyed: 'You mean—you know?'

'I don't know anything special. But I did, of course, notice she'd altered. She's made a tremendous effort. I appreciate that.'

'Then you don't know about Jules?' he asked—on a note of relief.

'You seem to forget. I've been away.'

Duncan told him that Jules was really fascinated by Kate. Harvey took this in, with apparent calm.

'Well, how do you feel about it?' Duncan finally asked.

'I don't know. I suppose I ought to be upset. One never is what people expect,' he added, with his kind of self-complacency. 'Whatever it is,' he went on, 'I suppose, considering the way I've gone on, that it's what Kate's entitled to.'

'The fact of the matter is, you don't care—that's all there is to it,' Duncan said, suddenly spiteful.

'Oh yes, I do care.' Harvey regained his seriousness. 'But you see, I trust Kate.'

At this, Duncan looked depressed. Harvey, as so often before, was aware of pressure being brought on him, pressure that appealed to his sympathy. Duncan's bossiness and malice were only a thin cover over desperation: and now that he was quite happy managing Kate in Paris, Harvey was letting him down. It didn't really seem fair. The way out was to feed him with the Harvey Granville Story which might have been invented by Duncan himself, but didn't have to be invented because it happened to be life. He was a True Life Story-Teller for Duncan's special entertainment.

So as often happened in their conversations, he started improvising his feelings to satisfy a need in Duncan, and then having said what he felt, it seemed to become true. At any rate he could not remember the state of unconscious innocence he had been in before he said what he felt Harvey wanted him to relate.

'As a matter of fact, I won't be awfully sorry for Kate to be taken up with something other than me, for the next few days.'

'You won't! Really! Why not?'

'It's difficult to explain. But for one thing, I want just to walk along the street in Paris and touch the walls of the buildings. I want to run my fingers along the lines of stones that remain in place, to make sure that they are really there. Not just the walls either, Duncan. I had the same feeling of wanting to touch a wooden hoarding by the Rue du Bac, on which there are all sorts of posters of things that one can really buy and enjoy here.'

Duncan Ballard sat up and looked intently, with widening eyes, at Harvey Granville. His eyes shone in the way they did when an authentic fish bit. He suddenly saw into the machinery of Harvey's mind. 'The

reason why he'll never be able to write,' he thought,
'quite apart from his lack of education and his ignorance
of what writing is about—is that he can't distinguish
between the metaphorical and the literal.' What Harvey
had just said was a nice way of showing his nice feelings
about the ruins. But that he should imagine that he
literally wanted to touch the walls, and that he could
drag Duncan along with him in this fantasy—that was
acting out false literature. 'I must write to George
Wurlitzer about my new Harvey Granville discovery.'

'Another reason is this letter.' Harvey felt in his
pocket, and Duncan reflected chucklingly that their
meetings were really getting too stylized for words.
At a certain stage, it seemed, the letters, the docu-
ments, had to be produced. He indulged in a weary,
patient sigh. Checking himself, Harvey said abruptly:
'After all, I haven't got it on me. Anyway, all it said
is that if I can meet her with a taxi at the Gare de l'Est
and take her across Paris to the Gare du Nord, where
she and her sister and mother get on another train—she
will arrange for the other two to traverse Paris together
without her.' He paused, then he said solemnly: 'It will
be the first and only time outside the camp that we shall
ever be alone.'

Harvey went back to the hotel. Kate and he dined at
one of the restaurants high on Harvey's list of recom-
mendations.

They talked of what she had seen and done in Paris,
how kind Duncan had been, what Len and Ed were
doing, whether little Duncan would be influenced for the
worse by Geoff. They were strangely constrained with
one another. Although he knew that Moura and he,
who had never completely met, must separate, and that
now there would definitely never be 'anything between
them', he felt it would be disloyalty to tell Kate this—
at all events before the meeting of tomorrow that was

filling his whole mind. Strange that what he so easily said to Duncan Ballard he could not tell Kate.

And there was a barrier which she used to protect herself from him. Yet he knew that it was meant as much to help as to resist him: resisting him, until tomorrow, was helping him.

'We must wait,' he observed suddenly.

She looked at him in silence. Then she asked: 'By the way, did Duncan speak to you about Jules Alain?'

'You mean the medical student? Yes, he said we were going to meet him for supper tomorrow night. Who is he?'

'Well, it seems you know. He's all right, I think. Duncan says he's very clever, and very poor. He seems to have been something in the Resistance. I don't know much about that. Then some professor, who was also in the Resistance, took him up and sent him to college. He seems quite a nice sort of fellow.'

'What language do you talk with him?'

'Oh, he speaks a bit of English, and I try some of my French, now and then. I seem to make myself understood, whatever I want to say. I told you, when you were away I did a bit of studying an Easy French Course, and then I listened to conversation lessons on the wireless, in order not to let you down. Oh, Harry, I did work hard.'

He put his arm round her waist as they walked back to the hotel.

The next morning they went to the Louvre and she showed him the paintings she had seen with Duncan. She told him what it was Duncan said made Géricault such a good painter, and what you ought to like and not to like in Corot. She really saw the point in what Duncan had said.

They went on talking about paintings and other things that she had seen. They got on very well, as though they had met for the first time. But combined with this sense of newness, there was also a sense of staleness. As they talked there was a feeling that they might be using up all the things they could say which lay between them and come to a terrible gulf which had on one side of it boredom, on the other, passion; and that finally, when all the conversation was finished up, they would have to choose which side to be on. He was aware also within himself of something very perverse: a conviction that the relationship which was going to end that afternoon was sacred and demanded a fidelity which he could never give to marriage. It imposed a freezing chastity on his real marriage. Or which was his real marriage?

He told her vaguely and in a very general way that he had to report in the late afternoon to some sort of Headquarters, where he had friends who expected to hear his impressions of the D.P. Camp. She accepted this with so little demur that he felt a bit ashamed he had offered any reason at all. He could just have taken her to their hotel door and said: 'Good-bye, I'll see you this evening at the Flore.'

All the meetings of this week took place in exceptional settings, as though they had been dragged out from the environment which was so much part of their needs and circumstances that it seemed an organic part of themselves, their home being simply the impress made on a tiny patch of the world by the mould of their lives. But now they met in scenery which seemed artificial to them, as though they had been suddenly called on to act out their story in front of cameras which saw them in the kind of settings the movies choose. This dramatized themselves for themselves, so that when Harvey appeared at the café which was prelude or backcloth to the restaurant, his mind was filled with a photographic image of Moura in the taxi: a close-up of her face against the inside of the cab, with the traffic flickering outside the window, and at the back of the stream of street, famous buildings—the Madeleine, the Arc de Triomphe and the Eiffel Tower.

In the restaurant, for a long time, he noticed Jules Alain's face much more than what was said. Pale and wrinkling and intelligent, it was an old-young man's face, crossed with contradictions. It was frank, opening and smiling when he looked at you, withdrawn, rather bitter and alone, in repose. His features, with wide open eyes and a nose whose tip was drawn down somewhat over towards the upper lip, were of a blond Northern Italianate kind, seen in certain Renaissance medallions. He had an aristocratic disdain and yet also a plebeian ingratiatingness. There was something of the pastry cook's son who becomes a Pretender in his wavy hair, his rather coarse mouth, and most of all in the look of unresting resentment which lay just under the surface of his gaiety.

Jules looked across the table at Harvey with, as it were, an incipient shrug—as though he were about to spread out his arms and exclaim to Duncan—'*Le mari —voila!*' But it was a shrug verging on a smile of complicity, as though, between men, they shared a joke directed at Kate and, still more, perhaps, at Duncan himself.

The restaurant which was in a street leading into the Place Furstenburg, was chosen by Duncan because it was at once good, and inoffensive to Harvey's extremist politics. It consisted of one large plain room, low-ceilinged, with paper-covered tables, and wooden benches. The door from the street opened straight into this room. At the end opposite the street door was a hatch opening into the kitchen. Everything here was *en famille*, and workers mingled with bourgeois. The chef's assistant—his younger brother—looked into the restaurant through this hatch and took orders shouted to him by one of the two waitresses.

Kate didn't see much to the place, though she didn't mind the food. The meat was certainly excellent. Duncan was very much at ease here. Summoning the proprietress, whom he addressed as 'Madame', he ordered the inevitably right wine, the inevitably only possible dishes from the menu. Occasionally, out of courtesy to the one of his guests who was on native grounds, he consulted Jules who agreed, without showing much interest, in all Duncan's decisions.

When the food and wine had been ordered, Duncan set about getting Harvey and Jules on to the right kind of talking terms. 'Our friend Harvey Granville has just come from the American Zone of Germany. Doubtless he can provide you with information about the German workers.'

Jules, who knew very well where Harvey had just come from, said: *'Les Allemands, les Americains. Tout ça.'* He admitted that he had no great concern for the welfare of the Germans—not even for the German workers.

Harvey, making conversation, and playing up his rôle as an official of the Occupying Forces, asked: 'But as an internationalist, aren't you interested in the German workers?' which Duncan translated rather tartly, 'As a communist, shouldn't your sympathies be internationalist?'

Holding his head down and looking up under his eyebrows so that his forehead became wrinkled in a way that somehow had a touch of pathos about it, Jules wagged his forefinger and said: 'Ah, you forget! The Party line today is nationalist and anti-German! How you English love the Germans!'

Harvey started on a pedantically reasonable tone. 'We don't specially like the Germans, but we do happen

to be an Occupying Power—as are also the French.
Surely, M. Alain, we ought to agree that we are concerned with the welfare of the people in our respective
zones?'

'Of course,' said Kate. 'But that doesn't mean we have
to like the Germans.'

'D.P.'s happen to have been my concern. And they
were not Germans anyway.'

'But it was the Germans you were just defending,'
she insisted.

'Was I?'

'You send food to the poor German miners in the
Ruhr, while the poor French miners almost starve.'

Harvey smiled, quite the amiable officer conscious of
being British and shouldering responsibility. 'Well, we
don't happen to be occupying France, so we can't exercise our virtues here. Though we seem to eat fairly
well,' he added, putting a slice of meat into his mouth.

There are certain conversations which the act of
eating makes incongruous.

Jules looked as if he would be annoyed did he not
realize that it would be unintelligent to be annoyed.

'After all the Germans are human beings,' said
Duncan, bringing the conversation back to this simple,
controversial point.

'Are they?' asked Jules, with genuine irritation this
time. 'When the Germans occupied our country they
didn't regard us as human beings. They didn't treat us
as human beings, either. They didn't even claim to be
human themselves. They said they were superhuman
which seemed to be something quite different. And they
treated us as sub-human. Humanity was left out of it.'

'I'm sure you're right about your experiences,' said
Harvey, 'and of course, we all sympathize. But still, not
all Germans are involved. Some of them felt about it as
we do.' Jules Alain looked sceptical. 'If one happens to

have lived among them,' Harvey went on, 'one sees them not as "the Germans" but as individuals. Sometimes these individuals detested the Nazis.' He then recounted exactly, with perhaps too much feeling, the story of his visit to the diabetic Dr. Grosche. 'Wingfield, the Camp Director, said that Dr. Grosche was known as an anti-Nazi.'

'We have diabetics, and we are short of insulin too,' said Jules. And then, in his real effort to be amiable— not to allow the conversation to flounder in political imbecilities—he conceded. 'Anyway, conditions such as this exist everywhere under capitalism.'

'You mean to say, you think people are better off in communist countries?' sneered Duncan.

'If they aren't, that is also the result of capitalism. Your nice Germans invaded Russia. Certainly that has put the clock back for socialism.'

Kate said: 'I'm very bad at arguing, but it does seem to me, Jules, that all you're doing is to say that whatever happens your party must inevitably always be in the right and the capitalists always in the wrong.'

It took some moments to convey to Jules the sense of this. He looked at Kate, his head held sideways, an ironic melancholy expression in his eyes. Then he shrugged his shoulders and said: 'Quandmême . . . that might be true. I mean, it might be true that they were always right, and the others always wrong.'

'Really. In that case discussion is utterly impossible!' said Duncan, laughing with extreme irritation.

Jules looked at him as though to say, it might be true, discussion might be impossible.

'Making every possible allowance for the Russians, who certainly have suffered enormously,' said Harvey, 'and admitting all the things the Germans have done, nevertheless, we have ample evidence collected from D.P.'s that when they go back to Russia or the East, the communists behaved to their own people almost as savagely as the Nazis behaved to them.'

'Yes! Tell him about what happened to your friends!' said Duncan.

Harvey told the story of three women, a mother and two daughters, at a camp where he had worked on the staff, whose cases he could vouch for. They had gone back to the East and been treated there as suspects, subject to the brutality of the inquisition or the concentration camp.

'That is the story—isn't it—of a great friend of yours whom you trust—absolutely?' asked Duncan, as though he were some kind of magistrate presiding at an *in camera* tribunal.

Jules lifted, very high, an eyebrow, and looked up in that curious way, holding his head down. It was almost as if he were winking.

'It is your very great friend and her family, of whom you are speaking—the one you call the Princess?' pursued Duncan.

'At the camp we have every reason to believe her story though there is some doubt what is meant by her being a princess.'

'Oh but surely she was a princess!' exclaimed Kate warmly.

Jules raised his forefinger again, wagging it maliciously at Harvey. He was shaking with laughter. '*Quandmême les princesses sont d'habitude assez réaction naires*—the aristocrats—are they not a little bit reactionaries?'

Harvey didn't reply. Then Jules said, seriously this time: 'Even in Russia, you know, there were Fascists and people who hated the regime. Personally they may have been sympathetic and intelligent—but *objectively*, just the same . . .'

'I'm sure she was completely truthful!' Kate said

angrily. 'What she told Harvey is that she was beaten, assaulted, by the soldiers on their way back and then sent to a camp. Do you think that is right, to come home and be sent to a place worse even than the D.P. camp you came out of? You can't get away with saying that poor poor Russia had to be protected against three helpless women.'

'She was only one among thousands,' said Jules, 'and I do not deny that in her case there may have been injustice. Exceptions of every kind are possible, under any system. Don't blame me for it. All I think is that it is not the exception that counts.'

'Perhaps what I think, is that it is the exception that counts,' said Kate.

'In any case,' said Harvey officiously, 'the incident is closed. The Camp Director managed to get her and her relations to Australia. They are on their way there this moment.'

Kate got up and said: 'I'm afraid I must go back to the hotel.'

Before any of them had time to do more than protest, she was outside the restaurant door, in the square. Harvey said: 'Excuse me, I'll be back immediately.' He jumped up and followed her. The little square seemed almost deserted, and in the middle of it were two immense trees. 'Kate!' he called. She ran along a narrow street into the boulevard. He saw her hail a taxi.

He caught her up and said: 'Kate, what's the matter? I thought you'd be pleased at what I told you.'

She seemed hardly to see him, but answered in a dazed way: 'Pleased? What do you think I wanted you to tell me? You'll please me if you go back, Harvey.'

'But, Kate, I must look after you. I can't let you go like this.'

'I'll be perfectly all right. Honestly I will, Harvey. Go back. If you don't, they'll be so upset. Please do.

You must go and talk to them. I'll leave the key in the door and go to sleep. They'll need you to tell them everything's all right.'

He didn't answer, until she said, on a different note: 'If you don't go back, I will. And then I don't know what I might not say.'

He saw that she meant this. 'All right then. I'll just quieten them down, then I'll come to the hotel. But I did want you to understand, Kate. Moura and I have finished everything. She's gone to Australia. This afternoon I said good-bye to her.'

'I don't understand why you're telling me all this. Don't you see, it's nothing to do with me? Why do you think I would be interested?' She said this in the quiet voice that he thought of as dangerous. 'You don't have to hurry back,' she added, quite calmly. And she got into the taxi.

Jules and Duncan were relieved to see him.

'Is Kate all right? Why did she go off like that?' asked Duncan. He did not seem really to care very much. In the restaurant the whole incident seemed to matter less, and Kate might have been just an English 'one of the ladies' leaving the men alone to sit round the table after dinner. The atmosphere was easy, quite cosy, now without her.

'*Ça peut arriver, mais quand-même, ça n'est pas grave,*' said Jules—things like that happen, and don't have to be serious. 'But all the same,' he added, 'if it happened too often . . .'

He became quite cordial with Harvey. 'I was perhaps a little rude. I am vairy sorry. We should not talk politics. It is always mistaken,' he said in English. Then to Duncan's interpreting, he became autobiographical. In spite of what he'd said, he by no means accepted the Party line altogether. Though he was a bit ashamed of this: he was a bad communist, like you can be a bad catholic. As far as he, Jules, considered as an individual, was concerned, the communist line was often very inimical to him. But then, he asked himself, how much should individuals count as individuals? When he thought of the 'poor masses' and then of those literary ladies and gentlemen who met at the Flore and who would certainly despise a little medico like him—then he asked whether their freedom to say whatever they liked was really so much more valuable than the scientific planning of society without regard for individual eccentricities. Still, perhaps he had the inferiority complex of the 'poor little man of science' in this world of France where everything was dominated in intellectual life, by Letters. In 1941, when he was sixteen, he'd been sent to work in the mines. And then he'd noted well that the miners were all anti-German whereas the bosses were mostly collaborators, working hand in glove with the Nazis. Now came his confession that went deepest. In 1944 he had the chance to join the Resistance. He had not done so till 1945. As a psychologist, he had to admit that one reason for his communism might be shame that he had not taken up a risky revolutionary position earlier on.

He looked up with his corrugated smile that seemed to cover over, like a roof, the suffering of an extremely sensitive intelligence. There was a look of excuse in his eyes.

Duncan started talking in English to Harvey, too fast for Jules to follow. 'What happened today?' he asked. Then shifted the direction of the question. 'Did you enjoy the Louvre?'

Harvey looked as though he knew he was now expected to be intelligent.

'If I hadn't relegated the uneven struggle to the more talented, my impressions might have formed a subject for my collected works.'

'What would that have been?'

'Nothing about the artists or the paintings even, really. About the gallery itself. The pictures looking at the people, the people looking at the pictures. It's as if the dead artists were trying to send messages which had been selected and hung by people who, without quite realizing what they were, knew that these were the most significant that had ever been made. The people in the gallery understand this too. They walk around or go away thinking that perhaps they ought to devote their whole lives to understanding what the pictures are saying. Or perhaps they feel that they ought to go home and plan to deliver messages to posterity themselves.'

'That could be a subject, though I don't quite see any conclusion.'

'Neither do I. But it makes pictures be like a kind of life which we look at and that doesn't quite succeed in communicating with our life, because our circumstances have put us out of touch. An art gallery is like a zoo. The pictures in their frames are the animals in their cages, that belong to their own world where they speak a non-human language that we don't understand. And yet we feel that if we did enter into a living communication with them, our world would be different.'

'How different?'

'Well, for one thing, we would understand about love.' He suddenly blushed violently, like a schoolboy. Then he went on hurriedly: 'We would have international understanding. We might have perpetual peace.'

The conversation had grown altogether too serious, in fact, intense. In the competition between Harvey and Duncan, it had somehow brought things full circle. Duncan was back at marvelling at Harvey, thinking there was something there after all—things he himself would never have been able, even so clumsily, to express. He broke through a circle that seemed to be enclosing him, with a question that cut a knot. 'How did your meeting with the princess go off?'

'Quite well. You've just heard what we talked about in the taxi. Thanks to you sending Kate to the Louvre, Moura and I talked about pictures. My dear Duncan, don't go away thinking that I have any original ideas. I always acknowledge my sources.'

He was beginning to strike his familiarly pretentious note, Duncan thought—the false cleverness that had been the poison Duncan, after all, had himself given him. Duncan said, a bit ironically:

'What marvellous conversations you must have had!'

'Yes. We did talk about a great many things,' Harvey said simply.

'And is that all that happened in the taxi?'

'Not quite all. I kissed her.'

'And how was that?' Duncan asked, feeling Harvey had challenged him to do so.

'Well, nothing much. It couldn't be. You see it was the first time we had ever embraced. All I noticed was the lobe of her left ear, and the traffic going past like a march of giant beetles. On the other hand, it was also the last time I ever kissed her.'

Duncan's very first impression of Harvey—so long ago, in the ward of the hospital—fused with this moment. The almost conventional features had made him forget how the eyes would seem to darken as though shot through with ink, and the mouth quiver. There was really nothing left for him to say, Harvey had told him everything. He was quite full, with the complete Harvey Granville Story. He turned to Jules, and made a show of bringing him into a conversation whose subject would certainly have to be changed now. Yet he could not think of a subject. He opened his mouth and said merely '—Er!' Harvey got up, as though this were the signal for him to leave the two friends alone. Perhaps it was. Their parting was exactly as if they had reached a point where the rest of their relationship could best be fulfilled in a farewell.

Harvey walked back along the Boulevard, past the cafés, the bars like over-filled cupboards, bulging and spilling their bright or soiled contents into the streets, past the lovers and the solitaries, all, in the Parisian manner, absorbed in thoughts that had surrendered utterly to the night. He felt unaccountably exalted, nervously at peace with himself, as though whatever might happen now, he was on the verge of his own truth.

He opened the door of the hotel bedroom. He saw, with something of a shock, that Kate had left the lights burning. She lay in bed with the coverlet pushed back, her head sideways on the pillow, an arm out over the side of the bed, almost touching the floor. She was breathing so quietly that, when he stood over, looking down at her, she almost seemed made of some motionless substance. Her face was extremely pale, her lips slightly apart. Every care, every wish, every word, every dispute, seemed to have been erased from her perfectly pure forehead. She did not seem to belong to any time or place, it was as though he had never known her, as though she stood always at the end of a long tunnel which was their botched marriage, and remained as she had been the instant before he first saw her, before she had been ruined by any glance from him. She was as outside his life now as irrefutable truth, or as one of the beautiful dead faces on a canvas in the Louvre.

He stood there absolutely filling his mind with her, sadly conscious of the strangeness, that this was his most intense communing with her, when he saw her truth, and she was unconscious of his terribly solitary thoughts. He was now perfectly free to be with her and yet entirely by himself, and to ask, without her perceiving what was in his mind, whether love was possible if it was only acknowledged on a level of scarcely attainable truth. At that moment she opened her eyes, looked at him with an extraordinary childlike smile of awakening and said in her original, first voice: 'Harvey!' Then she turned away as though to bury herself in a grave of sleep again. He put his arms round her and held her so gently as not to disturb her. Then he realized that she was moving in some kind of somnambulant half-consciousness, and that if she woke now she would not recognize him. She suddenly said, very distinctly: '*Mon mari est mon frère.*'

He was still in his exaltation, where the fact that truth spoke out of a First French Lesson book struck him as most lovingly comic. What she had said, coming out of an oracular state of consciousness, did not shame or surprise him. He simply accepted it as something which he had to deal with. It filled him, too, with a sense of her serious justice. He turned out the light now, and walked over to the window and looked out onto the street. His own particular kind of falsity which shut him out of all rooms and sent him wandering along streets and across roofs, was suddenly clear to him. In one of those flashes that seem perfect in their own instant and then meaningless immediately afterwards, his relationship with Moura, who had just gone away, and this other woman lying, like a princess, on her bed in the satin of her flesh, seemed identical. It was a kind of Nothing in himself that made them the same. Then he thought of their home, Dunky, Geoff, orange curtains, their day to day life together, and saw how, for a time, something came into his existence which could not accept his marriage. Yet underneath it all, Kate on the bed was no more like the superfice of their day-to-day existing, than was he himself. She stayed beneath and beyond it like a religion which he knew to be ultimately true, in which he ultimately lacked the faith to believe. Yet because he knew this, he could not know anything else, anything less than this. They had nothing except one another. He walked over to the bed, and very gently began to wake her.

(1946 and 1957)